She crept to the side of the bed

It felt treacherous gazing at Mickey. One hand lay open beside his face. His dark lashes swept against high cheekbones, making him look vulnerable and boyish. His magnificent shoulders were roped with muscle. A sickle scar marred his right shoulder, another, the tapering cobblestones of his ribs. Dark hair bristled from the confines of a towel secured around his hips, and the terry cloth had fallen away to reveal a thigh that had been honed by hard workouts.

Laura felt a mixture of emotions—a longing to touch that seasoned, slightly battered body that had conjured the fiercest pleasure of her life from her; compassion for his exhaustion and the monkish way he lived; curiosity to know the whole of him, intimately, from the thick black hair on his head to the tips of his tapered feet....

ABOUT THE AUTHOR

Louella Nelson's Scorpio personality and tastes are eclectic and formed in large part by travel. She moved from rural Maine, where she was born, to New Hampshire, Alaska, Hawaii and Mexico. Lou now resides in California. In *Emerald Fortune* she reprises a character from her first American Romance novel, *Mail-Order Mate*—hero Mickey Stone, truly a man with a mission.

Books by Louella Nelson

HARLEQUIN AMERICAN ROMANCE
214–MAIL-ORDER MATE

HARLEQUIN SUPERROMANCE
96–SENTINEL AT DAWN
128–FREEDOM'S FORTUNE

LOUELLA NELSON

EMERALD FORTUNE

Harlequin Books

TORONTO • NEW YORK • LONDON
AMSTERDAM • PARIS • SYDNEY • HAMBURG
STOCKHOLM • ATHENS • TOKYO • MILAN

To Stacee,
Daughter & Friend:
Go for your dreams

I wish to express my gratitude to Carl Baggett, Jr.,
for his encouragement, forebearance in the days
before deadline, and faith in my abilities. And to
Don Murdoch, lifelong friend, for insight into the
vagaries, challenges and glories of federal law
enforcement—the inspiration for this book. And to
the homeless, for their courage and for mirroring
our strengths, weaknesses and direction for growth.

Published February 1991

ISBN 0-373-16379-7

EMERALD FORTUNE

Chapter One

Snow iced the San Gabriel Mountains on one of the rare days when the saw-toothed flank of the Los Angeles metropolis was visible. Thirty miles south across a maze of freeways, factories and inner-city sprawl, the lords of the gem trade eked out their living in small locked-from-the-inside glass-walled cubicles. Their kingdom was the Jewelry Mart, a network of old brick office buildings, warehouses and high-rises surrounding the grass and shade of Pershing Square.

DANCING, read a sign on Sixth Street, half a block east of the square. The vertical capital letters were chipped and faded. They had the sad, lost aspect of a bygone era. The three-story building, with its corner shop full of dusty X-rated lingerie, no longer lured movie moguls and wealthy heiresses from the Biltmore Hotel on the square, to dip and swirl to big bands in the smoky, illusory privacy of a downtown ballroom.

A few feet along the sidewalk, an inconspicuous sign—gold leaf on wood scrubbed by the years—bore the name GARTH GEM BROKERAGE.

A strong sun shone through the dust and pollutants glazing the upper-story windows of the brokerage. Inside, the light cast a deceptively warm-looking tint on the grayed oak floors, the cot beneath the windows, and the planes and hollows of Mickey Stone's face as he worked at a scarred wooden desk canted free-style in the cavernous room.

Mickey Stone straightened up and rerolled the cuff of his white shirt. His gaze made a restless sweep of the desk. His green eyes narrowed, and a grimace of distaste deepened the grooves that months of deprivation had carved into his cheeks. Then he bent back to the task of filling out purchase orders for uncut emeralds, sapphire pendants, diamond-and-ruby rings—while the resentment roiled through him.

His chronic anger was fueled by his memories. And by the plastic-sleeved list under the telephone—names, dates, locations—leads on the Garden Emerald case, dead ends that galled him every time he picked up the phone to handle a gem transfer for Garth. Sometimes the anger choked him when he glanced at the stacks of notes and files on the corner of the desk: some of them read "Property of the U.S. Government—TOP SECRET—NSI." He'd pirated copies of the case files from the National Security Institute when they'd cut him loose. Now the files were gathering dust.

But when he rifled through them, it kept his hatred alive. It made the small-time deals Garth entrusted to him bearable, because one of these days—

The phone rang.

Automatically, for the thought of a break in the Garden Emerald case was a constant stimulant, adrenaline kicked into his bloodstream. He felt a thrill of eagerness. Solving the case might mean NSI would reconsider. God, how he needed the Institute to take him back.

When he picked up the phone, he had to force himself to sound matter-of-fact. "Garth Gems," he said.

"So who died," said his ex-partner at NSI and best friend—only close friend, these days.

"Why?" Mickey asked. "You going to change your ways and pay your respects?"

"That's rich. You've been acting like the dear departed far too long to deserve any special treatment."

Mickey's lips thinned. "Yeah, well. What's up, Clint?"

Clint's raspy tenor voice tweeked a note. Mickey sat up. Everything else about Clint's personality, including his computerlike brain and his ability to handle himself with the brass, made him a good career man. But that odd high note gave him away to Mickey, who'd known him since they'd been undercover for the San Diego P.D. more than fifteen years before. Clint had something explosive under wraps.

"Meet me at Harry's Seafood in an hour," Clint said.

Hackles prickled the back of Mickey's neck. He had half a dozen purchase orders and three calls to gem dealers to finish before he'd quit for the day. But Clint's tone and his abruptness cleared Mickey's schedule for him. He half rose from the maple chair.

"What's up?" he said again, his breath shortening.

"Be there," Clint said softly. "That tall bag of bones you call a body? I'm about to resurrect it." He hung up.

HARRY'S SEAFOOD WAS a fish-and-chips joint that faced north onto the park, centrally located yet discreet enough that the most paranoid dealer could let his belly hang over his belt. Mickey pushed through the glass door. Inhaling the sweet musk of fry oil and the stench of fried cod, he adjusted to the dimness. The place was nearly empty.

Taking his spot at a booth where he could watch the front door, he ordered coffee and waited. In a short while he spotted Clint outside, dodging traffic and heading for the restaurant.

Backlit, Clint came along the row of booths, his shoulders looking full back, his sandy hair grayed by the dim light. He wore the regulation medium charcoal suit, black dress shoes and conservative tie of the government agent. A folded *Times* Classifieds peeked out of his right pocket, adding to the mock-Wall Street image. *There, but for the grace of God*— Mickey thought wryly. His own slacks and open-necked dress shirt were a sight more comfortable. Not that he wouldn't trade them in in a heartbeat.

He allowed himself a split-second of hope that Clint had brought him news of a miracle: the Institute had decided to reinstate him. But there were no miracles in Pershing Square or Greater Los Angeles or all the realm; not anymore.

In spite of his nervous anticipation, Mickey grinned, stuck out his hand. "Big Daddy still dresses you funny, you old lifer."

"Glad to see you, too," said Clint, shaking hands, sliding in and commandeering the coffee cup. He took a drink, did Groucho with his eyebrows. "Real java. Harry come into some money all of a sudden?"

Behind the Formica counter, Harry was wiping down glasses. The restaurateur sucked on the last inch of a dead cigar while he worked. Sweat sheened his jowls, and his biceps and breast flesh jiggled, burgeoning beneath a tan shirt that he should have bought at Big & Tall, but he never wanted to pay the extra ten bucks. Still, the big guy had a soft spot for folks who didn't eat right. That made him special in these parts.

"Harry's a wise and generous man," Mickey said to Clint. "He's given me a meal or two in the lean times. But he's a careful rustler, too, you know?"

"Yeah. I get giddy thinking of the knots he'd tie in the Bureau's finest, trying to pin him down." His hazel eyes glowed for a moment, then Clint quirked his mouth in derision. "Did I tell you the FBI wants full disclosure on the Aracino case? Full disclosure! On a case as sensitive as that! Paranoid bunch of mama's boys."

"The dance doesn't change, just the music," Mickey said, taking back his coffee, tasting it—doing his part to ritualize the mind game that he and Clint played in a place that could be miked.

The dinner-shift waitress pushed through the café doors. She was half his age, perhaps twenty; blond, curvy and kittenish. She glanced at him, smiled, tucked her white blouse more neatly into designer jeans. Mickey indicated coffee for Clint, and ordered the salmon for dinner. She delivered the coffee, filled Mickey's cup, cocked her hip and gave him her best man-watcher smile.

"Thanks," he said, lifting his mouth but glancing away. She wasn't his type. He hadn't met his type in many a moon.

Looking disappointed, she went to the counter, poked at the cash register.

Mickey wanted to get to the point of the meeting, but his ex-partner took out a Marlboro, lit it, exhaled sharply. "The FBI wants to know who I talked to in Guatemala," Clint said with a good show of exasperation. "Hell, Mickey, I was operating on a need-to-know deal down there, and as far as I'm concerned, they don't need to know crap. Let them figure out the network Stateside. That's their bailiwick. I'm not burning my bridges so they can look good at the next presidential."

Talking about the Aracino case was no breach of national security. Clint had brought in indictments last month on Aracino and his son-in-law. Only the bit about the FBI's frustration over not being a part of the action was news. Harmless detail that didn't affect the case, if anyone happened to overhear the conversation.

Mickey fidgeted with the pepper shaker. He wanted to know what Clint had under wraps, wanted to get to it and devour it like the pizza and beer he loved so well. "So what's coming down?" he asked for starters.

Brakes squealed outside and both men looked up. Rush-hour was in full swing.

Clint evidently was distracted from answering by the flash of the sun-shot door as it opened. A couple of gem lords came in, took a booth, ordered food.

The waitress brought the salmon to Mickey's table, bracketed the dinners with silver and napkins, and set down a basket of bread. Refilling their coffee cups, she hustled back to the kitchen. She wasn't a glutton for punishment, Mickey thought sourly. No man-watcher smile this time.

The dinner consisted of french fries, tempura broccoli spears and grilled salmon. Oil-rich as it was, at least it had food value. Mickey tasted the salmon. It was sweet and moist, grilled to perfection. He ought to want to wolf it down, but he didn't. Clint stubbed his cigarette and dug in.

Mickey pushed some broccoli to the edge of his plate. "We going to play cat and mouse all night or what?"

"Thought I'd at least let you get in a last good meal," Clint said nonchalantly. "Before I send you off the deep end again."

So it was something big, and it had to do with the stolen eighty-eight-carat emerald. Mickey's fork clattered to the plate. "Lay it out," he demanded, his heart ricocheting.

Clint gazed at Mickey's nearly full plate of food. He looked into Mickey's face, studied it. "It's killing you. You know it is."

Irritated, Mickey let out his breath. "Save the sermon. If she'd been your wife, you'd want her to pay, too."

They locked gazes for another electric moment. Then a dullness came to Clint's eyes; defeat slumped his shoulders. "Maybe that's why I'm here. They wove us out of the same stuff." He sighed, reached into his pocket, hesitated. "Just promise me one thing, Mickey."

"Give it a shot."

"Keep me posted on this one."

Again that zing of adrenaline. It made Mickey's voice thready, soft. "What do you *have,* for the love of God? The space shuttle's got nothing on you for building to a climax."

"Just . . . keep me posted."

Mickey nodded curtly. "Yes, all right. Just give."

Clint drew yesterday's *Sunday Times* Classifieds from his pocket and laid it open to the Personals. It took Mickey a moment to find the bombshell. And then it leapt at him:

$10,000 reward for information leading to recovery of Garden Emerald stolen from L.A. Jewelry Mart seventeen months ago. Contact L.J.M. c/o Grosvenor House, London.

His hand curled around the paper, crushing it. The air thinned. He felt vapor-locked, his gut sucked in. The clink of glass, the hiss of searing fish died away and a leaden silence caught him, reeled him back in time.

Johnson at headquarters had called him on the car phone, asked him to come in—*ordered it,* though Mickey outranked him. A flood of memories . . . the professionally neutral expressions of the captain, the internal security man, the investigating officer. Questions that flayed him alive . . . "Did you ever have reason to suspect your wife—Veeta—had a . . . had affairs? Did she exhibit behaviors that made you think she was criminally larcenous? Was she being blackmailed? How do you explain her involvement in the theft of the emerald? Where do you suppose she is?" The questions had seared through him, numbed him, torn his guts out. The more because he couldn't answer them.

"Just a lousy relationship," he'd said. "We were . . . closed off. Veeta complained about my being gone all the time. So I got her a job at the Jewelry Mart, with Garth."

Silence. The security man and the captain exchanged glances. "How did you know Garth?"

"Met him at a cocktail party when I was on the Smith arms case. We hit it off, played some golf together. He was looking for office help in his brokerage, so I set him up with Veeta. It gave her something to do."

They'd cross-examined him endlessly about his relationship with Garth.

Then they'd focused on Veeta again. "We had separate lives," he'd insisted. "I—didn't know her, I guess." *Didn't know she'd destroy me like this,* he wanted to scream.

Then he'd faced the humiliation of being put on temporary leave. The erosion of trust between him and his fellow officers robbed him of sleep. He was tortured when his private life was turned inside out as the Institute and the FBI both conducted investigations riddled with one-upmanship and petty suspicions.

They couldn't implicate him, but they couldn't clear him, either. So the Institute cut him loose. "In the interests of national security, to protect the Institute and the people of the United States from possible compromise at a later date—" It was a long speech that said, basically, We can't trust you anymore. You're fired.

End of a career. He could never understand why they'd fire one of their top agents because his wife was a sneak thief. It made no sense.

Garth had been sympathetic; but it had also made good business sense to show his concern by hiring him. When he hired Mickey, he got a trained bodyguard, a green gem dealer with a quick mind and a built-in suspicious nature, and a man with a vested interest in retrieving the emerald. The tediousness of the job still galled Mickey, but the money had funded his private vendetta until the leads ran out.

But now—now he'd been handed the first legitimate lead in nearly a year.

The hatred and vengeance sparked through his brain, and the half-dead hope that he could clear himself, go back to the Institute—to *life*—brought him to his feet.

"Telephone," he muttered. "British Airways' last flight is—" he checked his watch "—ninety minutes from now."

"Mickey," Clint urged, getting up. "London could be another dead-end. A trap, maybe."

Mickey's brain spun. He needed to pack a suit; Grosvenor House was a world-class hotel. He'd better take a few phone numbers so he could contact Garth's customers and put them off for a couple of days.

"Mickey—"

He turned. Clint was handing him a lump of something folded into a white napkin.

"What's this?" Mickey said, taking it, coming back to reality.

"Your lunch," Clint said, jerking his chin toward the door. "G'wan. You'll be late for school."

It struck him like an uppercut: Clint was the best thing in his life. Clint had fought the Institute to keep him, he'd punched out a fellow officer in a dispute over Mickey's character, and he'd bucked up Mickey's spirits with war stories about ongoing cases. But most of all, Clint had trusted him. It had kept him sane.

Mickey gripped Clint's arm and pumped a grin onto his face. "You're all right for a lifer. Best they come."

Clint's mouth worked. "G'wan," he said. "Beat it. Let me finish my dinner in peace."

"I'll call you," Mickey said, already striding down the line of booths. Ducking out the door, he began to run down the block toward the gem brokerage.

"L.J.M.," he mused. Who the devil was L.J.M? In London, tomorrow afternoon, he'd know.

A sweet sharp pain went through him, an ache of longing for revenge. Then there was only the thrill of knowing the chase had begun again, and he was alive with it.

Chapter Two

Beautiful, Laura thought, gazing down through the dining room window of a suite in Grosvenor House. Hyde Park was all velvet with the mist falling on the trees. Twenty years of English gardens and landscapes, and still the lushness was startling, compared to the parched tans and sage greens of her Southern California birthplace.

Drawing a breath—inhaling serenity and lodging it inside—she settled her shoulders. Ten minutes to go. Ten minutes, and then maybe the specter of John's death would begin to recede.

The hotel staff had handled everything—taking Stone's phone call, arranging the meeting time, the light lunch, the flowers, the protocol to be followed when Stone arrived. Jimmy Welch, the world-renowned front hall manager of Grosvenor House, would personally ask for identification, phone the suite, escort him up. And Hendley would be here to admit him.

Mingling with the fragrance of roses from the centerpiece on the table, a brisk scent of sliced lemon wafted to her from the silver tea service. Everything was highly controlled and elegant.

That was partly for impact. Most Americans, like herself when she'd arrived in London as a young newlywed twenty-two years ago, loved to experience a "proper" English moment, and she wanted the benefit of impressing her guest, if that were possible.

On the other hand, booking a suite in one of London's leading hotels minimized the risk of danger to herself. What kind of man was Stone? She didn't know, other than that he was connected to, or interested in, a very rare stolen emerald worth a million dollars. The solicitousness of the staff, the elegance, the presence of Hendley and, because of the status of the hotel's clientele, the unstated notion that police protection was a phone call away—all were intended to intimidate a ruffian, impress an average Joe or allow Laura to hold her own with a dignitary. Used to a protected and dignified life-style, Laura assumed, then, that she was armed to meet any personality who walked through the door.

Yet she shivered as another tremor of anxiety ran through her.

Hendley's Oxford accent came to her from the doorway of the servant's quarters. "Is everything to your liking, Mrs. Marley? Will there be anything else?"

Laura turned to the rangy Englishman who'd served ten years as director of operations for Marley Enterprises. There was a London *Times* tucked under his arm. He'd come prepared for a long wait.

"Just that I'm grateful for your understanding," she said. "Getting the emerald back is crucial to me, to the company. With that infant-care order from Brit Hospital already under our belts, if we get the emerald back to Mr. Sutama where it belongs, we really will be in the black, Hendley. We won't have to struggle for every deal we close. They'll believe in us again."

"Not to worry, Mrs. M.," he said gently. "And I'm with you one hundred percent, whether we get the jewel back or not. You know that."

"I know. That's what I'm trying to say. If you weren't here, or weren't so very good at handling things with the clients while I'm picking away at this gem situation, I'm afraid I'd be a bundle of nerves. Especially about meeting Stone."

Mischief danced in his tawny eyes. "Shall I hover? Play the eavesdropping butler? How should you like me to play it, Mrs. Marley?" He grew mockingly pensive. "Actually, I rather like playing Watson to your Sherlock. We'll sell the rights to the BBC, shall we, after it's over?"

Laura knew instantly that he was telling her to relax, loosen up, stay with her strong suit, which was running things. She smiled. "Hover, I think, Hendley. We'll want Mr. Stone to feel your protective presence but not have to deal with it, if you know what I mean. I would have you sit in with us, but that might inhibit candor."

"Quite right. Hovering it is."

"Good. I'll go and look properly engrossed in my work until you announce him."

A last apprehensive look out into the park, and Laura went into the sitting room. Shipping contracts she'd been working on earlier were stacked beside her open briefcase on a Louis XIV lamp table. The lamplight cast warmth over the papers, the pale gray carpet, the blue-and-gray floral pattern of the couch cushions, the landscape above the fireplace. Her personal decorating taste was more eclectic, more relaxed, but she felt confident among the cool blues, the dark woods of this hotel room that had housed nobility and celebrities through the sixty-odd years of its history.

As she sat down in the chair and picked up a shipping agreement, she fanned her royal-blue silk skirt around her, tucked up a tendril of fine-spun brown hair and began to read.

But the coming meeting with Stone distracted her, the importance of it harassed her composure. The insurance company, with whom her late husband, John, had dealt, had paid the claim for the missing gem. Their detectives had tried to trace it, had failed and given up, and her Japanese client, Sutama, had bought a villa for his betrothed instead of the emerald. Still, Sutama had lost face. As a result, he had cut back the number of containers of stereo systems and clock radios that Marley Enterprises brokered for him worldwide.

That had dealt a serious blow to John. He grew morose. He mumbled. He refused to answer Laura's concerned questions, refused to see the children, refused to eat decently. He stayed out late and came home with a stubbled face and haunted eyes.

Remembering, Laura cringed inwardly. In personal terms, losing the gem had cost them so very much. And *why* things had ended so tragically was still a haunting mystery. A nightmare of unanswerable questions and guilt.

If she could shed no light on John's misery before he died, at least getting the emerald back would change the financial picture.

Something in her refused to believe the gem was lost forever. Somehow it must be recovered. And she must be involved; that seemed essential to her, though she couldn't explain her obsession to Hendley, who'd raised his eyebrows when she'd resorted to placing the ad.

She'd had two other calls before Stone's. A vague tip from a furniture rep in Los Angeles—still a Marley client—and another from someone wanting to open negotiations in case the emerald was recovered. She'd put the latter man off. She needed to keep focused. This man Stone might be the only concrete lead she'd get in time. She had to handle the interview with supreme tact.

A tightness gripped her chest. It was as if the long period of mourning, the guilts, the excruciating dullness of her life despite the pressures of running the business alone—all of it—was like a long-held breath she was about to expel. How would it be to breathe again? To feel alive? Her brow creased. Would Stone be her ticket back to vitality, to life?

She needed him to be, she thought. She was only forty-two but felt much, much older.

She needed to get out into the world, fill up the emptiness of herself, find the emerald—and still the demons of her conscience.

Terrible to put such importance on a meeting with a stranger. But he *had* come all the way from California in response to her ad. Surely that meant he had something significant to tell her.

Waiting like this for Stone reminded her of the nights. Some of them were nightmares while she waited for sleep. After an exhausting day at the office, not even a hard workout at the health club or an evening at the Barbican could stop the loneliness from dropping over her like a sodden wool blanket. She lay in the king-size Queen Anne four-poster, sleepless, restless, her insecurities like pitchforks jabbing her in the airless cocoon of her isolation.

It was then she dreamed of the emerald. Large as a fat, juicy key lime, perfectly faceted, it cooled the cup of her hand. She held it up to the sun and it gleamed with a rich kelly brilliance. She envisioned traveling to Japan, handing it to Sutama, the man who wanted it for his fiancée; imagined his smile, his gratitude at regaining face, his awe at the magnificence of the gem. She conjured up the satisfaction she would feel at completing the task that had seemed to emotionally cripple John Marley just before his death.

She would personally hand over the gem. Surely then her demons would retire to hell.

A knock on the door in the foyer startled her. As muted voices completed the introductions, Laura settled her gaze on the columns of figures in the contract—and fought the urge to stop breathing.

THE ENGLISHMAN WHO'D introduced himself as Hendley behaved like a butler: bowing Mickey in, not offering to shake hands, taking his raincoat—but Mickey sensed the astuteness of a Wall Street banker in Hendley's scrutiny. Something about the moment made Mickey glad he'd worn Italian leather shoes that shone and a Bijon silk-wool suit of subdued charcoal and black stripes. The suit camouflaged the weight he'd lost in the past seventeen months, and gave him the air of a wealthy businessman making his last call of the day before heading for a snifter and cigar at the club.

Approval seemed to flicker in Hendley's fawnskin gaze. Then, folding the coat over his arm, the man said in Oxford tones, "This way, Mr. Stone."

Mickey followed him through the entry into a dining room smelling of roses and the cloverlike scent of scones and cream. It stirred memories of his childhood in the Hill District of San Francisco. He noted the familiar formality of silver serving dishes, gleaming candelabra, white linen. L.J.M. indeed went first-cabin, he concluded; even to the artfully arranged pastries and crustless sandwiches cut into rosette and diamond shapes. The spread would rival his mother's panache in laying out lunch.

Despite his outward demeanor, Mickey felt uneasy. He'd been valuable to the Institute for many reasons, not the least of which was his ability to maneuver in any setting. But his ex-wife's betrayal had changed all that. Now he felt more at home slithering among the dregs of society, and that only because a gut-gnawing revenge made him fearless in his pursuit of her. Tense with unaccustomed restraint, he resolved to override the reserve this formal setting required and get to the purpose of the meeting.

The memories and feelings flashed through him, and then Hendley was ushering him forward into a living room done in muted blues and grays. A marvelous landscape focused the eye over the fireplace. Beyond the couch and coffee table, a woman sat working beside an open briefcase.

"Mrs. Marley," Hendley said with somber respect. "Mr. Stone is arrived."

Mrs. Marley was a still life of mature beauty and flawless composure as, ensconced in a wingback, she studied some typed pages. Royal-blue silk draped around her slim wrists and fell in folds to perfectly-matched silk pumps. Lighted from behind, her profile was pale and smooth and reminiscent of a fine cameo. Her neck curved downward to

the task of reading, and the sweetness of the curve, graced
by tendrils of brown hair, tugged at Mickey.

A moment longer, and she looked up. "Thank you,
Hend—" she drew a small breath as her eyes met Mickey's, and then she finished, "—Hendley."

She put away the papers and allowed herself a brief scan
of Mickey's appearance. Her gaze came back to his face.

"Welcome to London, Mr. Stone," she said, sounding
American.

Her eyes were startling: blue as a desert sky, alive with
intelligence and perception and curiosity. But there were
shadows beneath them, as if she needed to rest. He logged
in this detail.

Mickey came forward, stopped in front of her, offered
his hand.

Without hesitating, she reached up. Her fingers were
cool, smooth and strong; a welcoming but reserved greet-
ing. Small stains of color tinted her cheekbones. Perhaps
he hadn't noticed her true coloring from across the room;
or she had just reacted to him in a very feminine way.

"L.J.M.?" he asked softly.

"Yes," she said. "Thank you for coming."

She withdrew her hand, then gestured toward the couch.

Hendley cleared his throat. "Will there be anything else,
Mrs. Marley?"

"Coffee, please, Hendley. Or perhaps Mr. Stone would
like tea? A cocktail?"

"Coffee, thanks," said Mickey, settling into the cushions and girding his emotions. Mrs. Marley was a siren in
a silver setting, he decided. He wanted her, Mr. Marley or
no, and that was a complication he could not permit.

While Hendley brought in the refreshments, set out
plates of sandwiches and pastries, and poured coffee, Mrs.
Marley asked about Mickey's flight.

"Uneventful," he responded. "I slept a little. Treated
myself to the Underground, since I had the extra time before our meeting."

"Your first time on the Underground?"

"No. I've been in London several times."

"On business, Mr. Stone? Or vacationing?"

"Business."

She glanced down and he got the impression she was pleased. *Yes, Mrs. Marley,* he wanted to say, *we're equals.* At least intrinsically. Mickey decided he would cut through the preliminaries as soon as the servant was gone.

She accepted a cup of black coffee from Hendley. The man's back was turned, and Mickey noted the fit of his brown suit. Well-made, perhaps even Savile Row. And no bulge where a gun might be.

Hendley served Mickey. Then he glanced toward Mrs. Marley. She nodded, dismissing him. Hendley bowed deferentially and went toward the dining room.

Mickey heard a door open. It didn't close. Not only doting, Mickey deducted, but protective—from a respectful distance. Adding cream and sugar to his coffee, he mentally shook his head at the assumption the wealthy made about their own safety. He could have been an ax murderer.

Picking up his coffee cup, he said to the very pampered, proper Mrs. Marley, "I take it your husband won't be joining us," and took a drink, watching her.

Her eyes darkened. "No," she said, clasping her hands in her lap. "My husband...died a year ago last November."

A widow. Three months after the theft. Mickey thought back. He'd been on that wild-goose chase in Alaska—Anchorage, Sitka, a puddle jumper to Juneau in midsnowstorm to deliver the Teals' wedding ring—wrung out, strung out, full of rage. It had been his first errand for Garth, complicated by a false lead on the emerald.

And she'd been dealing with death. "I'm sorry," he said, feeling a mixture of sympathy and suspicion.

She inclined her head. Took a breath. "Mr. Stone. Let's get down to it, all right?"

"I'd like that," he said, surprised.

She smiled—a radiance tinged with vulnerability. "Good. Recovering the emerald is important to me, crucial to the family business. I'm hoping you'll be the key to its recovery."

Exactly my hope about you, he thought. "What kind of business is it?"

"Marley Enterprises wholesales goods internationally. Furniture, electronics, inflatable toys, clothing."

"What's your connection to the Garden Emerald?"

She straightened her back, a sign she chafed at his taking charge. "Mr. Stone, what is your connection?" she asked bluntly.

"Mrs. Marley, we could play croquet again, or we could cover the ground we need to cover in order to find out how we can help each other."

She bit her lip. Abruptly she rose, and Mickey tried not to be distracted by the shimmer of blue silk over wonderful curves as she began to pace in front of the table. "It began as a personal favor, really," she said. "John mentioned the gem to a Japanese client of ours, a wealthy man who wanted the emerald as a betrothal gift."

"John?"

"My husband."

Present tense. He noticed how softly she spoke about him. There was feeling there. It bothered Mickey for some reason, and he sounded abrupt even to himself when he said, "Go on."

"Mr. Sutama, my client, put a substantial deposit on the stone. When it was stolen, it put a black mark on the reputation of my company. I want Mr. Sutama to have the emerald."

"How'd your husband know about it?"

"The Demude family of Amsterdam owned it. John's father had known the senior Mr. Demude for years. The Demudes were in financial trouble and decided to liquidate their assets, the emerald included. They asked John to handle it."

Recognition stabbed through him. "The Garden Emerald has been in the Demude family since the forties," he said. "I wondered why it came on the market."

She stopped pacing to stare at him. "You know the history of the gem?"

"Some of it. Demude was involved in the early German V-1 and V-2 rocket programs. That piece of business allowed him to hold on to the emerald during the war. Afterward, Demude cut a deal with the U.S. to help deliver intact the technology of the German rocket program. Bingo, his assets solidified again and, no doubt, his fortunes increased. Evidently his luck didn't hold."

Laura came within two feet of him, sending him the scent of a dreamy, feminine perfume. But there was nothing feminine about her eyes. They were icy with suspicion. "Who are you?" she demanded. "What is your connection with the gem?"

He gave it to her straight. "My wife helped to steal it."

The cameo lost a layer of pink. She backed up a step. "Helped...steal it?"

He stood up. "No conclusions without the facts, Mrs. Marley, if you don't mind. I was an agent for the National Security Institute at the time." His voice grew harsh. "Her involvement cost me my career."

"How was she involved?"

"She was a girl Friday for the Garth Gem Brokerage. Evidence suggests that when the gem was delivered by courier to the brokerage—where she was a trusted employee, I might add, since I was a top-security agent—she simply signed for the gem, took it into a stretch limo parked down the alley and drove off into the sunset. Her accomplice was a criminal known as The Tape. He's a sleaze bucket who deals in blackmarket videos and runs a number of fronts from pizza parlors to food concessions all over the Southwest."

She gave a small laugh of doubt. "This criminal was a friend of the wife of a government agent, Mr. Stone? It stretches credibility."

"Does it?" he snapped. "The Institute gave me heart-burn over that, too." He smiled bitterly. "That was before they laid it out for me. Come to find out, Mrs. Marley, Veeta and The Tape were lovers, not just friends."

"Lovers," she echoed. But she was not scandalized, he saw; only shocked. That meant she hadn't been buried alive in the social register. She took a few steps, twisting her fingers, maybe attempting to weigh his probable guilt against his losses. "Then," she said, glancing back at him, steering directly into his most bitter memories, "it cost you your marriage, too?"

"Only in fact."

"What do you mean?"

"I filed for divorce, but it was a bad marriage, anyway."

"Of course. Otherwise, why would you put the emphasis on career. The important loss was your job."

"It was much more than a job, Mrs. Marley."

A second passed. "Laura," she said, suddenly moving to her chair, sitting down, arranging her skirt. "My name is Laura. We both have a great deal to gain by getting the emerald back. And we both know crucial bits and pieces about the theft." She took a breath, then beckoned him to be seated. "Shall we compare notes and decide what to do?"

Mickey was taken off guard. He had to relax his stance, unbend stiff muscles, loosen the determination on his face. He walked to the fireplace, put an elbow on the mantel and studied the brush strokes in the landscape. Did she believe him that easily? Or did she already know who he was and plan to use his contacts to get the emerald back so she could restore her company's reputation? But that gave them a common goal, didn't it? Her surprise at his knowledge of the gem's history and her shock at his ex-wife's involvement seemed genuine. What was making him hesitate?

Finally it surfaced. He'd known Demude was the seller, Sutama the buyer and Garth the middleman. Who had left out the Marley link—Garth . . . or the U.S. Government?

To answer that crucial question and get the gem back, he needed Laura's cooperation, not her animosity. He'd better play along.

Behind him, silver clinked against porcelain. "Turkey or creamed cheese sandwiches, Mr. Stone?" she asked, her voice trembling slightly.

So she was unnerved, too. Playing the hostess to regain control. It gave him a nudge of self-confidence. But he wished she was a street urchin, greedy and lacking the subtleties of breeding, instead of self-contained and surrounded by the armor of wealth and protocol. Even her name had class. Things were simpler on the streets. The Achilles' heel was easier to find. What was Laura's weakness? he wondered.

"A sandwich, Mr. Stone?" she repeated.

Running an impatient hand through his hair, Mickey faced her and said, "One of each and a beer if you have it."

She arched a brow. "Since we need each other and may be working together, shall we switch to self-serve? It'll save time." She used a pair of serving tongs to point toward the dining room. They shook slightly. "Bottles of Guinness and cans of American beer in the cooler on the sideboard. Opener on the tray next to them."

"I bet you run a mean board meeting," he said, heading for the beer.

Hendley materialized in the doorway to an adjoining room. Mickey saluted him and said, "We're on self-serve now. She wants to get down to brass tacks."

He thought he saw the ghost of a smile at Hendley's mouth, but the man only said, "Very good, sir," and bowed out of sight.

Mickey dug a can of brew out of the ice and popped it open. He considered using one of the glasses on the tray, but dismissed the nicety and took a slug from the can. It bit his throat on the way down, then jolted him with a refreshing zing. "God love you, woman," he muttered and returned to the sitting room.

Laura nibbled at a sandwich. "I heard yesterday that the emerald was coming back into circulation," she said around a morsel of food.

Mickey stopped dead, his heart rocketing crazily. " 'Heard' it was coming on the market? Just like that?"

"Mmm." She put down the sandwich and looked at him. "Through the grapevine. You know, a rumor from a friend of a friend. In response to my ad."

He set down the beer. "Where? When? Is the source reliable?"

"I don't know. Yes, probably. It's a rumor, no detail, no certainty. I got the information from a client—a furniture rep who knows a man in the gem business." She laughed. "Mr. Stone, we're both Americans. We can dispense with last names, can't we?"

"What?" he said, his mind running.

"What's your first name?"

"Mickey, it's Mickey. Where can I find the furniture guy?"

"Where can *we* find him, Mickey. *We* are going to find him in Los Angeles. Tomorrow, if all goes well. I'll pay all expenses. Have a sandwich. We'll make a plan."

Mickey was reeling. She'd hit him with zinger after zinger—news of the gem, going back to talk to a lead that had been right under his nose in L.A., her tagging along. He was losing his objectivity.

He turned, glanced into the dining room. Hendley was fiddling with dishes—listening in because of the raised voices. But not armed, and therefore of little threat should they argue about the plan of attack.

And they would argue, he knew. Laura was a wealthy woman who had time but no wedding ring on her hands; a take-charge kind of woman who thought it was her duty and her right to go gallivanting around the world in search of the emerald, the dangers be damned. Oh, yes, they would argue. The anger was already flaring through him.

He didn't trust her. Was she a thrill seeker, like Veeta? Was she ambitious, like Veeta?

One thing he knew: She was the first woman in years to trigger every male start button he possessed. She was beautiful, feminine, seemingly vulnerable. His shoulders and thighs felt like granite boulders near her fragility. Something urgent turned inside him when she moved.

Beautiful woman... money... gem. Despite his training as an agent, that combination had duped him before, ruined him. No woman was going to get her hooks into him like Veeta had.

If this London-based American widow could help him get the gem back, avenge himself with Veeta and clear his name, he'd use her. If seduction was a bonus he could pay himself, all the better.

But success depended on running the case his way. No interference. Optimum cooperation.

He let the information he'd learned about her filter through him for a moment longer. Then he asked the question hovering there, needing to be asked. "Mrs. Marley... how did your husband die?"

Utter silence. He took his time turning around. Looking at her, he felt a pull in his gut. It was as if he'd struck her. Her fingers whitened as she gripped the plate of food. Her face was bleached marble. Her eyes were lavender, wide with memories so painful they engulfed her spirit. Guilt, horror, loss. He read each emotion and recognized it, felt it rip through him.

Still he held her gaze, demanding an answer. "How did he die?"

Chapter Three

Stone's question jammed Laura's mind with painful memories: her daughter Jessica's grief-ravaged face after the funeral when there was nothing for it but to accept that her father was dead; John, Jr.'s pale face, a mask stretched over muscles that refused to bend to the grief, because the sudden, useless death made her son question his self-confident belief that the world was solid, safe.

This past fall their marks at university had dropped off, and lately they'd been too busy to come to Sunday dinner, being wrapped up, Jessica explained, in school activities. Laura didn't begrudge them the social life; she was glad they had friends and a place to fit in. Yet she knew they were covering up isolation and confusion, just as she was by working even longer hours than when John was alive.

Why did their father die? Laura asked herself for the thousandth time. Had she not made him happy enough? Surely she'd hidden the occasional boredom and loneliness she'd felt during the precious years they'd been together. She'd been as stiff-upper-lipped as her English counterparts, the women famous for their forebearance, when John had taken those endless business trips and left her home, wishing she was with him, longing to live the adventurous life by his side.

She and John had been friends; as close, anyway, as she imagined was possible in partnership types of marriages. She missed him as she missed the loving support and understanding of her parents, who'd died five years ago of complications from the Asian flu.

How did your husband die? The tall man with the fire in his green eyes waited for her answer. "It was a good relationship," she whispered. Yet John Marley had wanted to die. *Why?*

Laura searched Mickey's face, the craggy lines shaded by that inky ruffle of hair that seemed to crackle with vitality; the complexion weathered by stress and experience, the generous mouth tautened by bitterness. Everything the opposite of John, who'd had a banker's hands and an intellectual's hairline and the smooth face of an aging adolescent. Stone's face was too demanding, too harsh. There was no understanding in him, only an angry impatience. And yet . . . her son sometimes looked like that, and she knew the good in him.

How hard it was to tell this aloof, predatory man about John! She couldn't. The words stuck in her throat. Her eyes wanted to brim over with grief and guilt, but she managed to stem all except a vision-dulling dampness, a sugary hoarseness in her voice. "I don't know why he wanted to die," she said, feeling shame heat her face. "We'd had some minor financial setbacks, but it was nothing that couldn't be righted with some restructuring in the past year. I just don't know."

"Suicide," Mickey Stone murmured, and it was like a spear thrust through her.

He seemed cruelly familiar with her demons. It took Laura some moments to realize how he'd put his uncanny perceptiveness to such devastating purpose. Then anger at his callousness stiffened her back. "Yes, suicide," she bit out. "And there's an end to it. We'll discuss the emerald, but my marriage is off limits. Agree to those terms or leave this room."

With the grace of the predator he was, he moved to the couch, sat down. "Laura, this obviously hurts you," he said with a softness that was almost a purr. "We'll take it in stages, all right? Tell me whatever you can."

For a moment, his kindness took her off guard and she let out a relieved breath. Then her instincts flashed a bright message: Danger.

Stone was too knowing, too clever, too manipulative. He was desperate to find the gem, more desperate than she, an inner voice said. He had nothing to lose—he'd lost nearly everything of importance to him—and he'd stoop to any manipulation, no matter the cost to others.

She was in a fight to regain something lost in herself, as, perhaps, he was. But she had a great deal to lose if he destroyed her: she had children and clients and employees relying on her. Getting the emerald was to restore her business reputation, but more than that, it was to be a catharsis that made her whole. She wouldn't step on people to reach her goal. And she refused to be crushed by Stone's ambition.

Laura put off answering by sliding the plate across the table, reaching into her briefcase for a tissue. She folded it, refolded it, thinking....

Stone's investigative skills and contacts might have saved her some time, but she didn't *need* his help, she decided. Sending him packing didn't mean the end to her quest. She could contact his former employer, ask for their cooperation, piece the case back together on her own. She could go to Los Angeles and trace the link to the gem dealer. And perhaps others would respond to her ad.

Yes, Stone's abrupt gentleness only underscored the danger he represented. She couldn't possibly chase down the emerald by his side. It would be like handing her damaged inner self to the jackals. The U.S. government didn't trust him, and neither could she.

She put the tissue aside.

"Mr. Stone," she said cooly. "Obviously you didn't come to give information but to get it. I'm deeply disappointed, but business has taught me to cut my losses and find alternatives to reach my goals. Thank you for coming all this way." She stood up. "I wish you the best of luck in pursuing the gem on your own."

"Now wait just a minute—"

"No, you wait." As he rose to face her, she held his incredulous gaze with all the anger and disappointment she felt. "You're here under false pretences. You led me to believe you had information leading to the whereabouts of the gem. That's what I advertised for and that's what I expected of you. Not some personal—" she wound her hands together "—interrogation of my private life." She glanced toward the dining room. "Hendley—"

He appeared in the doorway. "Yes, Mrs. Marley?"

"Please see Mr. Stone out and then call for the car. I'll be going to the office for the rest of the day."

Beside her, Stone muttered an expletive. "Hendley," he said with a wave, "hold on a sec."

Hendley looked at Laura. "Mrs. Marley?"

"Mr. Stone is leaving," she said.

"No, I'm not, Hendley," Stone said, sending her a level look. "I don't think Mrs. Marley fully understands what my leaving will mean to her. I doubt, for example, that she'd have much time for business if I leave here now. She'll be too busy answering inquiries by MI5, MI6, NSI, the State Department and any other government agency in Holland and Japan that I can interest in the international conspiracy that obviously took place in the case of the Garden Emerald."

Hendley looked askance. "Perhaps we should hear what Mr. Stone has to say, Mrs. Marley?"

Laura's anger seethed and boiled against the injustice of being threatened by Stone. She held herself very erect, stared hard at Stone's craggy, smug face, and spoke through a jaw clenched with indignation. "You must be deluded by the depths of your personal loss in the case, Mr. Stone. What 'international conspiracy'?"

As in-command as a defence attorney who finally has the attention of the jury in a murder trial, Stone bowed slightly, walked to the fireplace and faced them. "Do you want him to hear this?" He indicated Hendley.

"Hendley is my managing director," Laura said bluntly. "He'll stay."

Stone smiled a private smile that said, I never supposed he was a butler. He said, "Very well, why do you suppose I never heard the Marley name while investigations were in progress on the case?"

"I presume because you were a suspect," she said.

His face darkened but he continued levelly, "I had access to all evidence up to the time I was released from service. None of it mentioned Marley as the middleman in the gem transfer. Demude, Garth, Sutama. That was the progression."

The implications of what Stone was saying chilled her blood. Laura walked to the window and gazed with blurred focus at the park. She rubbed her arms.

The governments of Holland and Japan might create unpleasant controversy for Demude, a family friend, and Sutama, still a valued client. News of that might erode the reputation of the company even further. And Britain might misconstrue John's role in the gem transfer. Who knew but that they might change their mind, take it in a bad light, his involvement, his later suicide. Perhaps even Jessica and John, Jr. would be interrogated, harassed by the press, scorned by their peers. That was unthinkable!

Her instincts about Stone's jugular methods were confirmed, and she felt dragged against her will to the lip of an abyss.

Ridiculous turn of events, she railed. She was not one to feel victimized, usually, but the reins of control were slipping away and she felt the heady frightening rush of vertigo—as if she'd stepped over an edge she could not see and was reaching for a branch that was invisible but there, somehow there.

Above all, she felt the quicksand-like chemistry between them, she and Stone: subtle crosscurrents of desire, sparks of excitement; challenge, wariness, intelligence, personal needs—mixed up in them and between them and around them, like volatile fumes waiting for the match to strike.

Sleep, that treasured fugitive, would be elusive this night, she realized.

"Mrs. Marley?"

"Yes, Hendley," she said without turning around. She drew a deep breath, willing the serenity in, trying to expel the confusion and fear.

"May I suggest we sit down and discuss the situation. See what can be done?"

"Yes, of course. I was only—" she lifted her shoulders, faced them "—thinking of the children. I haven't told them yet that I'm leaving."

Abruptly Stone stepped away from the hearth. "That won't be necessary," he said. "I can look into things in L.A. Let you know what I find out."

Laura stared at Mickey Stone in silence, as if debating the wisdom of his plan. She had expected his resistence; already knew what her answer would be. She let the silence lengthen until the tension vibrated in the room.

"Mr. Stone," she said at last, with a hard edge to her voice. "We'll go to Los Angeles together. We'll chase down leads together. We'll compare notes and decide what to do next—together, is that understood? Until the gem is in my hands. We'll do that or I'll go completely on my own. I'll call on your friends at NSI. I'll visit the L.A. contact myself. I'll piece things together alone, and you can whistle 'Dixie' for information. Your threats about international conspiracies be damned!"

Hendley looked to be keeping a "jolly well put!" in check. He beamed at her.

Stone's eyes glittered dangerously. "NSI wouldn't let you through the door. You need me for that. Besides, I have most of the pertinent information, anyway."

"Classified information?"

"You could call it that."

"Isn't that illegal, Mr. Stone?"

He smiled slowly. "Are you thinking of blackmailing me, Mrs. Marley? I let you be the boss or you'll tell on me?"

"Extortion was what you had in mind for me, wasn't it? Why should the rules change now?"

"In that case, you might as well make a citizen's arrest now and be done with it." He grinned widely and held out his arms, wrists together. "You have to read me my rights, otherwise it isn't legal."

Hendley was vastly amused by the verbal swordplay. He practically croaked aloud. Laura shot him daggers, and he did a nimble about-face, saying, "I'll just get my brief-case, shall I?" He disappeared.

Laura was stunned by Hendley's behavior and felt be-trayed. "Excuse me," she muttered to Stone, and walked as regally as possible into the servant's room.

"Hendley," she said tersely, coming up behind him. "Whose side are you on, anyway?"

"Why, yours, Mrs. Marley, as always."

"Then why are you behaving as if every word Stone ut-ters is bloody Shakespeare?"

"Have I done?" Hendley met her irritation with aplomb. "I do apologize, immediately. It's just that, well, Stone's turn of phrase isn't bad, is it? 'Read me my rights,' and so on. If we're going to the BBC with this when it's over, we'll need those crusty bits, won't we?"

"Hendley, if you continue with this, I'll—"

Hendley stuck his wrists out. "Cuff me?" He chuckled. "Look, Mrs. M., you couldn't have ordered up a better accomplice for your adventure if you'd had the queen's command, now could you? A top-flight investigator!"

"Ex-investigator," she pointed out, beginning to lighten up.

"With a macabre sense of humor and enough macho to—"

"He's dangerous," Laura countered.

"Very," Hendley agreed, tucking a note pad under his arm. His eyebrows crept into contact. "I'm told one fights fire with fire, Mrs. Marley. *Criminals* have the emerald. And you're at checkmate with Stone, who's got all the proper credentials to get it back."

She pursed her lips, thinking aloud. "I'll have to smooth his bloody ego, I suppose."

"Mmm, yes, definitely. Over lunch?"

"Right. I'll agree to introduce him to Gregorgi in L.A., and to let him—no, not let him. I'll *rely* on Stone for the strategies. As long as he agrees to keep me completely informed of the strategies and let me—" she said this last with distaste "—let me play a small but active part in finding the emerald. That ought to be enough female dependence to put Stone's macho ego into retirement, Hendley."

"The perfect amount, given your position, Mrs. Marley. Shall we?"

Laura headed for the living room with what she hoped was an adequately humble demeanor: a slight but conciliatory smile and the words, "We need each other" at the ready. And she prayed Stone was a man of his word.

IN THE MANOR HOUSE, in a bedroom that felt like spring with its purple-and-white-and-green decor and its vases of silk flowers, Laura packed at a furious rate.

Stone had said, "act the rich widow." Into the cases gaping open on the four-poster bed went a burgundy-and-black designer suit, rubies and diamonds for accent. In next, a navy-blue Johnathan knit, natural pearls, matching heels and clutch purse; an extra traveling suit; a dinner dress with a black-lace décolletage; slacks, sweaters, sleeping attire. Too much, she thought, unpacking and repacking it all.

The shoes! she recalled, panicked that she might forget something he would think was important. Comfortable walking shoes, but elegant, he'd said. She packed low-heeled kid pumps from Spain and Paris. And jogging shoes for good measure.

One after the other, the accoutrements of an elegant-but-stifled life—folded and tucked and scented with sachet; packed and unpacked, deliberated upon and packed again.

She remembered her passport and went back to the safe near the dressing room door. Thank God she'd gone to Germany this year to talk to the hospital baby-bed people.

Otherwise she'd have had to update it for the trip to Los Angeles.

Where was he right now? she wondered, thinking of Stone with more warmth, now that she was well and truly going with him. He'd refused to sleep in one of the guest rooms. Preferred to get a quiet bed-and-breakfast, he'd said. Get a look at Old London. Wander a bit.

She'd had a meeting with Hendley on the Brit Hospital account, and she'd had to rush to the bank to arrange a transfer of funds to Los Angeles per Stone's instructions. And she'd had to pack, of course. That was an hours-long project in itself, as it turned out.

She should have insisted he stay here, she thought, locking up the cases. A twinge of conscience tried to wend its way into her flighty good spirits, but she dashed it properly with a reminder: Stone was a desperate man and entirely too appealing. If she wanted to come home to London better off than when she left, distance and decorum were her best policy. Let him have his night of solitary London, she reiterated, this time with finality. She had phone calls to make to the children, a nice cup of Earl Grey to sip by the fire, and a wonderfully exciting imagination to carry her through till morning.

At 8:00 a.m., the car would come and she'd be on her way to Gatwick and the great beyond. Stone would meet her at the check-in desk.

Unbidden, a brief joy darted through her and she hugged herself. *It's not because I'm going to see him tomorrow,* she told herself. *It's because of the great adventure ahead. That, and the prospect of getting the emerald back.*

After months of loneliness, guilt and self-doubt, the veil of darkness had risen from her shoulders and she felt, this night, young and free.

Chapter Four

"Maybe it was a hit," Mickey offered quietly.

"Preposterous," Laura responded as the jet taxied to a stop at the gate at Los Angeles International Airport. "It was an overdose of sleeping pills that killed John. Let's leave it at that, okay? We've had a lovely flight. Let's not spoil it now. Besides, we've got to get off the plane."

"Off?" Mickey blinked and narrowed his eyes toward the sunshine outside. "Right," he said as if coming out of a spell. He ducked down to his carry-on satchel and tucked away a tattered *Field & Stream* magazine that he'd evidently planned to read. He'd never even opened its cover.

To Laura's relief, there was no more time to continue the discussion about John that Stone had abruptly begun moments ago, after hours of really delightful chit-chat. She and Stone debarked, cleared customs and took Mickey's blue six-year-old Chevrolet to her hotel. Stone saw her checked in, then left for his office.

At Stone's suggestion, Hendley had booked her a suite at the prestigious Los Angeles Biltmore Hotel. It was a four-star hotel, eleven stories of brick, with beige keystones at the seams of the three wings facing Pershing Square. Frescoes, murals, cherubs and angels adorned the public rooms, putting Laura in mind of fourteenth-century Italy. Conveniently, her rooms looked on the square, and the Garth Gem Brokerage, Stone's headquarters, was only a block and a half away.

Hendley had also arranged with the management to in-
stall a small computer, telex, fax machine and second telephone so she could conduct the business of Marley
Enterprises during down times in the Garden Emerald case.
The office equipment would be set up tomorrow while she
and Stone were visiting Gregorgi at the Los Angeles Furniture Mart.

Laura unpacked, changed into a white shell beneath a
chocolate-brown cardigan and slacks, and put on walking
shoes. Slipping money and credit cards into a brown velvet
clutch, she locked the suite and came down to the street to
take a look at the famous center of the gem trade in Los
Angeles, Pershing Square. He'd made it sound glamorous,
Stone had. She couldn't wait to explore the neighborhood.

It was sunset and the strips of glass in the high rise facing the Biltmore across the square blazed with magenta.
Other city buildings rose above the four streets that framed
the square; entire five- and fifteen- and twenty-story
buildings filled with precious gems and jewelry. She looked
above her. Floor after floor of locked glass offices har-
bored gem lords and their caches of riches. That's what
Stone had described to her on the plane. And she was here
to find the prize of them all, the Garden Emerald.

She felt a sudden gratitude toward Stone. After they'd
agreed to the terms of their association, he'd become almost chivalrous—offering suggestions about where to stay,
explaining the basics of the gem trade during the flight,
seeing her moved into the suite, then discreetly disappear-
ing while she unpacked and freshened up. He'd made the
trip seem like a vacation, so far.

She wished he'd agreed to come back to show her the
square. She wanted to see a dealer "memo" a white packet
of gems to someone, and wasn't sure she'd recognize the
transaction unless it was pointed out. But Stone had said he
wanted to touch base with a few of his people, so she was
on her own.

Nothing new about that, she told herself, listening to the
familiar roar and squeak of the city she and her older sis-

ter had shopped in as young women, before Laura had moved to London with John, and her sister had settled in New York to design women's fashions. She was used to being alone, Laura mused—after fourteen months of it. But she still didn't like it.

She tilted her chin, recognizing the scent of diesel and smog and wealth that belonged uniquely to Los Angeles. Tomorrow would be the beginning of the great hunt for the emerald. They'd strike out on the first lead. Stone had agreed they'd trace the first ones together, with him acting the wealthy widow's protector.

No one but her would know how truly contrived the wealthy part was. And no one knew yet, especially not Laura, whether Mickey would turn out to be protector or predator. All she knew was that, albeit unwillingly, he'd given her a second chance at life, and for that she was grateful. She virtually tingled with the excitement of it.

From beneath the arch of the hotel entrance in the middle wing, Laura watched men with briefcases hurry out of the buildings and disappear into underground parking. Sleek women in designer suits clutched their purses and glanced apprehensively toward the square as they made their way toward the safety and splendor of the Biltmore.

The square itself warranted a certain paranoia, Laura supposed. It looked romantically decadent in the late afternoon. Spiky shadows fell behind bronze statues. Out toward the center, a great tiled reflecting pool seemed filled with red ink, and patches of dirt in the lawns looked like stepping stones scattered beneath palms and giant magnolia trees. The unemployed lounged along the concrete walls of the square, smoking and gesturing against a lacework of bare rose bushes, stubbled faces and rumpled clothing softened by the gloaming.

Then she saw Stone and her heart ticked with pleasure. He was several yards into the park, leaning against the trunk of an elm. He was talking with a huge, cigar-puffing man wearing a cheap tan shirt. Stone looked whipcord in comparison; he'd changed into a red golf shirt and dark slacks that billowed slightly in the breeze. The twilight gave a ruddiness to his normally pale complexion. Ruggedly handsome, she thought, so eager to see him she had to sprint across Olive Street to avoid a barreling taxi.

She entered an opening in the abutment of the park and made her way along a concrete path. All the while she mused about the contrasts in his nature. Demanding and harsh when she'd confronted him at their first meeting; even frightening. But there had been an appealing courtliness about him when, on the plane, they'd discussed the European Common Market, America's staggering trade deficit, the aerospace display he'd seen at the Smithsonian four years ago. He'd shown her a passionate side, too. She smiled, remembering his barely-muffled expletive when they'd touched on how slowly America's war on drugs was progressing. And his hands had carved arcs in the air when he described where to find the best pizza and beer in major U.S. cities. Enigma, she thought, relishing the romantic sound of it. Enigma described him perfectly.

Dodging a cluster of men who eyed her hungrily and murmured when she passed, Laura congratulated herself on coming to terms with the hard-nosed ex-agent. While she couldn't quite trust Stone because of a certain ruthless quality and because he had the circumstantial black mark of the theft against him, she looked forward to working with him.

She glanced into the distance and saw him blazoned with the last rays of sunset. Stone had presence. He looked as if he could take on the world and enjoy the challenge. She'd read about his type in bestsellers but never dealt with his kind as a woman, and the prospect excited her as she hurried toward him.

She heard a rustle behind her and felt a tug on her left arm. She was jerked around. Then something brushed her right hand. Her purse—stolen!

As she whirled around, disbelief went through her. Then anger—a fierce explosion of it that spurred her forward. She'd lost her husband because of a thief. The theft had brought her nights of agony, months of loneliness...the shame and pain and loss of dealing with suicide. All of it flashed through her again and a hatred like acid spread into her midsection, burned into her blood. Maybe it's him—the same thief, she thought. *I'll kill him!* And she pounded after the man.

He was fleet. A slight man with shaggy dark hair, he bounded around a rose bed and darted for a knot of men ahead. His black windbreaker ballooned, and Laura drove herself after it. He dove through the crowd. The men scattered like dry leaves.

"Thief!" Laura shouted, tearing into the melee—angry with herself for musing mindlessly about Stone, being caught off guard. "My—purse!"

She heard laughter as she plowed through the mass of unkempt sour-smelling men. Fury took over. "Move!" she muttered, shoving aside a man in a filthy orange sweater. "Where is he—"

Ten yards away, the thief glanced over his shoulder—and tripped over the lip of a fountain. Miracle! He went down. A yelp. He'd landed hard, elbow first on the tile of the shallow pool, his feet kicking air. Her purse went flying—into the pool, naturally. A two-hundred-dollar velvet clutch from Asprey's.

Rage whipped through her brain. Theft—*theft*—her nemesis. Cost her so much. Injustice of it! She hated the fallen man, and burst toward him. She stomped over one of his feet, heard him yell. "Good!" she grunted, pounding both hands on his shoulder. "How—dare you steal—from—me!"

He raised his arms to protect his lined gremlin face. She glimpsed his eyes—white bands of fear, irises huge with it. "Disgusting!" she said, and thought she heard raised voices—cheering! But she remembered the clutch and scrambled past him into the pool to snatch it up. It streamed water. The red gauze choked her this time. She spun around—"Bastard!"—and whapped him with the purse, again and again, water spraying everywhere.

He yowled, cringed, splashed to get away. She flung the purse down. Grabbing his leg, panting now, she held him fast. She had not so much a clear view, as a sense of a crowd gathering behind her. Shuffling feet. Grunts of approval.

"Police!" she screeched.

Objections clattered up into the twilight.

"You doin' just fine, sugar," said a gravelly voice. "No need to bring the *man*."

She cursed in frustration.

"She some hot pussycat, ain't she?" the man praised.

"Do something!" Laura demanded, voice ringing.

A tug on her arm. She was dragged backward. "No, not to me," she wailed. She fought to reach the thief again, flailed to get at him. "Call the police."

She heard, ". . . kill the guy . . . locked up for murder."

"Yes," she said, heaving in gulps of air. "Call the police."

"I mean you."

She canted around, arm raised to strike her second assailant. "Stone!"

He snatched her wrist in midswing.

Men clapped, whistled. "Tame her, Stone, if you man enough! She beat poor Fast Eddie to a pulp."

"You all right?" said Stone, keeping his mouth straight in an effort not to grin.

"Yes—"

Splashing, in the pool. She turned to look. The thief was cowering away, crab-stepping into the men. "He's getting away!" she said, craning to reach him.

Stone had a firm grip on her and pulled her back.

"Damn you, Stone, he's a thief!"

"Yep," said Mickey, and his eyes gleamed.

"What," said the beefy man he'd been talking to, "she a friend of yours, Mickey?" The big guy clamped his cigar in his teeth and grabbed a wad of the thief's black jacket. Water trickled from the grip. He hauled him up close and cuffed him open-handed on the cheek. "Whadya clippin' this lady for, Eddie? Huh? Only a snivelin' old dog snatches ladies' purses. Anyway, ya don't scalp a friend 'a Mickey's, f' cryin' out loud.''

Fast Eddie whimpered. ''Just gettin' by, you know.''

''Gettin' by?'' demanded the giant, straining the buttons on his shirt as he took a tighter hold on the pickpocket Fast Eddie's collar, making his feet dangle. ''You gotta job! You done it yet? Huh, Eddie? You picked up the mushrooms at the Produce Mart like I told ya?''

''Aw, Harry,'' said Eddie. ''I was just on my way to tell ya—''

''That can wait.'' A cuff on the shoulder. ''You gotta make, what, restitution to Mickey's lady friend here.''

''Resti-what?''

''Apologize.''

''Aw, come on, Harry.'' Eddie eyed Laura.

''Do like I tell ya!''

Eddie rubbed his palms down his jeans. ''Sorry I clipped ya, lady,'' he mumbled. ''I thought you was, you know, free game.''

The men whistled in appreciation, purposely misconstruing his meaning.

''He don't mean nothin' personal, Eddie don't,'' Harry offered. ''Just greedy like the rest of us, right, boys?''

Chorus of agreement.

Losing some of her anger, Laura shrugged—the most she could offer by way of accepting Eddie's apology.

She felt Mickey stiffen beside her. He let her wrist go. Glancing up, she saw him gazing over the heads of the crowd. He was evidently trying to see someone in the shadows. She put her hand on his sleeve, noting the hard bands of muscle beneath. ''What is it?''

For a time, Mickey's profile was granite. Then he said, ''Nothing. Somebody I thought I knew.''

He looked down at her. During a long, quiet appraisal of her face, his obsidian gaze softened noticeably.

''Not only beautiful but brave, too,'' he said.

Laura's pulse picked up a notch, when it had just begun to settle down. She stared at him.

"Uh-*huh*," the gravel-voiced man remarked, clearly approving. He tugged at a stained gray fedora. "Stone the main man, uh-*huh*."

Mickey brushed some grass from her arm and said with evident concern, "Sure you're okay?"

Laura felt an old emotion beat its way like a great bird from the depths of her. Almost...happiness. She smiled crookedly.

"So, you visitin'?" asked Harry, breaking the spell.

She bent to pick up her purse. Mickey tucked her other hand into the crook of his arm, keeping her close. "This is Mrs. Marley, boys. She's here on business."

Murmurs of welcome, another wolf whistle.

"Business?" Harry prompted in a neighborly tone. "What line you in, Miz Marley?"

"Information," Mickey cut in. "Same as me, Harry. Only she's got deeper pockets."

"What type 'a info?" Harry asked.

"Big green bird flew the coop seventeen months ago. You know the one. Only bird of its kind. We're looking to net it. Pass the word."

Harry took his cigar out of his teeth and stuck a thumb in his waistband. He rocked back a bit, eyes slitted. He nodded silently.

"Take it easy, boys," said Mickey. He took Laura past the group and on down the concrete path.

At the line of palm trees on Fifth Street they cut left and headed for the intersection at Olive. "Who is Fast Eddie?" she asked.

"Eddie was born passed out," said Mickey, checking the traffic as they crossed Olive Street.

"You mean he drinks all the time?"

"No, I mean his mother did. She was drunk in the delivery room. Eddie was born blacked-out on vodka and reds. The street people have known him all his life. They say he lost maybe forty percent of his IQ before he took his first deep breath. That still left him close to average."

She felt shame for the intensity of her hatred toward Eddie. She blushed. "I hit him. Hard."

"Look, Laura." He stopped her, took her shoulders. "I warned you. This is a bad area. The Biltmore is an oasis. Out on the streets, life isn't worth much, so take tonight as a lesson and watch yourself. Just so you know. There's a code we live by here. You look after yourself first and your buddies next. If there's a conflict between the two, you opt for number one. Understand?"

She nodded, feeling loneliness knot inside her. She wanted Mickey to go on talking, holding her arm—anything but let her go back into the cocoon of the grand hotel where she'd be safe but alone.

"The men respect you for it," Mickey was saying.

"For what?" she asked.

"You took care of number one." Mickey smiled. "And you made me look damned good into the bargain."

"Because they think I'm your girlfriend and I follow the code?"

He smiled his private smile. "Something like that."

And then he walked her into the marble lobby of the Biltmore and said good-night.

Chapter Five

A blocky building of beige stone, the L.A. Mart rose thirteen stories above South Broadway and housed three hundred fifty showrooms filled with the latest gift merchandise and home furnishings. Mickey ushered Laura into the lobby, where, prearranged by Hendley, they obtained passes giving them access to the showrooms.

As they crossed to the elevator, Mickey looked behind him. The entrance was vacant. Perhaps they weren't being tailed, after all. He'd thought a man in a tan coat, collar turned up, had followed them in a black Riviera from the Biltmore to the Mart. But when he and Laura pulled into the parking lot south of the building, the sedan had driven on past. Mickey had stalled around, locking his briefcase into the trunk of the Chevrolet, buttoning his gray sport coat, giving the man in the tan coat plenty of time to park, but he never showed up.

Just being paranoid, Mickey reasoned, punching the button in the elevator. Last night in the square, after Laura's mugging, he'd seen the shadowy bulk of a man who looked like Sledgehammer, a known underworld thug. It had set off his internal warning system.

Laura smiled up at him, one of those friendly eager looks that made him think of bobby socks and apple pie. She wore a clingy white blouse tied at the throat with a multicolored scarf that picked up navy blue in her pleated skirt. Her hair was drawn into a severe bun that showed her classic features. Her eyes were luminous and very blue. Just the right amount of feminine conservatism, he thought. Appealing.

If he didn't have such pressures about the case and Garth's business, teamwork with Laura could be fun. Mickey gave himself a mental shrug. Ease up on the paranoia, he told himself. The emerald was still a long way out of his grasp.

They left the elevator and came almost at once to Yugo-U.S. Tucked between a lounge-chair manufacturer and a line of mock-marble tables, the exhibitor's cramped floor offered a selection of modern hardwood benches and chairs. The only decoration was a travel poster of Belgrade taped to the slate-green walls. The beige carpet looked threadbare enough to have been requisitioned from a military dining hall.

"He's overstocked," Laura commented.

Mickey had to follow her single file through the maze of furniture to get to the sales rep, who was pouring himself a disposable cupful of Evian when they approached.

Half a dozen issues of *Furniture Today,* a folded, marked-up *Times* Classifieds, a stack of new purchase orders and a few Bic pens cluttered a table against the wall. Gregorgi spent a lot of time in the showroom without much in sales to show for it, Mickey concluded.

Laura had related little about the rep other than that she'd met him four years ago at the Marley offices, when her company had been contracted to broker worldwide shipping for the small Yugoslavian company.

In fact, the man reminded Mickey of the Alfalfa character in the old Our Gang series. A gangly fellow of about thirty-five, Yrov Gregorgi wore baggy trousers and a tie of bold geometrics that repeated flecks of red and blue in his sport coat. A cowlick rose from a crop of dark straight hair that bounced when he set the bottle of Evian on the table.

"Ah, Mrs. Marley," he said. His voice was thin, almost squeaky, and heavily accented. He pushed up round spectacles when he glanced at Laura, and took both of her hands in his. "A pleasure to see you again. I hope I can be of help to you and—" he reached to shake hands with Mickey "—Mr. Stone."

"Appreciate your time, Mr. Gregorgi," Mickey said pleasantly, glad the showroom lacked trade.

"It is nothing. I realize Mrs. Marley has had a difficult time. Anything I can do to help, I am glad to do it for the sake of friendship and goodwill between our companies. That is why I telephoned. But please—" he indicated benches "—sit down, sit down. May I offer you some coffee? A drink of water?"

They declined and took seats on the floor samples, forming a triangle with the furniture merchant at the apex.

Gregorgi opened the discussion by lamenting about the difficulty of establishing new outlets for the Yugoslavian line during a prolonged slowdown in furniture sales. He said he wished headquarters would let him advertise in the trade publications. But the company maintained that it was a "people-to-people business," which was why they had installed him at the Mart.

"They consider that advertising is an unnecessary expense," Gregorgi finished, his expression one of frustration.

Laura sat quietly for a moment, then said, "Perhaps Marley Enterprises could provide funding for advertising on a cooperative basis. Would your people be open to it?"

"Why, yes," said Gregorgi, patting the stack of blank purchase orders, making his cowlick waver. "They are disappointed that business is slow. They might agree if the costs were shared."

"It would be helpful to have a press release prepared, perhaps even one a month, to support the advertising," said Laura. "New product introductions, news of your involvement with the trade and business associations, that kind of thing."

"I have a source for such work," said Gregorgi, enthusiasm making his voice crack. "For lack of budget, I have kept all the information in the files. Now, I will be in business!''

Laura smiled. ''If you'll forward costing information to the Biltmore, I'll look it over and ask Hendley to finalize a proposal. Both of our companies would benefit by increased sales in the U.S.''

Impressed by Laura's business skills, Mickey let her complete her public-relations mission, then turned the conversation to white-collar crime. Gregorgi took the hint.

''So,'' said the Yugoslav, taking a drink of Evian. ''You wish to know about the emerald, correct?''

''Yes,'' said Laura, leaning forward. ''You mentioned that it's coming on the market. When? Where?''

The rep held up his palm. ''I wish I knew the details. All the more since you have been so generous this morning, Mrs. Marley. I do not, I am sorry.''

''Anything would help,'' said Mickey.

''Yes, of course,'' said Gregorgi. ''I am happy to tell you what I know. Yesterday I went to Sam White—he is the arcade manager on the ground floor. We lunch together occasionally. It is he who heard the rumor about the emerald. I asked him to tell me how he knew about it.''

''And what did he say?'' asked Laura.

''He said he had met a friend at the boxing match. Nothing arranged in advance. Just a chance meeting. Between rounds, the friend mentioned that he had what the street people call 'inside information.' ''

''About the gem?'' Stone asked.

''Yes, precisely. It is rumored that a famous emerald of enormous size will be for sale soon. On the black market. I do not know if this is the emerald you seek, Mrs. Marley.''

''But perhaps it is,'' she said, her eyes lighted with excitement. ''It was a lucky break, you seeing my ad.''

''Yes,'' Mickey cut in, using a tone of approval. ''How in the world did you realize it was Mrs. Marley who had placed the ad about a stolen gem?''

Gregorgi smiled at Laura in reminiscence. ''Did not your late husband refer frequently to his partner, 'L.J.'? I was surprised, and delighted, of course, to learn on meeting you four years ago that you were Mrs. Marley, as well."

Laura's cheeks pinked. Her glance cut to Stone, fluttered, and went to her hands. "Yes," she said awkwardly. "He called me L.J."

Gregorgi blinked and looked at Mickey with an apologetic expression that said he was sorry if he'd upset Laura. "I have a—what is the word—obsession with reading the Personals section in the newspaper," he hurried on, hands spread in an appeal for understanding. "I am a foreigner, Mr. Stone. I have much time on my hands and I wish to learn about my customers."

"Naturally," said Mickey. "And you saw Mrs. Marley's ad?"

"Precisely. When I saw the advertisement by 'L.J.M. at Grosvenor House,' where Mr. Marley and I had lunched, I remembered hearing of his troubles with a certain famous emerald." He braved a look at Laura and found her composed. "I concluded that it might be you who placed the ad, Mrs. Marley. I immediately telephoned you. And as you were in the office at the time, your Mr. Hendley put me through to you at once." He glanced at the stack of purchase orders and sighed. "If only my headquarters in Belgrade would listen when I tell them the power of advertising in this country. It is amazing, is it not?"

"You had no trouble getting the information from Mr. White?" Mickey asked to keep the discussion on track.

"None at all. I obtained the name of a coral merchant in San Pedro."

"Wonderful," said Laura. "If we retrieve the stone, you'll be rewarded, just as I promised in the ad. That is—" she gave a somber glance to Mickey "—I was thinking it would be fair to split the reward between you and Mr. Stone since he's providing crucial insight and time in getting the gem back."

Gregorgi shrugged with deferential solemnity. "Let my contribution be a gift," he said. "It was not for the reward that I telephoned you, Mrs. Marley."

"Of course, Mr. Gregorgi, but I'm grateful, just the same. You shall have your half."

Sealing the agreement as firmly as a government contracts negotiator who'd closed a billion-dollar deal for aerospace, Laura sat back and looked at Mickey.

Mickey took the opening in his teeth, diving back into his mission. "What did the coral merchant have to say?" he asked.

Gregorgi's shoulders rose in apology. "I would have visited him, but..." His gaze encompassed the wall-to-wall tables and benches. "I am married, as they say in America, to my inventory."

"We understand. Did you tell Mr. White why you wanted the information?"

"As Mrs. Marley and I agreed last night, I told him a business associate in London needed to dispose of a surplus of funds and might want to consider procuring a valuable gem."

"Perfect," said Mickey. "How is White connected to the coral merchant?"

"That I did not ask. I am sorry."

"That's okay, you did fine." Antsy to have the lead, Mickey suggested politely, "The name may be a great deal of help."

Dutifully Gregorgi reached into his coat pocket and withdrew a white scrap of paper, handing it to Laura. Glancing at it, she gave it to Mickey. A nerve twitched in his jaw as he read Paulo Paishon's company name and address. He tucked it away. Maybe there were miracles, after all.

Gregorgi picked up the plastic cup and turned it for a moment. Then he said, "May I ask, Mr. Stone, what is your association to the...to the situation?"

"Mrs. Marley's company takes a great deal of pride in fulfilling its contracts, as you must know from your long and successful relationship. Her client has been cheated of the pleasure of owning the stone. I'm simply trying to assist her in locating it."

He felt Laura's gaze on him. He smiled at Gregorgi and stood up. "You've been a big help. Mrs. Marley and I are grateful."

They shook hands, and Gregorgi accompanied them to the front of the showroom.

"One other thing," said Laura, turning back to look at the furniture. "Americans love a sale. Perhaps—in addition to the features and benefits of your line—you might want to offer a small discount in the ads?"

"You're right, Mrs. Marley!" Gregorgi's smile went ear-to-ear. "You have a—what is it—flair for marketing. Would you like to look over the ideas I've outlined for advertisements?"

"Delighted to. Send them along with the media information and I'll be in touch."

She turned, putting her hand in the crook of Mickey's arm.

As he led her from the room, he felt a sudden pride in her abilities and a mild concern for her mood. She was almost grave in her personal business style, he mused, heading for the elevator. Maybe she'd adopted the conservative, diplomatic mannerisms of the London business community. But he didn't think so. Her gravity seemed rooted in the emotions, and that was a temporary condition. Maybe seeing Gregorgi had brought it on. Still, despite her pensive aspect now, in the meeting she'd used her knowledge and experience with a warm, subtle strength, and that was the source of his pride.

His appreciation was replaced almost immediately, however, by a driving eagerness to see the coral merchant.

En route to Terminal Island

MICKEY WANTED TO STOP by the arcade to meet Sam White to see what he could learn about Paishon. Laura quietly acquiesced.

Unfortunately, Sam White had gone home early. Toothache, they were told by the girl in the ticket booth. Mickey would have to gather his own intelligence at the meeting with the Portuguese coral merchant.

In minutes he and Laura were back in the Chevrolet and heading out the Harbor Freeway toward the waterfront.

It was convenient that Laura didn't seem to want to talk, because Mickey wrestled with his earlier suspicion: being followed. It wouldn't do to be careless now. The emerald might be closer at hand than he'd guessed.

For ten miles along the congested I-11, he checked his rearview mirror for the black Riviera. Then he saw it and his insides did a nervous jig.

Keeping seven or eight car lengths behind them, the driver drove sedately to avoid attention. What the devil did he want? Was the government still on his back?

But in maintenance-surveillance—as it would be at this point—an agent would probably have driven a more conservative car. The heavy luxury car was more likely owned by a well-off businessman . . . or a crook.

What the heck, Mickey decided. Test the situation.

He cut in front of a red Toyota pickup, dodged a pair of motorcycles, and sped ahead. Suddenly erratic, the pursuit vehicle jerked around a white limo, then buried its nose in the tailgate of a vegetable truck. The bumper and a wedge of ebony paint edged out into the next lane occasionally as the driver tried to keep tabs on the Chevy.

Mickey smiled grimly. He had a choice to make.

Where they were headed, it would be a cinch to duck a tail. Sloping into the Los Angeles Harbor from the prestigious Palos Verdes Peninsula, San Pedro, with its irregular boundaries, reminded him of a jigsaw puzzle half put together.

He and Clint had spent plenty of time on stakeouts and interviews in Worldport LA, as the commercial area was now called. Losing a shadow would be easy.

On the other hand, it would be enlightening to know what the creep behind them wanted. In reaction to the tension building in him, Mickey's biceps flexed. He'd pull into an alley in San Pedro, roadblock the sedan. Drag the chump out by the scruff and shake some information out of him.

Thinking to alert Laura, he glanced at her. She looked downright glum. She stared out the window, but her head didn't turn with the sights. Come to think of it, she'd been quiet since they'd left Gregorgi's showroom.

"You okay?" he asked.

She didn't respond.

"Laura?"

"What?" She turned quickly, as if he'd startled her.

"Penny for your thoughts," he said.

"Oh," she waved, looking sad and lost. "Just . . . thinking."

He had a hunch. "Remembering, you mean?"

She nodded.

He shuttered an alien jealousy, and said quietly, "You really loved him, didn't you?"

She searched his face. He had to look away, check on the sedan. It was six car lengths back, tailgating the red Toyota. He looked at Laura.

She nodded. "We were best friends. It's the way I lost him that's so hard to accept. So many unanswered questions."

He thought about Clint—what it would feel like to lose him, permanently. Can't even imagine it, he thought.

His brother, two years older, had died of pneumonia when Mickey was eighteen months old. He had vague memories. A tussle of some kind, maybe over a toy. A moist hand holding his, the hand not much bigger than his own. There was no pain associated with Bobby's death, just a void. But Laura had had a lifetime with her husband, and she really liked him. What must that have been like, he wondered.

"We used to go for drives every Sunday after dinner," she said, her voice dreamy and her gaze focused ahead, as if the windshield were playing family movies. "I imagine the talking we did then held us—"

She stopped, bit her lip.

"Held you what?" Mickey prompted, as gently as he could given that he was concerned about the tail.

"Held us together," she said in a tiny voice.

He felt that lurch in his gut. The same one he'd felt when he'd demanded to know how her husband had died, back in London, and she'd had all that pain in her beautiful eyes. So they'd had problems, too. Things weren't perfect in paradise. He found himself reaching for her hand.

It was as if she'd been needing his touch, because her fingers curled around his, tight and shaking.

"Easy," he soothed. "It'll be all right. Let it pass."

She scooped in some air, let out a long breath.

"Thanks," she said, letting his hand go. "It's always unexpected."

"What, us holding hands?" he said, teasing her.

"No—well, yes, that, too." She made a poor attempt to smile. "My mind gets to running in circles, faster and faster—all the things I should have done differently, the good times, the—all of it. Something sets it off, like the L.J. business, and I can't shut it out."

"Now, there's something I understand," he said.

He felt her sudden interest, her probing look at his profile.

"What gets to you, Mickey?"

"The grand funk. But I have a cure for it."

"What's that?"

"Pizza."

"Pizza?"

"You bet. A fourteen-incher with everything, and maybe a good game of darts. Makes me forget all my troubles. You know, get out of myself."

"That's it? That'll cure the blues?"

"You bet. If you say 'a world without love,' I can live with it. But if it's a world without pizza, forget it. I'm outta here."

She smiled at him. Almost as an afterthought, she frowned. "I was really asking what puts you in a funk."

Sobering, he nodded. "Some other time. Right now, we've got a tail to lose."

"Tail?"

"As in, black Riviera that went from the Biltmore to the Mart, just like us. And it's heading for San Pedro, just like us, if my hunch is right. Nice of him to wait while we visited Gregorgi, wasn't it?"

She glanced out the rear window. "The guy with the turned-up collar, sunglasses? Doing a poor imitation of Columbo?"

"Right."

"I'll be . . ." She sat back in her seat. She scanned the urban sprawl as if expecting highwaymen to come thundering toward them out of the canyons of the city. "What does he want?" she asked—and it seemed to Mickey she was too eager and naive.

"I don't know," he said.

"Let's find out."

"Out of the question." In the past few minutes, feeling her fingers shake as he held her hand, he'd felt a rub of conscience. What had he been thinking of, scheming to pull a Dirty Harry move on the tail and maybe put Laura in jeopardy? Thugs were unpredictable. You didn't want to bring a society woman anywhere close to them. "I'll lose him before we go down into San Pedro," he said firmly.

She canted toward him. "Mickey, he might be someone important to us—to the case."

"No," he said.

"But—"

"No, Laura. That's final."

She flopped back in the seat in apparent disgust. "Mind if I ask why?"

"Could be dangerous."

"We're in the midst of twenty million people, in broad daylight. He wouldn't dare hurt us. We *need* information, Mickey."

She was right. Damn that she was with him. He cursed aloud.

"Maybe he knows where the emerald is," she said, digging deeper into his frustration. "Maybe the people in the square tipped him off and he's waiting for neutral ground where he can approach us. At least let him follow us, will you?"

He set his chin, knowing it looked stubborn as hell. He said nothing.

"Talk to me, partner," she urged with a slice of sarcasm.

He gave her a hard glance. "You want to bring trouble down on Paishon? A law-abiding citizen, for all we know? This Columbo character could be lethal. Thugs are nasty beasties."

She pursed her lips. "I didn't think about that."

"I imagine not," he muttered. "He might be armed, might be a lunatic who took a fancy to your figure when you walked through the lobby—we don't know. He could be anybody, anybody at all."

"You're an agent. I thought you could handle people like that."

"Hellfire!" He slapped the wheel. "I'm not God, thank you very much. On a meet, the idea is to meet them on your own terms—choose your ground, get the odds in your favor. There's nothing in my favor right now. Believe me, honey, you're my biggest liability."

Laura choked back some obvious indignation. Before she could take a deep breath, she was thrown sideways against him as he swerved across two lanes and took the Artesia Boulevard exit. Horns moaned. Laura jerked away from him, clung to the door. With her left hand, she grappled with the seat belt to get it cinched.

So what if she was angry, Mickey thought. Good. Maybe now she'd realize things got dangerous in his business. Maybe she'd quit arguing with him and let him do his job— a part of which, dammit, was seeing that she didn't get killed while they chased down the emerald.

He drove the Chevy like a blue comet along the boulevard and hooked a right on Vermont Avenue. A wedge of

the South Gardena Park whizzed by in a green blur, then
town-house developments nicked by. He checked the rearview. The black Riviera bucked to a stop at the corner of
Artesia and Vermont, then screeched onto Vermont and
came after them like a hunting hound to the scent.

Mickey picked up speed and did a squealing left onto
168th. Laura kept her mouth clamped shut, for once. He
sped past stucco cottages in pastel colors, swung left on
Raymond and found, to his chagrin, that his escape route
dead-ended at a school yard. Kids swarmed over the playground. Innocents, he thought, ducking west on 170th,
images of a tragic collision adding to his urgency to pass the
scene.

Having greater horsepower, the black car stayed with
them. Mickey muttered in frustration. Darting down Nor-
mandie, he decided a large yellow *carnicería,* advertising
the sliced Mexican steak called *carne asada,* was as good a
landmark as any, and he ran late through a turn signal to
get beyond it on his way down 166th Street.

And then the break he needed appeared. Ahead, orange
cones x'd out most of the right lane and a street crew jack-
hammered the pavement. A semi was hogging the divider
line, though, at barely twenty miles per hour.

"Hold on," Mickey said, and swerved across the yellow
stripe to overtake the truck.

In his peripheral vision he saw the bonsai pines and pa-
goda of a Buddhist temple. With perverse timing, Laura
took the Lord's name in vain.

His eyes widened at the reason: a twenty-foot black-and-
orange bobtail van barreled toward their front bumper. His
heart hammered in panic. The van honked. Mickey
crowded the semi. Just in time, the van slid out of his way,
forcing a dented station wagon to move over. Mickey heard
curses. Brakes squealed on the cargo truck as it geared
down to a stop. The van came to a shuddering standstill in
its own lane. The station wagon fishtailed sideways and
stopped, nicely closing up the street. A horn blared, and

Mickey knew it was from the black sedan, corralled in the vehicular snare.

The armpits of his white shirt stuck to his skin. His hands trembled. Gripping the wheel harder, Mickey burned rubber to get to Western, a wide avenue that led back to Artesia. Columbo didn't make the cut.

Cracking the window, he luffed the lapels of his sport coat to cool himself, and angled a glance at Laura. Her fingers were white as she clutched the blue fabric seat and the arm rest of the door. *Okay,* he thought. *Point made.*

"You can relax," he said, shifting his shoulders to loosen the tension.

She gingerly let go of the door and sat back, eyes front, mouth firm.

Mickey felt a nudge of regret. He had a hard side that took its toll on others. The immediate danger was over, and now he remembered the trusting way she'd put her hand in his. It had stirred something in him—a long-forgotten compassion, perhaps.

"I was a little rough on you back there," he said, voice grating over the unfamiliar humility. "I'm sorry."

She turned her head, looked at him steadily. Then she nodded. "Thanks," she said softly.

"Okay."

Relieved, he shifted his weight, settled, concentrated on the road. He worked his way back to the Harbor Freeway, and on down to the I-47 connector in San Pedro.

Without further event, they crossed the Vincent Thomas Bridge enroute to Terminal Island. Sapphires of sunlight trailed in the wake of the container ship *Plantin* out of Antwerp as it lumbered beneath the bridge, its mammoth stern deck stacked with at least a hundred and fifty containers of goods, Mickey figured. Docks patchworked the edges of the harbor. Huge cranes spiked the sky, like giant space-age praying mantises waiting to winch up the containers from the vessels. What was once a small regional harbor had grown into one of the leading passenger and commercial-fishing ports in the country, and the leading

West Coast port for automobiles, gasoline, jet fuel, cotton and other products. The port was the most profitable in the United States. That was just counting the legal trade. Despite stringent controls, huge amounts of black-market goods, including weapons and drugs, passed in and out of the port every month.

Paishon, their contact, could be clean. On the other hand, Mickey knew, he could be as dirty as the worst low-life black marketer. He'd ask Clint to run a printout on him.

On the downside of the bridge, Mickey turned onto Terminal Island, and the hair on his arms bristled. The paranoia characteristic of the men of the flat dusty peninsula registered at least eight on the Richter scale of his nerves.

Paranoid men were unpredictable under stress. They were dangerous. Because Laura was with him, he hoped Paishon was a pussycat—a B-type personality with a good memory. That would be a real plus.

Mickey followed Earle Street, past groups of squat round storage towers, stacks of containers, parking lots jammed with dusty new cars—all surrounded by the symbols of that paranoia: high chain-link fences topped with barbed wire, guard shacks and locked gates.

Nearer to Fish Harbor, the breeze stank of fish slime from the boats and canneries and cold storage facilities along Wharf Street, their destination. At 700 Tuna Street, a humble white building bore the sign TUNA COMMIS-SION. Dead ahead, a fifty-foot tuna boat, the *Katherine M,* white with black trim, ground against the dock, lifting and settling with the swell.

He parked close to the corner, facing the *Katherine M.* A two-story building sheltered them from most of Wharf Street.

"I'll ask the questions," he said. "Paishon's not expecting us, so at least we have the element of surprise."

"Right, boss," Laura said, and gave him a smirk that reminded him of a political cartoon. Her mood had evidently improved.

She collected a navy-blue leather purse, slipped the strap over her shoulder, and they both climbed out.

Laura's chin lifted as she tested the sea air. "Mmm," she breathed, sounding pleased.

It was cleaner here, the breezes coming right off the water.

She gazed at the gulls keening overhead, and Mickey thought she looked fresh and lovely against the whites and blues of Fish Harbor. Too clean for the business they were about.

He was aware of that bright spark of intelligence that made her so capable in business. She exuded a confidence that only success could bring. Yet she was vulnerable; had shown her vulnerability twice. For some reason, that vulnerability got under his skin, made him react from protective instincts.

But something else about Laura held him riveted to the street, watching her. There was a side of her that *longed* for something. What was it?

She looked almost wanton: tendrils of her chignon trailing in the wind, her lips parted to taste the salt air—as if she were reaching for life, maybe. Fulfillment.

The high-necked silk blouse clung to her breasts. The navy-blue skirt outlined her figure to the hip, where the pleats kicked free and rippled with every movement. The breeze lifted her skirt, and Mickey caught his breath at a brief stretch of her thigh that curved out of sight, as smooth and lean as a model's. What he wouldn't give to love her.

No, *have* her, he corrected. Even for a night, and then never again.

He frowned. Fantasizing about her had no place in his world. It had slipped right in there unannounced to fly like a bright kite among memories of the smugglers he'd known; it disrupted his plans for the interview and relegated to meaningless, just for an instant, his desperation to find the Garden Emerald.

He knew, suddenly, why men gave up fortunes and fame for a woman, and he was chilled. Laura Marley epitomized everything that had destroyed his life. He'd already decided that. Abruptly he turned to lock the car.

"Let's go," he said, and started forward at a brisk pace.

"Coming," she said, and easily kept up with him.

Nobody was about. Mickey could understand why; it was unseasonably hot for January, even at midday. The crumbling sidewalk at the corner of Tuna and Wharf reflected blindingly into his eyes. Even the real Columbo character on TV would have more sense than to wear a trench coat on a day like this, he thought. Obviously their tail was trying to disguise himself—or hide a weapon, as Mickey was. He repeated the license number of the Riviera to himself, which he'd read during the chase, then bent his concentration to the meeting with Paishon.

They walked past several fishing boats, and down the length of a three-story wooden cannery painted robin's-egg blue. The clank of equipment and the grunts of men doing physical labor filtered to him. Steam huffed into the air from a cold-storage facility somewhere down the street. At the end of the cannery, they stopped to peer down a narrow alley. Forty feet or so into the dimness, a sign read ASIAN CORAL IMPORTS.

"Bingo," said Mickey.

As they headed for the entrance, he patted the lump under his sport coat, where his Walther was holstered. The weight and shape of the .380 caliber handgun always reassured him. "Odd place for a coral merchant," he observed.

"Why's that?" Laura asked.

"On the back side of a cannery? Think about it."

"Oh, of course," she said. "But they both come from the water."

Fish and coral, she meant. He smiled dryly to himself. Laura was trying so hard to be savvy. But her naïveté was a serious liability. He could never lose sight of that.

They stopped beneath the sign. "Ladies last," he ordered, and tried the door. When it swung open, the hinges squeaked from salt corrosion.

Stepping inside, arms curled for quick reaction, he automatically scanned for possible danger. Nobody in the reception room, which smelled musty, like dried mushrooms.

As Laura stepped inside, he took inventory. Oak floors, dark and scuffed. No windows. Two bare light bulbs in the ceiling illuminated a beat-up surplus-style desk holding one item: a sixties black telephone. The door in the opposite wall was closed. A mirror stretched along beside it, maybe two-way. Two chairs flanked a dust-grimed showcase, its few token coral formations arranged on the top shelf.

Static crackled. The faint beat of a country song filtered into hearing. Behind their heads, the biggest baritone voice Mickey had ever heard boomed through a speaker. "We're closed. Who is it?"

Laura gripped Mickey's arm, then moved away as if she were embarrassed to have been so easily startled. Mickey didn't blame her. His nerve ends danced with the crackle of the sound waves.

"Michael Stone," he said. "Sam sent me."

"Sam who?" said the huge voice.

"White."

The hiss of amplified breathing, the whine of a steel guitar. Then, the baritone, "Have a seat."

Mickey and Laura exchanged glances. Her eyes were huge; he read a naive excitement. They wandered to the coral display, looked at it in silence.

The doorknob warbled in its casing and the door opened. A frail woman with straggling hair and a faded print dress touched her throat. "Come in," she said, and ducked out of sight.

They went down a hallway, through another door, angled left and came to another room. Thumping, overhead, meant they were beneath the food-processing operation. The sour scent of fish permeated the air.

They followed the woman through a warren of partitioned spaces containing cartons tattered at the edges and spilling over with invoices and letters. Broken arms of coral poked out of a grocery cart parked in the aisle. In one cubicle, an Asian woman stared zombielike at a computer screen, her fingers dancing incessantly on a keyboard. In the adjacent space, desks and chairs were stacked up at haphazard angles, like cast-off metal in a scrap yard.

They came to the end of a zag in the zigzagging tour, facing a heavy door. Pressing bony fingers against the base of her throat, their guide said, "Mr. Paishon's in there." She opened the door and stepped back.

They went in. The door closed behind them with a solid, well-fit clink. Mickey felt slightly suffocated, as if he'd walked into padded, airless silence. The country music had been turned off. The air smelled faintly of musk cologne.

He took in Paishon's den—for it was that, being dim, and softened by Persian rugs, leather furniture, a zebra hide on the left wall between two doors. An eight-foot saltwater tank, set into the wall to Mickey's right, was so dimly lighted that the big shark circling among the coral fans and bridges appeared as a dark blur. If Laura needed further cautioning, the shark would do it for her.

Across the carpet, subdued light from an Etruscan-based lamp radiated down over a mahogany desk and credenza carved with curlicues. And the glow thrust upward to ivory the tusks of a boar's head and gleam in its glass eyes. But it gave away nothing of the expression of the giant behind the desk.

"Do for you, Stone?" boomed the faceless behemoth.

Mickey pressed Laura's arm to keep her in the shadows, and approached the desk. It held an intercom, a five-line memory telephone, a handsome leather desk set; no paperwork. Messages were impaled on a gold spike protruding from the breast of a nude figurine. The pink coral gave her skin a webbed texture that seemed overly fragile in contrast to Paishon's broad swarthy face. He wore a good suit.

"Paulo Paishon?" asked Mickey, extending his hand. "Sam thought you might have some information for me."

"Doubt it." A beefy palm snaked out, gripped hard, withdrew. "I'm a busy man."

"I pay my way."

"Sometimes that's good. Sometimes not. Depends." Heavy black eyebrows rose above eyes not unlike the boar's, small and unreadable. He glanced behind Mickey. "Who's that?"

Wary of Paishon's carnivorous tendencies, Mickey decided on the girlfriend routine.

"Laura, say hello to Mr. Paishon, honey."

"Hello, Mr. Paishon," Laura said with the right amount of bored, tagging-along-on-the-business-call respect.

Paishon stared toward her for a moment, then glanced at the coral figurine. "What is it you want, Stone?"

"I'm looking for something."

"Lost it, did you?" A sonorous rumble passed for laughter. "I don't lose crap. I worked for what I have, see, and I pay to keep it, if you get my drift."

"Sometimes that's good." Mickey arched his eyebrows to ensure the parody he'd launched would draw a response. "Depends."

Paishon eased back in his chair—minutely. "You a smart ass, Stone? I don't have time for a smart ass."

"No offense. Just so we're on the same wavelength. Sam—"

"Sam never heard of you, Stone." A deadly quality laced the caveman voice.

"We have a mutual friend." Mickey put a lid on his irritation and said, "Look, I get the information I want, we might be friends, too."

"I don't make friends easy."

"I take good care of my friends, Paishon. But I've got an agenda that would put the Pope on sick leave, so let's cut to the chase." He put his palms flat on the polished mahogany desk and leaned forward, so close he could see the facets in Paishon's diamond tie pin. It was at least two carats of blue blue fire. He knew his gems. Mickey set his jaw, locked gazes with the man, and said quietly, "I'll pay. Big. I want the Garden Emerald."

The giant had nerves of pure anthracite. The only tip Mickey had to Paishon's sudden excitement was the movement of his right eyebrow. The bushy caterpillar leapt. Once. *Paydirt,* he thought, keeping a thrill lodged deeply in his heart.

"I don't know emeralds," Paishon said, wheezing. "I deal in coral."

"Not interested," said Mickey. It was time to play hardball. He straightened, turned his back. All he could see were the whites of Laura's eyes and the glow of her white blouse. He walked toward her.

"Stone."

It was a command. He stopped and turned around.

"Where can I reach you?"

Mickey's heart catapulted against his ribs, wildly, as it had when he was coming down that first drop in his first roller-coaster ride, in Santa Clara, when he was ten. *A break. An honest-to-God break in the case.* He could taste the sweetness of it on his tongue. He swallowed and realized his mouth was dry.

Slipping his wallet from his hip pocket, he withdrew a card, replaced the wallet. He walked to the desk and stopped, looking into the beady unreadable eyes. He flipped the card into the air. It circled and fluttered down.

Paishon's hand snaked out, caught the card. Mickey smiled.

Then he turned, collected Laura and went back into the fish stink of Paishon's warren.

Chapter Six

At 1:25 a.m. the next morning, Laura lay on the bed in her Biltmore suite, watching a television special about housing the homeless in the U.S. The remains of her dinner, a Cobb salad and chocolate-mousse pie, lay wilting on plates arranged on the linen-draped table beside the bed.

She glanced at the service-for-one and frowned. Mickey hadn't shown up for the outing they'd planned at his favorite pizza parlor. He'd stood her up.

She toyed again with the idea of being angry, insulted. Yet instinct told her he wouldn't simply not show up. Something had detained him.

She thought back over the afternoon and evening. He'd brought her back to L.A. after the meeting with the Shark Man, as she'd nicknamed Paishon. Dropping her off at the Bank of America, where she'd had her London bank open an account for expenses and the reward money, he'd driven off on his own errands. He'd said he had to get a purchase order signed by a jeweler in the Broadway Shopping Plaza and take care of some other business for Garth.

She supposed he was under pressure to get as much of his paycheck work done as he could when he wasn't on the gem case. While they were waiting for Paishon to call them back, he had to work.

She'd whiled away the evening calling her sister in New York and watching television, but still he hadn't arrived. Famished by eleven o'clock, she'd ordered room service. At eleven-thirty, being too keyed up to finish the dinner, she'd changed out of her street clothes to relax on the bed. So far, she'd watched a cable program on saving America's forests, a half-hour commercial on applying makeup, which you could order by dialing a toll-free number, and Dolly Parton's life story on Nashville Network.

Now Laura tried to concentrate on the final comments of Senator Janes (D) New Jersey. In a tight camera shot of his Kennedylike face, he declared war on homelessness. He begged Congress to make it a "non-partisan victory for the homeless of America."

"Amen," said Laura, thinking of Fast Eddie and the others roaming the streets below her room.

Stop-action on the senator's face. Roll credits.

Laura's concentration wandered. Should she be worried about Mickey? He hadn't called her, hadn't answered the messages she'd left on his answering machine.

Thinking of the phone, she glanced at her watch. Nearly one-thirty. In London, it was 9:30 a.m. Time to get the last of her phone calls done. She'd already reached John, Jr. at his flat, and Jessica, who had asked her to bring home a T-shirt from L.A.'s famous Hard Rock Café. Laura had also telephoned the housekeeper, who'd reported there was nothing much of interest in the mail.

Now there was only Hendley to call. He'd be through with any return calls he had to make for the day, and just now would be having his morning tea and biscuits. He was a precise man and never missed his morning cookies. It was a good time to reach him.

Belting a short white satin kimono, she went through the main salon and into the second bedroom, which the Biltmore had converted to an office. She flipped a switch. Lamps highlighted a corner grouping on the far side and an L-shaped computer desk next to the window.

Minutes later she was saying to Hendley, "Can you believe Paishon keeps a shark in his office?"

"Muggings, car chases, sharks—all in the first twenty-four hours," he said, properly amazed. "I do hope you're taking notes for our teleplay?"

"I'm reporting in so I don't have to, Hendley. You're the one with the ear for prose. You must write the story."

"Oodles of thanks, Mrs. M. We aim to please." He paused, evidently to sip his tea. "Listen, perhaps you should reconsider. Let Stone do most of the interfacing for you—hold on a sec. There's another call."

Hendley put her on hold.

It was good to talk to him, to hear his paternal advice and be rescued from seriousness by his "witty bits," as he himself would call them. Hendley was a treasure of a right-hand man.

Prying open the shutters, she peered down at the park. It looked sinister. Lights from the city buildings sent streaks of red and gold across the reflecting pool. A couple of dark shadows moved into the pitch-black protection of the trees. The scene was unsettling; it made her think of Mickey out there in the night-city, tackling a tail in some dark alley. Shivering, she closed the blinds. Surely he was all right.

Hendley, for the love of God, hurry, she thought. *Waiting is so unnerving.*

She needed to focus on happier thoughts; that would help. Her gaze roamed the suite.

The flower arrangement on the coffee table contained fresh irises and pressed oak leaves, an unusual, striking combination that reminded her, despite the sunshine earlier today, that it was winter.

Things had changed in the last year, what with the necessity of trimming her living expenses, but in former years during the dormant season when she couldn't cut from her gardens, she had arrangements delivered for the main rooms of her home. And around Easter, she bought nosegays of violets and baby's breath that gave life to her purple-and-white bedroom, sitting room and bath.

But it was the computer at her left, the fax and telex machines and note pads and paper clips, the accoutrements of business, that really eased the isolation she felt being away from London.

Last night, after the mugging in the park, she'd felt desolate. She'd slept poorly. Waiting for Mickey tonight, she had felt lonely, edgy. Now, although she was worried about him, she felt less adrift with these familiar objects around her and a good chat with Hendley underway.

If he would just get back to the phone. His other call seemed to be taking forever.

While she waited, she mused about Mickey. Two things about him had revealed more of his character, and she told herself she had to take the good with the bad.

In a startling move in the car, he'd taken her hand to comfort her from memories of her marriage. It was a warm, loving gesture . . . and God knows she'd needed that lifeline then. She remembered feeling grateful for his understanding. She remembered liking him immensely in those moments.

And then he'd jerked the lifeline away by his insulting, harsh assessment of her as a liability. She'd been terribly angry at him. He'd also taken their lives in his hands by that nightmare of a car chase. But she hadn't had a chance to stay angry because he'd apologized, sounding gruff and sincere.

So, all in all, how did the ledger on Mickey Stone balance out?

To his credit, he was a wily investigator, a street-smart survivor, a man capable of handling himself anywhere, anytime—a combination Rambo/Bond type who made her feel safe. And he showed glimpses, few though they were, of gentleness.

Taken together, his qualities added up to . . . a desperate, rather dangerous, sometimes sensitive man.

What was the limit of his desperation? What would it cost her emotionally to be involved with him?

Suddenly she sat back, her jaw slackened. How odd that she would think in terms of the emotions, personal involvement. She analyzed her inner, deeper reactions to him.

Was she involved? Already? Wary, yes; fascinated, yes; drawn to him, certainly. What about the thudding of the old ticker when I see him across a grassy, sunset-tinted square? she wondered. *What about that silky feeling I get when I imagine him holding me?* she thought with dawning realization. *What about* those *feelings, Laura Marley?* Never in memory had she reacted so strongly, in so feminine a way, to a man she'd known briefly.

"Hellfire," she murmured. She *wanted* him.

What would it cost her? He was a desperate man with nothing to lose and everything to gain in their quest for the gem. How desperate? How dangerous?

Hendley would tell her not to worry about it. Stone was an agent, he'd say, and good at his job. The kind of man to get the emerald back. That, Hendley would point out, was the goal.

But it worried her, his not calling. It worried her, caring so much about what had happened to him.

"A SNARL IN THE OLD knitting yarn, I'm afraid," said Hendley, coming back on the line.

"What is it?" Laura asked.

"Brit Hospital."

Laura felt sudden alarm. British Hospital Supply was a ten-year-old Marley account worth millions in revenues over the years. Recently they'd ordered five million dollars' worth of highly sophisticated infant-care incubation units for several of their hospitals, from the source she'd located in West Germany.

"The shipment didn't arrive?" she asked.

"Oh, it arrived, all right. It seems the production models aren't meeting test specs. They're failing."

"That's impossible." She tried to quell the panic, tone down the high notes in her voice. "The samples passed with flying colors," she protested, clenching her fist.

"Indeed. But something's amiss on the production models. The life-monitoring system seems to be failing at room temperatures above eighty-five degrees. Brit Hospital rightfully says they expect room temperatures at some hospitals will get above that point on occasion.''

"Of course. What did you tell them?''

"That I would make it top priority and look into the situation.''

"Excellent, Hendley." *Calm down,* she told herself. Hendley was a top-notch director. "What's your game plan?''

"I'll have a look at the manufacturer's production setup. As you know, a manufacturer's samples aren't always made with the identical materials and methods that their production models are made from.''

"I know. Careful not to tweak their noses, though. The baby-bed folks take an awful pride in their work, Hendley. That's why we went with them.''

"Utmost diplomacy, Mrs. M., not to worry.''

"Right, Hendley. Oh, and get a copy of Brit Hospital's test results, too, will you? They should be checked meticulously.''

"You just take care of the sharks and thugs, Mrs. M. I'll keep the home fires burning nicely, you can rely on me.''

She chuckled, if for no other reason than to inspire his confidence. "You're a saint, you really are. Sorry I'm not there to watch over things while you're in Düsseldorf with the production people. I know it's a lot to handle.''

"Well, then," Hendley said, sobering. "Perhaps if things get rough, you'll consider letting our man Stone carry on without you for a few days.''

So Hendley *was* worried. "Let me know if you think I must, Hendley. Getting the emerald back is terribly important, but we can't sacrifice the company to do it.''

"I'm sure we'll put things right, really.''

"Of course. And Helen can be relied on at the front desk. You'll brief her?''

"I'll do that now, ask her to take all our calls while I'm gone. I'd better get to it, shall I?''

She told him to keep her posted and hung up.

The life-monitors failing! It was perfectly unexpected...and scary. It meant a half-million-dollar loss in income if Brit Hospital cancelled the contract. It meant greatly more than that if old BH lost faith in Marley's production sources and stopped buying through them. And if they did ask for a new source of supply through Marley Enterprises, it meant taking the time to find and test other products, arrange licensing and importing, and dealing with a host of other red-tape restrictions and problems. It all meant time. It meant money. It meant the whole nine yards, and she, the C.E.O., was chasing down an emerald in America.

The guilt washed over her, but she didn't have time to dwell on it. Someone knocked on the door.

She cast about the room for something more concealing to put on, but she'd closeted her pleated skirt. No time anyway, she thought, hurrying into the shallow foyer.

She opened the door and peeked out.

"Mickey!" she said, relieved to the core that he was all right, yet aghast that he would come at this hour. She supposed she had to let him in. She was dressed decently enough if one didn't count bare legs. Stepping back to admit him, she said, "It's, well, it's too late to go out. I've had dinner."

His gaze brushed over her figure. Instinctively, she closed the lapels of her kimono to the throat. She needn't have bothered.

He scrubbed a hand over his face, and the act said only one thing: exhaustion.

As he looked around, conducting that security check he always made when he walked into a room, she studied him. He was very slim, it seemed to her now. His face was deeply lined, as if he'd worn himself down to the last shred of his stamina.

"Sorry it's so late," he said, facing her, eyes bleary.

She wanted to wrap him in her arms. Instead, she gathered her wits. "Something hot to drink, Mickey? I could call room service."

"No time," he said. "I'd better get a couple hours' rest. I just came by to tell you to get packed. We're going to New Orleans."

Her eyes widened. "But I've got problems with Brit Hospital! I can't just—"

"Who's Brit Hospital?"

"One of my biggest customers. The incubators they ordered don't work."

"Incubators?"

"For babies."

"Ah. Babies. You'll have to take care of something that important." He sighed, looking weary but pleased. Too damned pleased. "Fine, then," he said. "I'll just call you if something comes up."

Realizing she'd painted herself into a corner, she bit out, "Like you did tonight, for instance?"

His eyes flashed sudden anger. "Did you consider it a date? It was business. I was unavoidably detained."

"By what?"

He glanced above her head to the crystal chandelier. With a grating bitterness he said, "Veeta."

"Your *ex-wife?* But, has she been arrested? What's happened?"

"Look, I'm exhausted. I'll explain later. I picked up my messages by remote phone, and Paishon's directive to see a man in New Orleans was one of them. Are you coming with me or not?"

"For how long?"

"A day, maybe a few days. I don't know." The look he gave her was bright with challenge. "In my line of work, you never know."

She took a breath, settled her shoulders. "I'm coming."

"Fine. Be ready to roll at six o'clock."

"A.m. or p.m.?"

He glanced at his watch. "In four hours. Now, if you don't mind, I've got to go."

She trailed him to the foyer. Her thoughts slipped back to an earlier conclusion—wanting him. As he opened the door and stepped into the hallway, she realized he had not had to come by at all. He could have gone to New Orleans without her. Or phoned her from his office, at the very least. But he hadn't. He'd stopped by, exhausted as he was. A tingling went through her. He'd wanted to see her, too, obviously. Not that he'd ever admit it, if he was even aware of it.

She smiled up at him. "Mickey?"

He gave her a tired, resigned look. "Yes, Laura."

"Wait a minute." She hurried back into the bedroom. With a tablespoon, she scooped up chicken, bits of blue cheese and avocado and lettuce and mounded them inside a large flaky croissant. She wrapped it in a linen napkin and took it to the front door.

"It's not gone off," she said, handing him the package. "It's only been three hours."

He took it, looked from the gift to her.

"Thanks," she said.

"For what?"

"For being a man of your word."

A kind of struggle seemed to possess him. He stared at her a long moment, emotions like doubt and surprise changing his eyes, pulling at his generous mouth. Finally, his expression told her he was grateful. Then he simply lifted the sandwich in a gesture of farewell and walked down the hall.

MICKEY HAULED HIMSELF UP the stairs and across the warehouse floor to his desk. Tiredly he tabbed in Clint's phone number. On the second ring, there was a grumbled response.

"Clint, come awake," he said.

"Mickey?" Clint cleared his throat. "What's up, buddy?"

"Gotta go to New Orleans."

"You calling from London?"

"No, my office. This is the first chance I've had to get back to you. I need some favors."

"Hold on." Clint was interrupted by Mary, his wife. She complained in the background. "It's Mickey," Clint said to her. "Go back to sleep."

Mickey could hear the bumps and scrapes of Clint picking up the phone, getting out of bed, probably walking into the den. His friend said, "What happened in London?"

Mickey took a deep breath, summoned the threads of recent events together and hit the high points. "L.J.M. turned out to be Laura Marley. Marley Enterprises brokered the emerald for Demude, the Dutch arms mogul. Sutama, the buyer, is a Marley client."

"What the devil? Where's Garth come in? What was the gem doing in the U.S. if it was a Euro-Asian connection to begin with?"

"All very valid questions," Mickey said drily. "I called Garth in Singapore this afternoon. He claims Laura's husband, John Marley, contacted him and asked him to handle the transfer. Said since Marley stayed entirely out of the deal, there was no reason to bring up his name."

"Therefore, no reason to mention Marley during the investigations," Clint concluded.

"Right."

"His story's a little thin, don't you think?"

"It stinks to high heaven," Mickey said in disgust. "When I pressured him, Garth said he brought the gem into the U.S. because it was couriered with some documents he was bringing in."

"For who?"

"About the time I asked him that, he said he had to go. I've never heard about any documents. Have you?"

"Not a whisper."

Mickey sighed. "I gave him heat about never telling me any of this, and he said the foreman of the mines was waiting to see him, he had to go. However, not before telling me to handle his end at the show next weekend."

"What show?"

"Big gem show in Santa Monica. He usually covers the Santa Monica show himself. But he says he's leaving tomorrow for Bogatá, won't be through there for three weeks."

"Conveniently absent. What about New Orleans?"

"Coral merchant I visited on Terminal Island left me a message earlier tonight—" he realized the time "—last night. Anyway, his name's Paulo Paishon. Ring a bell?"

Clint said negative.

Mickey said, "Paishon told me to talk to a guy in New Orleans who supposedly knows when and where the big stone is coming on the market. Guy named Luis Delarein. Supposed to be the plumbing contractor for New Orleans's big hotels."

"You think the tip is legit?"

"I don't know, but what choice do I have? I have to check it out."

"Where'll you be staying?"

"The Hyatt Regency, across from the Superdome."

Clint whistled. "Garth's going to hit the roof."

"Why's that?"

"He never paid first-cabin before."

"It's not because of me, it's for Laura. She's used to first-cabin."

"You've got the Marley woman with you? She have one of those open marriages or something?"

"No, it's not like that, Clint. Her old man's been dead for over a year. Suicide."

"Holy crow. The plot sickens," Clint murmured, evidently recognizing the abundance of coincidence. "So . . . you felt sorry for her or what? It's not like you to compromise an operation with excess baggage."

Mickey cursed. "Look, I know it's not like me. I had no choice in the matter, okay?"

"All right. Take it easy."

"About those favors."

"Name 'em."

He asked for a rap sheet on Paishon, and a whereabouts on Sledgehammer—in case he wasn't imagining having spotted the thug in the square last night. Finally, he asked for a DMV on the black Riviera. "It was tailing me this morning," he added. "Driver was male Caucasian, about my age, my coloring. Couldn't really see his size but I'd take a wild guess at smaller than me, maybe five foot ten, a hundred seventy pounds. Laura said he looked like Columbo."

"Got it. Give me a few days to see what I can dig up. Oh, by the way—" Clint indulged in a noisy yawn, then ahemmed himself and spoke again. "When you get back to California, you ought to call Rusty. He was the best double-jeopardy guy this country ever had. Remember him?"

"Yeah, he turned in reports on that hit in the presidential suite in South America. Retired early, as I recall. What's he doing now?"

"Fishing, I guess. He lives up on Big Bear Mountain. When you call, tell him I said hey."

"If I call."

"Do it if you've got the time, Mickey. There're aspects of your case that may interest him." He yawned once more. "I gotta get my beauty sleep. You take care, buddy."

"Thanks, man. Hang in."

He hung up and stood there, waiting for the energy to collect in his legs so he could walk to the shower and climb into it.

Chapter Seven

Her companion did not ask Laura about the death of her husband until they were flying above the ranches of West Texas. They had breakfasted aboard the jet, Mickey subdued throughout the meal, and Laura fretting inwardly about the glitch with the baby beds and her newfound, disturbing desire for the man at her side. But the hiatus came to an end when they'd handed their trays to the stewardess and were settling into their seats to relax. He brought back the past in a tone gentled, she wanted to think, by concern for her feelings.

"I know it's difficult to think about John's death," he said, turning to her. "But we've got to talk about it. There may be something crucial in what you tell me. Crucial to the case."

Was Mickey employing those terribly subtle manipulation skills again, using John's name? she wondered, gazing out the window at the gradations of tan in the hills and flats, thousands of feet below them. Because saying John's name in that quiet almost loving voice made a difference. It made her *want* to tell him about everything, all the secret fears, the worry, the guilt. She wanted Mickey to have it all.

Yet it was difficult to begin. A leaden weight, a deep dread, settled in her, and she said reluctantly, "I suppose you're right."

Mickey took her hand. "A little at a time," he said. "Something good first. What quality did you like best about your husband?"

"His solidness," she said, going with the instinct to trust Mickey's motives. She smoothed out a fold in her gray worsted suit and sat back. "Until John went to Holland to get the emerald, he was the rock of the family and the business. He would always make time for the children's school activities. He loved having our friends over for tea or a party. He traveled a lot, but he always made time for those things."

"Did you travel with him?"

"Generally not. He took care of business development. I kept the home fires burning and looked after the office."

"Did you want it that way?"

"No, to be honest. I wanted to travel."

The stewardess returned, asking if they wanted a cocktail. They both declined.

Mickey encouraged Laura with a look, and she began again. "John would come home and tell me about the furniture fair in Milan, the jewelry show in New York, the electronics show in Las Vegas. All the glitz...the intrigues...the action."

She looked down at their linked fingers, seeing only her life with John. "He was the front man for the company. We'd agreed years ago it would be that way because the children needed me when they were young. John liked a schedule, a format for things. He felt comfortable with our arrangement."

"But you didn't."

"Not once the children were grown. John's adventures sounded so exciting, so exotic." She sought understanding in Mickey's eyes, believed she saw it there. "I wanted to *be* there, Mickey, not just hear about it."

"And now you can."

Now that John is gone. "Yes," she whispered. "Yes, now I can."

He traced her ring finger, where for twenty-one years, until the funeral, she'd worn a white-gold wedding band. When she'd said goodbye to John at the funeral home, she'd tucked the ring into his handkerchief pocket. Somehow the gesture said she was sorry for letting him down.

A lump formed in her throat, and she watched the burlap desert stretch below, struggling not to cry.

"What changed after he picked up the emerald?" Mickey asked, his voice low, his tone patient.

"Everything," she said, straightening up, getting a grip on her emotions for the sake of the case. "He came home from Amsterdam, and when I asked him if things had gone well with Demude, he snapped at me. 'Now you're on my back,' he said. 'What is it with people today?'

"It was unlike him. He was always considerate of people's feelings. Careful not to hurt them, especially me and John, Jr. and Jessica and the servants."

"He personally brought the gem to London?"

"Yes, rather than use the mails or a courier, he wanted to go himself so he could visit with his old friend."

"And he took it to the States, too?"

"No, he said he was going to courier it. Actually, he said an American colleague of his was in London on business and would take the stone there."

"Did John say why it had to go to the U.S.?"

"Because the colleague had to take some papers, some legal documents, I think, back home before he went on to Japan. That's what John said."

She thought Mickey found something significant in this because his eyes narrowed a bit. But evidently he was just formulating his next question. "I assume it was Garth who came to London?"

"I don't know. John went out to the bank to get the stone from the safety deposit box, and took it directly to the meeting with his colleague. I think it's strange, now, that he never told me who it was, never brought him home or to the office. After all, you wouldn't trust a treasure like that to just anybody."

"No," he said thoughtfully. "You wouldn't."

"Really, Mickey, John said very little about the transaction until the emerald was stolen. I might never have known even that, except for the timing."

Laura's fingers convulsed at a memory of John's reaction to the theft. She was scarcely aware Mickey had tightened his grip on her hands. She only knew his touch was there, keeping the memories flowing, keeping the worst of the pain at bay.

"Take a deep breath," he said.

She drew in hard, let it out slowly, felt stronger. "He got a call in the middle of the night when we were in bed. 'What do you mean, the emerald is stolen?' John said, and his voice went almost to nothing. He wouldn't tell me who had called. He refused to come back to bed. He changed completely after that. Morose, moody, irritable. He was beastly, compared to his old self."

Mickey rubbed her forearm, twined their fingers again, calming her. "You say he began to change the night he came home from Amsterdam. I wonder what happened?"

She shrugged. "I've agonized over that question. I just know that when he came home from Gatwick, or rather, from the bank, he looked a little like you did last night."

"How's that?"

"Beaten with exhaustion. As if the world had been too heavy to carry alone."

She looked at him, wanting to feel more connected to the living, to Mickey, whose gaze felt like healing sunshine despite his own bad memories. She longed to get off the subject of her past and get to know his. There was something about him that made her long to be closer, more intimate. "You saw your ex-wife, you said?" she prompted softly.

His eyes went to slits of green ice for an instant. Then he nodded.

"Where?"

"I was in the Broadway Shopping Plaza at a jewelry store. She walked by the windows as I was closing a sale."

"What did you do?"

"I didn't recognize her at first because her hair is black now, not blond, and she was wearing big dark glasses and thigh-high leather boots and a pair of torn jean shorts. She looked like a forty-year-old hooker. Maybe she is one now." He shook his head as if the possibility disgusted him.

"What did you do?"

"When it hit me that Veeta had walked by, just walked right by me, I ran out of the shop in the middle of the transaction. Couldn't find her anywhere. So I tore out the nearest exit in the mall. Outside, I saw her get into a black limo. I yelled, but it sped away. It was too dark to read the license plate. God, I was frustrated!" He cursed softly. "My car was in the parking structure, and I ran for it, but it was too late. I spent till one-thirty this morning driving around, trying to find them. No luck."

"Why didn't you call the police?"

"The police?" He chortled in derision. "Didn't you know? I'm blacklisted, Laura. PD, FBI, NSI, CIA—initials that spell what, to the average citizen? The finest law-enforcement agencies in the country. But they don't spell bunk for me. Not anymore. They'd love to find an excuse to lock me up."

"For the love of— Why, Mickey?"

"They've never found a trace of her, the limo, nothing. Unless I drag her bodily into a station house, they're not going to waste another man-hour trying to find someone they think I probably bumped off in the heist."

"Bumped off?" Her eyes widened. "Is that what they really think? That you killed your wife?"

"After all was said and done, believe me, the thought had crossed my mind." His eyes were narrow chips of resentment as he glared out the window.

He didn't mean that, she thought, frightened for him. "They'd arrest you?"

"No," he shook his head. "They're too afraid if they push me I'll compromise national security or something. Can you believe that?" For a moment, he lost the words. His hands carved angry, futile arcs. "The nation's finest," he managed. "All the agencies. They bicker with petty jealousies, back stab for power, climb each other's backs to get recognition with the muckymucks. But I'll tell you, when they think they've got a time bomb in their midst, they work hand-in-glove. They cut you dead. And if you're the time bomb, it's like the lights went out in your world. They've put feather pillows all around you, and six feet of feathers under your feet, and it's dark. You can't connect. The horizon is gone and you're on your own."

He sucked in some air, was about to say something, and instead, took another breath. "Those agencies," he said, almost in disbelief. "They put the case on ice months and months ago, said they had other priorities, more pressing cases. Said they'd get to it later. They're not going to get to it, Laura. That's just governmenteze for dropping the case." Mickey exhaled, sounding explosive. "They're not going to lift a finger to open it up again. Not ever. There are parts of this case that baffle me completely."

Laura sat very still for a moment, disjointed thoughts coming at her as his breath gusted, quieted, evened.

They both had been battered by the theft of the gem. The timing was incredibly coincidental, it struck her. The theft, the shredding apart of vital lives, relationships; the unanswered questions. Something familiar was swirling around her, something hard to name.

"Mickey," she began tentatively, laying a gentling hand on his coat sleeve. "There's some kind of parallel."

He pulled his gaze from the window to her face, saying nothing.

"What John and you went through—there's a link." She frowned, trying to sort it out. "What is it? He was bitter, like you. It was as if he'd lost his faith."

A spark of hope came into his eyes. He angled around to watch her face. "Tell me about the night he got home from Amsterdam. He was upset, you said."

"He was downright grouchy. Naturally I tried to soothe him, find out what was wrong."

"And?"

"He said the gem transaction was a nightmare of complications and he wished to God the powers-that-be and his friends and family would simply leave him alone. He said he was sorry he'd ever gotten involved."

"What powers?"

"He never said."

"Was he working with the government?"

Laura felt a coldness around her heart. "I don't know," she said, amazed that she didn't. "He never said he was. We never entertained any members of parliament or anything."

Mickey's dark brows furrowed. Absently he said, "Those documents. The legal papers. He ever say what they were about?"

She shook her head.

She got the distinct impression he was disappointed. Tugging thoughtfully on his ear, he said, "What else do you remember?"

"Absolutely nothing. He fixed himself a drink and went into the study. I heard him on the telephone, but I couldn't hear what he was saying. I never eavesdropped on his calls. I never felt I had the need." The guilt whipped through her suddenly, violently, without the buildup that would allow her to maintain decorum, and she burst out, "I should have, though. It might have helped. He needed someone—"

"Don't," Mickey urged, enclosing her fingers tightly in his. "It's obvious you cared, and he closed you out. That's not your fault."

"Do you think so?" she asked, needing his encouragement. She scanned his face, saw the experience in it, etched by the worry and pain and loneliness of his particular hell. "Do you understand what John was going through? Would you close out somebody who loved you and wanted to help you through a crisis?"

Mickey glanced at his knuckles. "Probably. When discovering secrets is how you make your living and keeping them is how you survive, you keep the emotions down deep.

You learn to hide what you feel, and that could save your life."

She wondered what secrets John had kept. "How do you stand it? How did he?"

"People adjust, Laura. I don't think about how I feel, usually. I just go with it. If I feel lousy, I assume it's because I haven't figured an angle right or I need some sleep. I don't take it further than that. I've never been one for the old heart-to-heart. Today's an exception."

Did he mean that he felt something special toward her? Was the emerging warmth she felt for him being returned? Immediately she discounted the idea. She was a good listener and he was tired. His protective barriers were down, that was all. "No heart-to-hearts with Veeta?" she queried. "In your early days?"

He laughed derisively. "Veeta didn't have feelings. How could she understand mine? She wants and she takes. That's all."

"But didn't you used to want to talk about personal things? Once? Ever?"

He wrinkled his brow. "Maybe. A long, long time ago."

And then, she thought, the reality of living together set in. She could relate.

"Well, John didn't talk about feelings, either," she said. "But I'm beginning to think that's wrong. I think it makes you sick to keep it all inside." She appealed to him, wanting to confirm her discovery. "People can't grow if they don't feel, don't express those feelings."

"You may be right. But if you don't feel, you don't hurt, in my book."

She bowed her head, nodded. "That's awful, but it's true."

"Hey. Enough of this droll stuff." He plucked at a tendril of her hair, smoothed it into place, until she looked up and saw a glint of humor in his eyes. "Like I said, a juicy pizza and a game of darts goes a long way toward curing the blues."

"I'll have to try that," she said, and laid her head on his shoulder because she wanted the closeness and needed to rest.

She supposed they'd talk about John again. But now there wouldn't be quite the pain. The man beside her could be gentle. He'd experienced terrible losses, too. She could tell him.

Mickey leaned down and pressed his lips against her forehead. Feeling safe for the first time in many months, she drifted off.

New Orleans

THE RAIN WAS SUDDEN. One minute Mickey could see the brown Mississippi earth steaming beneath black thunder-clouds. The next, a bright flash, a crack and rumble, and thick rain sluiced down to cool the ground and slick the highway. The heavy water grayed the billboards, blurred the car dealerships, diffused the housing of outlying New Orleans.

A truck whammered by, throwing a wall of oily water against the driver's window of the luxurious silver Lexus. The force of the blow-by shook the car, yet the big V-8 sedan purred on under Mickey's steady hand, making him feel insulated, pampered, in control. Instructing Laura to play the rich widow in case they needed credibility in deal-ing with the thieving perpetrators offered an unexpected side benefit, he mused. It gave his normally grim life-style a boost. Enjoying the rush of velocity, he whipped into the right lane and took the 610 toward downtown.

"How far to the hotel?" Laura asked, checking her seat belt.

"Maybe ten more minutes," he said, and grinned at her. "My driving scare you?"

"Ever been on the roller coaster at Magic Mountain?"

"Uh-uh."

"I haven't, either, but in comparison, I bet it feels like a mule train."

He chuckled, feeling good, feeling closer to Laura than to any woman in memory. Something had changed in him after they'd talked today. He was more connected somehow. More alive. There was even a little beacon of hope flashing around inside him. And it wasn't just because he'd gotten some shut-eye on the plane.

His mind relived how it felt to hold her while she took a nap beside him. Aroused was how he'd felt. Protective, too, but the key reaction was entirely male. The longer he was with her, the more he wanted her—not just once, but a thousand ways from Sunday.

He ought to get a handle on that kind of thinking; it could compromise the case. He knew it, and yet he half hoped this plumber, Delarein, was too busy to meet with them tonight. He'd like to make better use of the time . . . a good meal, some rest. Then a long, slow beginning that ended in a wild night of pleasure.

Laura was making him aware of how long it had been since he'd indulged his sensuous side. He liked taking her hand, tracing her skin. He liked watching her eyes as they changed like the weather with every new sight, every shift in her mood. Restraint was beginning to be difficult. A kiss on the forehead—what was that? Nothing. He wanted all of her. His libido strained at the bit to know the intimate shape of her, the taste of her—

He left that thought to overtake a car, and to reprimand himself as he moved back into his own lane.

Give it up, he told himself. This wasn't a vacation, it was a mission. If they slept together, it had to be taken lightly, in stride, like the airline flights and the car chases and the interviews—the small events that wove the fabric of his cases.

The problem temporarily seated in logic, where it didn't threaten his devotion to The Cause, Mickey bent his natural resources to finding the hotel.

They passed a mausoleum on the right, a cemetery on the left, and rounded into the city. The Superdome, out the driver's-side window, shimmered in the rain and seemed to hover like an extraterrestrial aircraft.

Laura was looking at a map. "It's the Superdome exit we want," she said. "It's coming up next."

Taking the exit, Mickey followed her directions, turning right on Girod, passing the high-end department stores and shops of the New Orleans Center and entering a tunnel. The whir of wet tires echoed off the walls. He took a left and drove across cobblestones and brick to the covered motor lobby of the Hyatt Regency Hotel, where fountains and hanging plants grounded the soaring glass highrise.

A doorman, red-and-black uniform trimmed in gold, beckoned an attendant to park the car. Then he ushered them toward the registration area. As Laura slipped her credit card to the clerk, Mickey gazed at the twin sculptures above them, rainbow cubes suspended from the ceiling. It was good to be traveling first-class again, he thought. He was beginning to lose the discomfort he'd felt at Grosvenor House in London.

Minutes later, the bellman, a black man with hair like a white lamb, unlocked Mickey's room and hung his traveler in the closet. He opened an adjoining door to Laura's room and carried her bag in. With Mickey and Laura in tow, he explained the in-room movie system, the hairdryer in the bathroom, the valet and food services of the hotel. Mickey pressed some ones into his palm and saw him to the door.

"I want a nap!" Laura exclaimed, and Mickey turned in time to see her flop like a rag doll onto the king-size bed. She waved her arms in the air and let them fall above her head, onto the rose floral coverlet.

At this evidently unconsciously provocative gesture, Mickey wanted more than a nap. The gunmetal-gray lapels of her suit slid open to tantalize him with a view of cranberry silk mounds. Her legs had the sheen of expensive hosiery, and one shoe slipped off to the carpet, baring a tapered foot that begged to be kissed.

"Lord, woman, you have no idea how cruel you're being," Mickey said, feeling as if his eyes and mouth and every tendon and muscle in him were straining toward her, devouring her.

She propped up and gazed at him, her expression surprised, then pleased. "Can't a girl relax around you?" she asked, smiling.

"Not when she looks like you do on that bed," he said, and edged toward the door to his room. "I've got to call Delarein."

"Guess I'll unpack," she said, not moving. She rolled her eyes at him. "The way you take care of yourself, Mickey, I don't know how you keep up the energy."

"Active libido," he muttered, giving her a parting half smile. "If it's ever fully activated, you don't have a chance in hell of getting any sleep yourself."

"Promises, promises," he heard her quip playfully as he shut the door.

He felt out of himself for a moment—as if he were married again, but in fairyland; not to Veeta, because they'd never enjoyed the easy rapport that seemed to flow between him and Laura most of the time. It was quite pleasant, he admitted.

Hating to break the mood by calling Delarein, he decided to unpack first. He shrugged out of his sport coat and laid it across the dresser; removed his shoes, socks, tie. He went to the closet, unzipped his bag, brought shaving and grooming things to the bathroom, still ruminating about Laura.

He'd never had a female buddy or partner before. Hanging around with her wasn't half bad. She was happy most of the time, reminding him by her nature to lighten up and live. Quiet, too, when the moment called for it. And good at conversation, good at listening, good at making him feel like what he had to say was important.

When he wasn't telling her to stay out of his business, that is. He grinned into the mirror. She hated that, being told he was in charge.

How far could he push her, he wondered? What was her dark side like? Veeta was almost entirely dark side—

absorbed in self, insecure, possessive, demanding. Laura, it seemed, was strong-willed but not domineering. Properly aroused, her darker side might be a commanding passion. He could appreciate a quirk like that.

"Mmm," he murmured, wishing he could climb into bed with her. Duty called, though. He couldn't afford to be sidetracked with so much at stake.

Reminded, he mulled over what she'd told him about the documents couriered with the emerald. He'd just about decided, after what she and Garth had both said about them, that the documents had been important. Highly important. Had they been key to an NSI operation? Secret enough to cost him his job when they were stolen, implicating him? Or had Garth gotten himself a client who needed the documents for clandestine reasons?

Suddenly he was weary clear to his bones with playing his habitual twenty questions. Maybe because Laura had gotten under his skin with her talk of marriage and family life and how it had all come apart, or maybe because he hadn't had a woman in so very long—tonight he didn't want to mull over the mysteries of the documents. He hungered for diversion.

In an act of pure self-indulgence, he checked his reflection in the glass above the sink. Thanks to the laundry on Fifth Street, his plum-colored shirt still looked fresh. He'd need to shave again before the meeting, though. The electric razor he carried in the Chevy didn't do justice to his black beard. He leaned closer. Laura had been graceful in hinting about it, but she was right. The strain of his lifestyle showed. The grooves around his mouth were deep, and his eyes were still a little bloodshot. *Need some decent sleep,* he mused, rubbing his chin. *Going to get ring around the eyeball one of these days.*

Sleep reminded him of Laura. *Right next door.*

"After the emerald comes home and Veeta's in jail," he promised himself. "Then we'll see about my English Sleeping Beauty." He clicked off the bathroom light.

On his way back to the closet to hang out his suit for the meeting, he eyed the bed. King-size. Nice playground. He shook his head. His biorhythms must be up around the genius creative level or something. With the rain drumming on the glass and a beautiful brunette lounging in the other room, wanting a nap, the thought of making that phone call and going out into the weather left a sour taste in his mouth. But it had to be done.

He dug out his wallet and studied the number.

Circling the bed, he picked up the phone and carried it to a round table backed by sheer drapes and that whirring curtain of rain. He punched in the numbers. Two rings, then—

"Delarein," drawled a mature male voice.

"Afternoon," Mickey said by way of a greeting. "I'm Michael Stone. I was told we could meet to discuss the emerald."

"Why, yes, Stone." The man's drawl intensified with interest. "I've been expectin' your call. When'll you be in N'Orleans?"

"Just arrived."

"Here already? Damn the luck, man, I've got meetin's clear through this evenin'. But I want to meet with you, Stone, certainly I want to meet. Let me check—" Papers rustled, a female voice murmured in the background.

Delarein was awfully friendly for a blackmarketer, Mickey thought. Awfully relaxed. Maybe it was just the man's personality. At any rate, it looked as if they'd do some good work together. He was just feeling a nudge of the old excitement when Delarein came back on the line.

"Stone?" he said.

"Yeah."

"At ten-thirty I'll be in the Quarter—" he pronounced it "quaaw-ta" "—meetin' some folks. I could scrape a few minutes off a nine-thirty conference call, I believe. How 'bout ten at the Cajun Room? It's a new club just down from Felix's—that's at the corner of Bourbon and Iberville. You know where it is?"

Paydirt. And so soon. Enthusiasm for his mission zapped back into place as if it had never drifted away. "I'll find it," Mickey said. "How'll I know you?"

"I'm a carrot top. My mama was a good Frenchwoman, best they come, but she had the hair of a jezebel." Delarein chuckled. "In these parts, I stand out."

"All right. Ten o'clock. The Cajun Room."

"Mighty fine, then. I'll wait for you on the steps. Glad to hear from you, Stone."

"Pleasure's mine."

They broke the connection.

Elated, Mickey slugged his fist into his palm. Laura must be his lucky charm. He swung around and plowed through the door to tell her the good news.

Seeing her, he stopped dead still, his mouth ajar.

Laura was nude—glistening, dripping from the shower.

"For the love of *God*," he groaned.

Lean and pale as a modern sculpture, lit from behind, she was just coming past the bed, a towel pushed against her hair to catch the drops of moisture.

Breathing stilled. They were caught five feet apart, both of them riveted by the accident of intrusion.

Longing crackled through him.

Beyond the sheer drapes of this rose-and-gray room, rain sheeted through an early Louisiana twilight. Drumming, beating, like the sudden heavy cadence of his heart. *Time,* was all he thought. *They had time to kill....*

She made a birdlike movement, hand across her breast, and it triggered him.

Mickey took two strides and stood before her. He molded his hands to her damp shoulders. Instantly he could feel the tremble in her. It made him hesitate, but his breath tore in little pent-up gusts. He hardened then, swelling as if the mature body inches away had joined with him already.

Her lovely gaze traveled up, up to his face, and clung there. "Mickey," she whispered in admonition, in uncertainty.

Again that little *pling* inside him, and he answered the need in them both by kissing her. Not some delicate feather touch, but heated, urgent, possessive.

The marble sculpture in his arms came alive. Her lips melted for him, gave to his invasion. The towel fell away. Her arms circled his neck and she came roughly against him, breasts as full and ripe and warm as he'd dreamed.

He kissed her there, hungrily, noisily, and she arched back.

Taking her by the torso, he bent to the shadow beneath a breast and trailed his lips, pressed his cheek there, dusted her skin with his hair, incessantly seeking, exploring. Her fingers tugged through his hair, and she shivered, moaned, pleaded, "Please..."

Was ever a woman ready for him like she? Never in memory. Before the thought was fully formed, he lifted her, slid her onto the bed, one hand tugging off his belt and loosening his slacks.

"Mickey," she breathed, "Mickey," and urgency beat heavily in his blood.

She hurried him, helped him, unsheathing his buttons, baring his shoulder and blazing a trail of moist kisses over his flesh.

As he skinned off his clothes, they moved in a kind of twining dance and there was no hesitation in her, none at all. Only an answering need.

He found that concave plain between her ribs that made her shiver when he kissed her there, and he did so, again and again. He found another tender area under the damp flood of her hair.

She crouched, arched her neck, whimpering.

Something made him open his mouth wide and press his teeth into her nape, and a tremor shook her entirely.

She changed then, came alive with feline power. Curling beneath him, she kissed him where his jugular throbbed. He caught a glimpse of her eyes. Midnight blue and glittering with hunger, half woman, half cat. Her lips curved and she drew her fingernails down the length of his back.

Fire ran to his gut, raged, exploded. He groaned. As he brought his mouth to her, he heard her laugh, triumphant and joyous.

She was a thing to be tamed. Wild, hot cat-woman in heat, and he felt the terror and the glory of taming her. Only need now, only an ache and a dizziness and the drive to conquer the she-cat who flayed his skin and breathed her musk and tore at him and thrilled him with her writhing.

Arching, she took his flanks in her hands, and he felt the comblike pricks of her nails as she held him. And that was the last of his restraint. They joined wholly, and again—again—again—

Chapter Eight

They slept as if drugged, deeply and quietly, half swathed in blankets, chests bared to the cooling air. Mickey's leg tented the sheet over Laura's thigh, and he was unaware of the darkness or the rain outside or the way time had escaped. Laura's hand lay against his face and she smiled in unconscious contentment.

A rattle of thunder woke Laura. She blinked in the dark, confused about the ache in her feminine center. There was an unfamiliar warmth beneath the back of her hand. *Mickey's face,* she thought, and lightning blanched their bodies, bringing flashes of recall about their tumultuous lovemaking.

Immediately she knew something inside her had changed. Irrevocably and shatteringly changed. She felt *whole.* United with herself. Complete. She was that prim Ellen Barkin awakened to womanhood by the steamy sexuality of Dennis Quaid in *The Big Easy,* shot right here in the rain and heat of New Orleans. Only, the name of her undercover cop was Mickey Stone, and he was real. And she was in love with him.

Feeling giddy with joy, she caressed his cool shoulder, felt the crisp delicate hair on his chest, ran her hand lightly over the protrusion of his right hip. *Incredible man,* she thought. *What miracles you perform.*

Her caresses disturbed him. He uttered a low moan and moved fretfully. Then his breathing deepened again. What

troubled his sleep? she wondered. Even while he had no
conscious thought, couldn't he revel in the same glorious
feeling of deliverance she felt?

Lightning frissoned, thunder grumbled, and she thought,
Poor baby, it's just exhaustion. "Rest, my love," she murmured, easing out of the bed.

Her thighs ached, too. Evidently she'd been doing the
wrong exercises three times a week at the health club. But
then, she thought, no workout in the world could have
prepared her for making love with Mickey Stone.

The clock on the nightstand read 9:15. Time enough for
a shower, and then she'd call room service and order dinner for two.

Mickey hadn't said if Delarein could see them tomorrow. If not, perhaps they could make their business calls—
she needed to phone Hendley—then roam around the
French Quarter, listen to Dixieland jazz, sample some Cajun shrimp jumbalaya. And go back to bed! She grinned.
They wouldn't be bored, waiting to see Delarein.

Laura hugged herself. *Tomorrow.* They had tomorrows.

Picking up the fuchsia sweater and slacks she'd intended
to put on hours ago, she went into the bathroom and
quietly shut the door.

A look in the mirror made her glad she'd decided to take
the time. Her mascara was smudged, her hair tangled, her
mouth swollen. "My my," she said to her reflection. "You
look downright ravished."

The shower warmed her and revitalized sore muscles. She
stepped out, gleaming and dripping and famished. She
wondered if Mickey would rather go out to eat. Someplace
casual and intimate. Deciding to be prepared in case he did,
she dried off and dressed. She was just blow-drying her hair
when there was a knock on the door.

"Laura?"

It was Mickey's voice, sounding urgent.

She cracked open the door and peeked out. Mickey was
dressed only in charcoal slacks, his dress shirt slung over his
shoulder, the subdued light from a lamp behind him out-

lining his lean physique. He looked like a seasoned Richard Gere; better, if that were possible.

"Hi," she said, grinning. "You look sexy."

"We've got to go," he said, already turning away. "Delarein's meeting us at ten o'clock in the Quarter."

She ducked after him, glancing at the clock enroute. "But it's twenty-five to. We'll just make it. I thought we'd eat. I didn't realize we were meeting him tonight."

He stopped at the door to his room, slanted a look at her, his gaze flicking over her figure. "Yeah, well. I got sidetracked."

She gave him a provocative smile. "I'll say."

"I should know better." There was disgust in his voice. "Look," he said sharply. "I've got to get showered and dressed. Be ready to roll in five minutes."

"Mickey, what—"

"Let's go, let's go. Are you coming along or not?"

Hurt, she lifted her chin. "Sure. Ring me up when you're ready."

He held her gaze for a moment. It was dim in the room, but she could see the lack of warmth in his eyes. They looked haunted. The desperation was back. He nodded, closed the door.

Baffled by his mood, she stared at the wooden barrier. The cloud she'd been riding evaporated and she landed with a crashing jolt back on earth, U.S.A.

She and Mickey had no future! Her transition from half woman to whole had been empowered by a stranger, a man driven by revenge, a man thought by his government to be a thief and a killer. Why had she forgotten his past?

As she turned to go back and finish her grooming, she knew, and her heart contracted with the shallowness of her self-deception. The afterglow she'd felt was not one of character metamorphosis, of reborn spirit, it was purely physical. Their intimacy had been an exorcism. She had needed to mourn the death of her husband, put their relationship in the past. She's needed to break free of his memory. And she'd needed, most of all, to satisfy a long-neglected hunger for a man.

Their interlude hadn't moved the earth for Mickey. He was obviously irritated by the whole thing. She was still a liability; even worse, a distraction that had nearly cost him the coveted appointment with Delarein.

She slicked on rose-red lipstick that exemplified the embarrassment she felt. Call the intimacy what it was. Body heat.

She finished drying her hair and flipped her head back to settle the fullness. There. Let it flow freely, she decided. For another hour or two, the wanton would play at being a spy, unmoved by the experience of bedding an American agent, a cop who'd fallen from grace.

In the bitter acceptance of what she'd done, she relished this spark of independence. *Let him see that this hasn't hurt me,* she thought, going into the bedroom and transferring identification and money from her purse to the pockets of a black raincoat, her movements quick and concise. *Let him see that it means nothing to me.*

No regrets, no questions, no ties, that's how to play it. Hendley would be proud of her.

The only future she had with Mickey Stone, she imagined telling her confidant and business manager, was short-term: finding the emerald together.

The adventure she'd dreamed of was here at hand. She would grasp it and wring from it every drop of experience it held, and let it last her a lifetime. Pay Mickey half the reward, say goodbye. Take the gem to Japan, deal with the insurance company, deposit her fee for brokering the gem. And then pfft—adventure over, time to go back to business as usual.

By the time the phone on the nightstand rang, Laura had composed herself. She smiled, if bitterly, and answered, "I'm ready."

They met outside their respective rooms and went wordlessly down to the motor lobby, where the car was already waiting. The rain had abated to a drizzle, but she still wished she'd brought an umbrella. The attendant ushered her into the seat and shut the door. She snapped on her seat belt in anticipation of their usual travel speed—full-ahead.

Mickey didn't disappoint her. Clicking on the windshield wipers, he revved the engine and swept out into the street. He sped through the traffic on Polydras to Carondelet, a left turn, his mood foul and impatient. Repeatedly he glanced into the rearview and craned to see the cars in front of them.

As they crossed over Canal Street to Bourbon, entering the Quarter, he muttered an expletive and took a snappy left on one of the intersecting streets. The wrought-iron grillwork of the local architecture looked misty in the drizzle. The street signs were barely visible through the blur on the windows. She wondered how Mickey could know where he was going.

He whipped down street after street, checking the rearview at every short straightaway. They accelerated to sixty miles an hour, whizzing past a ghostly mansion she would have enjoyed seeing.

Irritated by his behavior, she snapped, "Where are you going?"

"We've got a tail," he said.

"For the love of God, Mickey. This isn't Los Angeles, it's New Orleans. Nobody knows you're here." She had to grab the armrest to keep from going horizontal in another turn. "You think the world is out to get you."

"Quiet!"

"I—" She sputtered in fury, and then cried out with anger at this new insult and the hurt of her earlier humiliation. "Don't tell me to be quiet! You're a paranoid, overbearing egomaniac with no consideration for—"

"Dammit, Laura, hush up and let me drive. He's a sticky one this time."

"He's a—" She swiveled around. A dark luxury car swung around the corner they'd just passed. She blinked in the headlights. A chill of fear went through her. "What does he want? Why—"

Just in front of them a limousine edged into the street. Mickey swung around it, barely missing its bumper. Laura glanced down the tree-lined driveway. The mellow glow of lights shone eerily through massive moss-hung trees, and she thought of Tom Sawyer and the meandering Old Miss, blocks away.

Mickey zipped around the corner and took the next right.

Down the street, limousines and sports cars were idling around a driveway and sloping lawn, exhausts clouding up to fizzle in the rain. "Paydirt," he muttered.

She thought the party an obstacle to their escape; he evidently considered it a bonus.

Thirty, fifty miles per hour, they flew past hundred-thousand-dollar cars, inches from them. Then they were out into another street and heading back the way they'd come.

Laura looked back. No one followed. They'd lost their pursuers in the traffic jam and chaos of the party.

FIVE MINUTES LATER, at 10:10, they were parked at the mouth of an alley in the heart of the French Quarter. The curlicues of neon signs glowed eerily. Turn-of-the-century lamps glimmered along the sidewalk. Mickey trained his gaze across the street to a place called the Cajun Room. The stucco building was three stories high, with filigree around its balconies and a curving set of steps leading to open double doors.

A man stood silhouetted on the steps, his umbrella trickling water from its spines. He glanced at his wrist, checking the time, and looked up and down the street.

"That's our man," said Mickey, pulling the key from the ignition .

"How do you know it's him?" Laura asked, buttoning her coat, flipping up the collar.

"Told me he was a carrot top."

She glanced outside. Sure enough, Delarein's head had a rose glow about it, a detail she had missed.

A station wagon pulled up at the base of the stairs, and a girl in a pink patent-leather rain coat ducked out and ran up, waving back at the station wagon. It crawled away down the street.

"Shall we?" Laura asked, opening the door.

Mickey opened his own, letting in the tapping sound of rain and the rushing of gutter rivers. A trombone and a base fiddle warbled from somewhere down the street. "Yeah," he said absently, his eyes restlessly pouring over the scene. "Yeah, let's go."

He was being careful. Laura was grateful; her nerves still felt whacko from the roller coaster ride into town.

They met on her side of the car, beneath an awning. Mickey took her elbow and they turtled into their collars and began to run. Breaks squealed. Twenty feet away, a limousine pulled up, blocking the steps.

Mickey halted, pulling Laura awkwardly into a huddle against him.

A glance at his face, drizzled with rain and granite-still, made her look toward Delarein. Two men wearing Mickey Spillane hats, collars up and coats billowing, ran up the steps and grabbed his arms. Delarein yelled objections. They forced him into the car. Doors slammed. It sped away. The umbrella rolled, limping to a standstill in the street.

Mickey jerked Laura around and back to the Lexus. They climbed in, Laura looking askance at him. Mickey punched the accelerator, manhandling the car into motion. It slewed sideways into the street and righted. Laura clung to the dashboard.

The red taillights of the limousine disappeared down an alley with no sign to mark it. Mickey drove into the gloom after the large car. The taillights faded around the side of a brick building. Mickey doused his headlights. Slowing, he looked down the intersecting alley as they eased on past it.

"They've stopped," he said, voice grating with surprise and tension. "This is no simple kidnapping."

"What are they doing to him?" She choked down a rising hysteria. She cast worried glances at the wall against which he was parking, inches away. She felt trapped, panicked. Mickey pushed the shift into park. "Mickey," she implored, "What are you going to do?"

"Stay here," he ordered. "Don't shut off the car." He reached beneath his suit coat, drew out a compact handgun. It gleamed blue-black in the dashlights.

"Mickey," Laura pleaded, breath coming in gasps. She grasped his suit sleeve. It was damp, with only a hint of warmth beneath, as if to remind her that death could be seconds away around a stucco wall. "Don't be crazy," she said, the hysteria rising, rising. "Mickey, don't go. What are you going to do?"

"Get a grip, Laura," he said coldly.

"Get a grip? Get a grip, for the love of God! I can't—not here in some alley, miles from home. You—you with a gun!"

Suddenly he took her shoulders, his hold viselike. "You stay here, Laura. Stay here."

Like some puppy being obedience-trained, she whimpered—and then he was out of the car, into the pattering storm, shutting the door with a *snap,* crouching away in the darkness.

Laura dragged in the metal-tasting air. "Stay here," she murmured. Minutes passed. "Stay here, right here, it'll be okay. Stay—*no!*"

Before she could analyze what she was doing, she was running, splashing through puddles that surged into her shoes and splattered her clothes. She came to the corner and sank against the rough stucco, drank in a lungful of wet air, and peeked around.

The scene was Ciminoesque. A long brick wall. Trash washed up against tufts of grass. A lamp cast a misty yellow glow over a set of concrete back-entrance steps. Exhaust curled around the wheels of the black limousine.

And Mickey crab-stepped toward it, his gun drawn.

She wanted to scream; uttered a sob of fear and futility instead. What could she do to help? What if they killed him because she interfered?

Brushing a straggle of wet hair from her eyes, Laura gathered her courage to run forward if he got into trouble.

She sheltered her eyes with a hand. At that moment, the back door of the limo popped open. Something tumbled out—Delarein, clutching his midsection. He rolled into a puddle, legs churning for purchase on the wet blacktop. Muddy water sheeted from his brown, beautifully-tailored suit. The car squealed away down the alley. Mickey ran toward the fallen man, and Laura ran, too, though her legs trembled violently.

Mickey bent down, said something to Delarein. As Laura came up behind them, she heard the man curse and saw him push Mickey away. He clambered to his feet, water streaming from his clothes, his face. "Damm you, Stone," he said in an angry Southern drawl. "I want no part of your emerald. You can keep the unholy thing."

"Keep it?" Mickey gestured in confusion, evidently unaware he was waving the gun. "I don't have it, Delarein. What did those creeps want, anyway?"

Delarein backed away from him. "They warned me off you. They let me have it in the gut as punctuation. I don't need further warnin', I tell you." He stumbled over the steps, straightened, looking from Mickey to Laura. "Get away from me. The both of you, get away."

Mickey turned, reeled back at the sight of Laura standing in the drizzle, hand at her mouth.

"I told you to stay in the car!" he roared.

"You might have been hurt!"

"You'll follow my orders, do you hear?" He whirled on Delarein, waving the gun in fury. "What the devil do you mean, they warned you off me? I don't have the emerald. I came here to set up a buy from you."

Eyes huge with fear as he traced the path of the gun, Delarein glanced furtively toward the mouth of the alley. "I don't have it," he said, inching along the wall. "I wanted it, but I don't want it now."

Mickey looked down at the gun. Then he slipped it inside his suit coat. "Look, I'm no thug," he said. "Relax.

I'm a form—" he coughed, slurred 'former' so it sounded obscure, like a title "—agent with the National Security Institute and I'm trying to track down the gem."

Delarein stopped, evidently debating. He shrugged a shoulder at Laura. "Who's she?"

Laura moved toward him, her hand outstretched, a grim smile on her face. "Laura Marley, Mr. Delarein. When the emerald was stolen, my client was cheated. I'm working with Mr. Stone to get it back." She glared at Mickey. "His manners are gone, though, and he thinks practically everyone is either incompetent or a criminal. It's the stress of cracking all those international security cases, I guess. Can we give you a lift back to the club?"

Mickey's mouth was ajar. She smiled to herself.

Delarein gingerly reached out to shake her hand. His fingers were icicles. He snatched his hand back, wiped his mouth. His hand slid to his stomach and massaged.

"Are you all right?" she asked, solicitous.

"Little sore, is all, ma'am."

Mickey stepped up. "How does a plumber afford the Garden Emerald?"

"Plumber!" Delarein spat out some grit. "I'm no plumber, Stone. I'm in real estate. I own half this city and two more besides."

"A fake out," Mickey said suddenly.

"Now, see here," sputtered Delarein.

"We were both used," Mickey interrupted, eyes glittering. "And no license plate to trace the limo. Dammit! Somebody's going to great lengths to waste our time. Or worse. Come on—" he ushered them toward the Lexus "—we'll give you a lift to your car."

DELAREIN COULD TELL THEM nothing about his abductors. The backseat of the limo had been pitch black, closed off from the driver's seat by a panel, he said, and he'd been so taken off guard by the ruffians he couldn't give Mickey any details about them. *Wouldn't* was more like it, Laura thought. Delarein had been thoroughly intimidated. He probably wanted to forget the incident ever happened.

By way of explaining what brought him to his plight, the real-estate mogul would admit only that he'd gotten two anonymous phone calls about the emerald being for sale at far less than market price. On the second call, he'd agreed to meet Mickey Stone, who was supposed to be offering it for sale.

After dropping off Delarein, Mickey said he wanted to drive straight to the airport and have the hotel send their luggage home the next day. Laura objected. She reminded him that they hadn't had anything to eat since breakfast on the plane, and had had very little sleep into the bargain. At Laura's insistence—very much against Mickey's will—they ran by a Jack-in-the-Box, went to the hotel to collect their clothes, and rushed over dangerously flooded roads to the airport in hopes of getting the late flight to Dallas, where they'd connect for Los Angeles.

Two hours later, dealing with irate crowds, cancelled flights and unpardonable rudeness from Mickey, Laura's feelings had gone full circle. She felt she could easily hate Mickey Stone. She could imagine never speaking to him again.

At one in the morning, she seriously considered taking a flight to New York to visit with her sister, then a flight home to London.

Unfortunately, all flights were canceled.

Saturday, January 14—Los Angeles

HAVING TO WAIT AT the airport in New Orleans until six that morning before finally getting a flight that delivered them to Los Angeles had only fueled Mickey's simmering rage.

Paishon had purposely led him to a dead end. He'd run Mickey by that invisible ring in his nose, run him on another wild-goose chase that sapped his energy and made his gut feel like steel mesh.

As if that weren't enough, Mickey was in turmoil over his relationship with Laura. It had gotten out of hand. Now there were feelings of tenderness to deal with, heightened concern for her safety and questions—unnerving unexpected questions. Chief among them, would she betray him, too?

The relationship had sprouted like a cancer in the middle of the Garden Emerald case, and Mickey, tapped out, going on nerves, back to the wall in an essentially solitary effort to solve the case, felt panic.

At Laura's suggestion to return to the Hyatt or get a motel room to wait out the canceled flights, he flatly said no. He'd let his eyes tell her the idea was treasonable—*she* was treasonable for suggesting it. At her attempts to talk, he'd angled his body away and given her sharp one-word replies.

Laura didn't know he'd been shaken by their intimacy and again by her rashness in following him to Delarein. She didn't know the anger he felt at himself for letting their affair complicate the mission. She had no clue about the fear of entrapment that choked him when he remembered how cataclysmic they'd been together in bed. She knew nothing of any of this.

He knew it, though; and yet, through that long vigil in the airport, he'd treated her abominably, hating himself for doing so.

Eventually, coldly angry at him, she'd gone to buy a paperback novel, and sat for five hours in a coffee shop to read it, waiting, like him, for the first flight out.

Now, pulling up to the curb in the cavelike Grand Avenue entrance to the Biltmore, waving over a doorman wearing a charcoal-colored top hat and uniform, he felt remorse. The events of the past day or two had punched most of the fight out of her, and he'd beaten her spirit with his rude orders and chilling silences.

He slid the gearshift into Park and glanced at her profile. She was wearing the gun-metal gray suit she'd changed into at the Hyatt. It looked crimped across the thighs from sitting so long. Before landing in L.A., she'd freshened her lipstick and combed her loose-flowing hair, a style he liked on her, but grooming couldn't erase the lavender shadows beneath her eyes. As she collected her gray leather purse, he saw a going-on-nerves exhaustion in her face. All she had left was a gritty dignity.

And as she climbed out of the Chevy, showing the attendant her bag in the backseat, Mickey felt that unfamiliar tenderness sway through him.

"Get some rest," he said, his gaze going to the shadows under her eyes. "I'm going to see Paishon. I'll check in with you later."

"Go to hell," she said, and slammed the door. Nodding to the doorman to follow with her bag, Laura swept into the lobby.

His pride stung, Mickey jammed the shift into drive and swung out onto Grand.

Twenty-five minutes later, he was still fuming when he came to a sliding stop between a gold-trimmed Eldorado and a dented green pickup. There were several other low-end vehicles ranged haphazardly along the wall outside Asian Coral Imports. Mickey lurched out of the car, barely remembering to lock up. He pushed roughly through the entrance, passed the dusty display cabinet and went straight through the connector to the halls beyond.

Someone had pushed the grocery cart full of broken coral into the hall. Mickey shoved it out of his way. It went clanging into a door and bounced off. He side-stepped it and cracked open the door to the warren of cubicles, steeling his senses to the stink of stale fish.

The young Asian woman at the computer sent him a do-not-disturb grimace as he jogged by. He came to an open space with a desk, telephone. The frail office manager wore another sagging lavender-print dress, and her hand fluttered to her throat when he nodded curtly and went on by.

"Mr. Stone," she called, trembly voiced. "Appointment . . . ?"

"No appointment," he threw back. "He damned well better be in, too."

Around the last turn, Mickey spotted some beef. Evidently this time Paishon was expecting him. Two football types in polo shirts and jeans lounged in a cubicle to the right of Paishon's office door, shoulders crowding the breathing space. The guy with the pock-marked face was reading a girlie magazine, flicking ashes from his cigarette onto the floor. The other was amusing himself by thumping his size eleven wing tip on the partition wall to see how much stress it would take before falling over.

They didn't see Mickey until he was already opening the door to Paishon's den. They jumped up, but he was already in and closing the door again.

An Asian child-woman in a short red sarong was serving the big man stir-fry, chop sticks full of dangling, steaming vegetables. She jumped back as Mickey strode to the desk.

"Leave us," Mickey ordered, jerking his thumb toward the twin doors flanking the zebra hide.

She picked up the bowls and stood still, eyes huge with surprise.

Paishon's pig eyes glittered, but he smiled. Dragging a white linen napkin from his chest, he tossed it over her arm and waved the girl away.

She ducked out of the room.

At the entrance, the football types fell over themselves trying to get in first and apologize. They bristled around Mickey.

"Boss," said Wing Tip, "he just barged in."

If he weren't so angry, Mickey would have found the situation funny. But he wanted blood himself, and he braced for a fight and glared from them to Paishon.

Paishon scowled blackly at his men. "Get out," he thundered. "Useless scumballs."

"But, boss—"

Paishon rose like a Neanderthal from behind the desk, his fists clenched. His heavily-starched shirt popped out around the tightening suit vest. He seemed to swell in size and ferocity.

The men backed out of the room and closed the door. Gently.

Paishon lowered back into his seat. His head ticked to the side—settling his nerves, maybe. "Now," he said, eyeing Mickey. "How was New Orleans?"

"You know damned well how it was."

"Ah, well," he waved. "Lovely city. Sorry you got rained out."

"You get your kicks playing games?" Mickey demanded, spreading his hands. "What are the rules here? What was the point? We had business to do."

"You disappoint me, Stone."

"Yeah? You know what you can do with your disappointment."

Paishon tsked in mock dismay. "I thought we were going to be friends. Friends can play a practical joke now and then, can't they?"

"I've got no time or patience for practical jokes." Mickey leaned forward, pressing his palms on Paishon's highly polished hand-carved property, purposely goading the man. "Give me a clue, fatman. What the hell is going on?"

Paishon lumbered up out of the chair and faced off with him, their noses inches apart. Mickey could identify every wiry black hair in the caterpillar eyebrows. He was aware that he'd forgotten his Walther in the trunk of the car. He was aware that this Portuguese coral merchant had the strength to crush his chest. His preoccupation with Laura had taken its toll. But he was in it now, and there was no backing down.

"You've got a mouth on you, boy," Paishon growled. "You don't find some respect, you'll find yourself floating in that bay out there."

"You earn respect, fatman. Sending me on a wild-goose chase gets you no respect. Putting thugs on me gets you no respect."

"I had my reasons."

"Let's hear them."

"I had to check out your resources."

"You want proof of collateral?" Mickey snapped his fingers, breaking the tension. "Ask. It's yours."

Paishon pulled to his full height. "We don't want a paper trail, do we? Anyway, no need. Nobody flies around the country at the drop of a hat without resources. Not at today's air fares. Luxury car, class hotel, connecting rooms to preserve the lady's reputation." He did that tick with his neck again. "You put out some bucks, went to some trouble. I figure you're serious about our business deal."

"Which is coming down when?"

Paishon's gaze slid away. He wiped down his coat pockets. "I'll let you know."

"You'll let me know..." Mickey smacked his palm on the desk to express his frustration and distrust. Pivoting, he walked to the fish tank, leaned against the wall and watched the boneless shadow drift through coral. "What's the holdup?"

"There are details, other interested parties. Things I got to line up."

"I don't suppose, since we're friends now, you want to confide in me."

"Confide what?"

Mickey twisted to look across the gloom at Paishon. "Who's got the emerald."

"Forget it." Paishon sat down, pushed some papers around his desk. He picked one up, looked at it, glanced at Mickey. "You going to be at the gem show next weekend?"

"I'll be there."

"I'll try to have something for you then. Meantime, get your collateral ready."

"How much?"

"Three hundred thou."

Mickey stood up. It was eight hundred thousand under the market price. "That's a little steep," he said for form's sake. "Steep for a hot one."

"That's just for openers. There'll be a silent auction. I suggest you bring whatever else you think it'll take. You want in, that's the opening price."

"The gem's hot. Why risk a crowd? Why not come to a price and let's do it?"

Paishon shuttered his eyes. "Let's just say the seller gets his kicks from taking a risk." He glared. "You waffling on me or what?"

Mickey had to be careful. The man was touchy as a mule buck in rut. "No," he said firmly. "I'm in."

"Okay, then. It's a sealed bid situation, just the figure on cheap paper, your first initial on the envelope—no other identifying marks. Highest bidder takes it. Cash, all hundreds, no series."

"All right, Mickey said, confident again and hardening his tone to make a point. "But no more side trips like New Orleans, Paishon. And no more tails. I've lost my sense of humor."

"Cool down, Stone. You're in. The games are over."

Mickey saw that Paishon's hand was extended in a let-bygones-be-bygones gesture. Mickey came to him and shook. Steel in the man's grip. Mickey gripped hard and released. They stared at each other in prehistoric assessment. Then the challenge was gone, and Mickey left him.

Chapter Nine

When he got back to the office, Mickey phoned the jeweler he'd been visiting when Veeta had walked by and set up another appointment.

He also placed a call to Garth through the office in Bogotá. He no longer trusted his boss because Garth had known about the Marley link but not reported it to NSI. He certainly hadn't told Mickey about it. Therefore, Mickey reasoned as he waited on the line, he wouldn't tell Garth about Paishon or the gem sale. But he needed to clarify pricing on some shipments of sapphires and diamonds ar-riving at LAX this week, before he marketed the gems to customers or to other dealers at the gem show. And he wanted to know what kind of documents had been couriered with the Garden Emerald.

Garth, he was told by the telephone switchboard opera-tor, was still in transit to the office. He left a message for Garth to call back.

Then, wondering who had had him tailed prior to meet-ing Paishon for the first time, Mickey called his best friend.

Clint said he was expecting Mickey's intelligence reports to come in that afternoon and early tomorrow. Agreeing it would be easier to camouflage a rendezvous among the comings and goings of other hotel guests, they set up a meeting the following morning in Laura's suite, where they would discuss Clint's findings—and, only Mickey knew, make plans to recover the emerald at Paishon's sale.

As he broke the connection, Mickey felt uneasy about the meeting. Clint didn't know about the sale. He'd be amazed, concerned, pleased about the breakthrough. But he wasn't going to like what Mickey had to ask of him. There was no other choice, Mickey thought, tired clear to his bones. NSI had to cough up the money for the gem, the manpower to make the bust, and only Clint could pull the strings to make that happen. He had to.

Finally, his insides jittery with stress, Mickey telephoned Laura.

She sounded groggy when she said hello.

"Sorry to wake you," he said, keeping his voice neutral. "I'd like to set up a meeting in your suite tomorrow morning."

"What kind of meeting?" she asked, cool.

If he weren't so tired, her tone would have goaded him to anger. He said simply, "Planning meeting. My ex-partner, Clint, will be there. We'll check for bugs before we begin."

"Bugs? You mean microphones?"

"That's right."

"What time?"

"Ten okay?"

"Fine."

He hesitated, feeling uncomfortable with the distance between them.

"Anything else?" she prompted, sounding impatient.

"No, I guess not. Talk to you then."

She hung up, no goodbyes.

In a rush of temper, Mickey swatted at the paperwork on his desk. It fluttered to the floor.

Well, he thought, he deserved her anger. Better yet, he wanted it. It helped to keep his libido in check, helped him focus on business. He sighed. The honeymoon was definitely over.

The most immediate chores done, Mickey showered and collapsed on his cot. As he floated into that no-man's land between consciousness and sleep, he saw Laura's body beneath him, slick with moisture and over-the-edge in ecstasy. He uttered a low, unconscious moan and drifted with that image into sleep.

Sunday, January 15—The Los Angeles Biltmore Hotel

AT SEVEN-THIRTY IN THE morning, Laura dressed simply in a navy-blue knit dress adorned with pearls at the neckline. She clipped on pearl earrings and moistened her throat with Miss Dior perfume. She fussed with her hair, finally knotting it in a loose chignon banded by a thin strand of navy ribbon. Grooming complete, she paced restlessly, reluctant to return to the proposal she'd begun writing yesterday evening for Gregorgi's furniture business.

Finally, feeling caged and agitated, Laura went down to breakfast in the Court Café. Noted for its Sunday brunch and fine Italian landscape murals, the restaurant was already swamped. Laura stared at the crowd in dismay, but eventually was seated near some windows.

While breakfasting, she relived Hendley's middle-of-the-night call asking her to return to London.

"D'you suppose you could pop back to London for a wee bit, Mrs. M.?" he'd said—and Laura, already moody and sleepless over her mistakes with Mickey and her memories, had felt her heart plummet in fear. She'd listened to Hendley's rundown on the situation with British Hospital Supply, and agreed to take the red-eye to London that night.

But first, she'd have to get through the dreaded meeting with Mickey. After all, recovering the green masterpiece was crucial to her company, she reminded herself. She'd win back some luster lost since the gem was stolen. She felt a prick of anger at John Marley for deserting her in the midst of such responsibility, and realized the healing wasn't entirely complete.

Upstairs again, she saw that Gregorgi's advertising and P.R. materials stared at her from the tidy span of the desk in the converted office. She made herself sit down. Better to have busy hands than a bad conscience and a mind full of self-pity, she decided, taking up a pencil. Besides, when she returned to London, if the Brit Hospital account let her have any breathing space, she wanted to discuss Gregorgi's proposal with Hendley and ask him to finalize it.

For forty minutes, she sketched ads and jotted down copy, wrote headlines and outlined financing arrangements, trying very hard to keep Mickey's blaming, condescending expressions out of her thoughts. At last she managed the concentration and decided, as she worked, that it would be wise to ask Gregorgi what top-end budget he thought would be acceptable to Yugo–U.S.

But as soon as she heard a knock at the entryway door, her mind returned directly to the subject she'd tried to avoid all morning. She formed a picture of Mickey scowling at her in the airport, and the disappointment and hurt she'd felt through the aftermath of their lovemaking returned full flood. Emotionally, she felt like a schoolgirl weathering her first breakup, all nerve ends and whirling feelings.

She put down the pencil and rose to stand stiffly by the desk, girding herself for a confrontation.

What humiliation would he try to heap on her today in front of his ex-partner? She must be prepared to take the offensive.

What secrets would he keep from her about the case? She had to go to London because the survival of the company depended on it, but Stone had made a bargain with her, and if she had to leave, he'd damn well keep her informed about the emerald.

Walking to the entry, she felt her facial muscles go rigid with determination. If he hedged on any detail this morning, she'd bully him into keeping his pledge and above all, she'd demand some respect.

When she opened the door, she showed that willful, chilly expression not to Mickey but to a stranger with close-cropped sandy hair and an official-looking black briefcase.

"H-hello," she stammered. "I thought . . ."

"Mrs. Marley?"

"Yes. You're Clint?"

"That's right." Clint's eyes reminded her of birds' eggs, the hazel irises speckled with bits of black. "Am I disturbing you—here a little early?"

"Good Lord, no. I'm sorry. Preoccupied, I guess." She stepped back to admit him. "Come in, Clint. Call me Laura."

He smiled. It brought out the crows' feet around his eyes, placing his age at early-to-mid-forties. A yellow knit golf shirt and cotton trousers fit his compact body perfectly, and he moved like a younger man, doing that security check she'd come to expect from his profession.

As he set the briefcase alongside a wing chair, his glance took in the closed door to the bedroom, the open one on his right that led to the office. He walked between the dining table and the conversation nook to the windows. He grasped a wooden slat on the window shutters and pried open a panel to gaze at the park. "Where's that tall bag of bones, anyway?" he asked.

She smiled, and when he turned around, she said, "He's not here yet."

"What's funny?"

"He told me you'd check for bugs. That's what you're doing, isn't it?"

"Trying to be casual about it, but yeah. I should do a thorough check before we discuss anything sensitive." He smiled expectantly. "What do you think, so far?"

"About what?"

"Whom," Clint corrected, opening the shutters to run his hand along the window molding and peer into dim corners. "About Mickey. How's he holding up?"

"Holding up?" Disconcerted by the memories that rushed at her of New Orleans, the rain, the darkness and ecstasy, she turned away. *He's holding up fine,* she thought, *but it's taking its toll on me.*

She adjusted one of the dining chairs more evenly with the table. "He seems ... preoccupied, I guess."

"That's two preoccupieds and one out-on-a-limb."

"I'm sorry, I don't follow you."

He went to the couch cushions, pulled them out one by one and inspected the empty sockets with his hands, talking right through the exercise.

"Well," he said, bent sideways, "you said you were preoccupied. Mickey's preoccupied. That's two."

"And you're out on a limb?"

"I'm—" he patted down the sides of the contemporary couch and looked beneath the French Provincial coffee table "—sticking my neck out to help Mickey when I can. It all adds up to a can of worms."

"So why do you help him?"

Clint lifted a heavy glazed duck from the table and looked under it, studying the rough, unpainted base. He put it back. "Mickey's a good man, Laura. The best partner, best friend I've ever had. We have history."

She nodded.

Clint's flitting hazel gaze came to rest on her face. "He went through hell when the agency let him go. Faced with ostracism and a major investigative hassle and no end of personal persecution, he still stayed in L.A. Most men, most agents, couldn't have stood it. They'd have picked up and moved someplace where nobody knew them and started over, if they could. Or maybe died a slow death. Mickey just hung in, trying to clear himself and bring the thieves to the ground. He's either the most courageous man I've ever known, or the biggest fool. I haven't decided which."

"To tell you the truth, I haven't, either."

He studied her features as if her face were a stakeout map. He arched a sand-colored eyebrow. "His macho ego giving you some trouble?"

"God, he's unbelievable!" Laura strode to the windows, looked out and saw nothing, eager to vent her feelings to someone who knew the source of her agitation. "He makes me feel so unimportant, Clint. So in the way."

"That stunt Veeta pulled turned him bitter. He was never a very trusting soul to begin with."

She turned, her hands clasped tightly. "Why, Clint?"

"You have a newspaper?"

"News— Of course, just a moment." She went to the bedroom and retrieved the front-page section of the *Times*. Clint had put a chink in the armour of attitude she'd built up about Mickey, and now she felt uncertain. Was she wrong to be so angry at him? But no, she'd been devastated by his coldness, his rejection. She'd been insulted by his rude directives and inconsiderate dictates. It wasn't right to mete out that kind of abuse. Especially to a partner. They were supposed to be partners in finding the emerald, weren't they? How had Clint dealt with Mickey's ruthless side all these years and come away best friends?

Wanting to know what else Mickey's devoted friend could tell her, she hastened back to the living room and handed the paper to Clint.

He split the pages and put half on a dining chair, half on the table. Pushing back a huge bowl of irises and oak leaves, he climbed up and began turning the branches of the crystal chandelier, checking for microphones.

"He told me, basically, that being an agent taught him to hide everything inside," she offered.

"It does that to you, for sure," Clint mused aloud, still working. "But Mickey started out not trusting. Why? I don't know. He lost his older brother when he was still in diapers. That might have scarred him. He comes from a monyed family. He said he had a decent childhood, but I don't think there was much closeness. They rarely visit. His father was heavy into design engineering in Silicon Valley. A pretty cerebral guy, I hear. His mother's still doing a lot of social work. I figure Mickey was a lonely kid."

"They say if you don't have solid emotional support at home, you don't learn to trust others later on."

"Yep. I was lucky that way. When I was a kid, my house was Grand Central and my parents did stuff with us. Ball games, birthday parties." Crystals tinkled as he turned the light fixture. "We were tight, you know?"

"Yes, I do. My sister and I were close. We had to work for our allowances and felt persecuted for it. But, really, we never wanted for anything, and we all got along. And when my children were growing up, John and I gave them all the nurturing we possibly could. I've got some wonderful kids."

"Mickey tells me you're a widow."

She was surprised by the directness of his remark. For a moment, the black months after the suicide crowded her mind. But somehow, since she'd begun to tell the story to Mickey and now felt comfortable around Clint, it was easier to talk about John.

"My late husband took a lot of sleeping pills one afternoon at the office. He died of an overdose."

She waited for the humiliation to sweep over her, but she felt only a nudge of awkwardness and the sharp prick of an old loss. She glanced at Clint for his reaction.

"That's hard," he said, climbing down off the table, dusting his hands. Evidently the subject didn't provoke his interest. He scanned the room. "So far, no third parties. Clean as a whistle." He checked his watch. "He's ten minutes late. Wonder what's keeping him?"

The phone rang. "That might be Mickey," Laura said, hoping it was not more bad news from London or from Mickey. "Last time he was late," she added, "he'd seen his ex-wife and tried to track her down."

"Seen Veeta?" Clint faced her abruptly, his eyes wide. "Where?"

"In the mall," she said, indicating the ringing phone. "I'd better see who it is."

Clint waved her away.

When she picked up the phone, Gregorgi greeted her in that tweaky voice of his. She drew a breath of relief that it was a routine business call, and asked him to hold on for a moment. She came back to Clint, who was crouched down before the fireplace, scooping out its charred interior.

"It's a client," she said. "I'm working on an advertising plan for him and need to go over a few things." Clint craned around to nod, and she added, "I'll try to be brief, and then I'll order coffee—or would you like something else? Rolls, eggs, some juice?"

"Sounds good, Laura, if it's no trouble," he said. "I had some cold cereal at seven. But if I know Mickey, he won't have eaten before he arrives."

She rolled her eyes in agreement. "On the road, he's a madman, running on nerves alone. Or should I say, revenge. It's downright scary, sometimes." She gave Clint a what-can-you-do shrug and smiled, appreciating the openness between them. "I won't be long."

Garth Gem Brokerage

AFTER HIS WORKOUT and shower that morning, Mickey took more time than usual to dress for the meeting, choosing a suit, then discarding it and pawing through the scarred wooden wardrobe near the dresser to find and discard trousers, jeans, shirts. Irritated with himself, he pulled on comfortable black slacks and a forest-green polo shirt that uncannily matched his eyes. What could it hurt to play up his assets, he reasoned. He was tired of fighting.

Fighting with Laura wore on him, added to his anxiety. It tripled his resentment toward Veeta, with whom he'd endured years of nit-picking incompatibility.

Scanning the clothing and paperwork he'd scattered like fall leaves around his living quarters, he realized the mess reflected the chaos of his mind. In the past week, while he traveled to London and back and to New Orleans and back, dust and grit from the downtown traffic had filtered in through the windows, filming the vast hardwood floor. The bathroom needed a good scrubbing. Even worse, his files were in disarray.

Leave them, he thought, striding to the door, already running late. Besides, convincing Clint to rally the money and forces of NSI for the gem bust was far more important than maintaining his usual fastidiousness.

The Biltmore

TEN MINUTES LATER, HIS STOMACH acidic, he was knocking on the door to Laura's suite.

Clint opened it. As his friend stepped back to let him in, Mickey realized immediately he'd pulled Clint from his regular Sunday golf game.

"Hey, Clint," he said, shaking hands. "Where're your golf shoes and clubs?"

"In the trunk of my car."

"That's what I figured."

"If we're done by noon, maybe I can team up with another single and still play."

"No problem, buddy. We'll see that you do."

Mickey glanced around the suite. Both doors to adjoining rooms were closed, and she wasn't in the room. "Where's Laura?" he asked, walking to the shuttered windows.

"Talking to a client about some advertising."

Mickey listened, heard the faint melodic sound of her voice.

"She's a good-looking woman," Clint offered, hinting for Mickey's opinion of her.

Mickey nodded, slanting open the shutters to peer around the window molding, looking for microphones. It was clean.

"I've already done the windows and doors," said Clint. "The lamps, heating vents, chairs, drawers and tables. I left the flower arrangement for you."

"Thanks, buddy."

He went to the dining table and pawed as delicately as he could through the oak leaves and iris blossoms. He ran his finger around the inside edge of the bowl. He tilted it up and wiped the base with his hand. "Clean," he concluded. "What about the chandelier?"

"Already checked it out," Clint said. "Nice piece, isn't it?"

"Mmm."

"Laura's a winner, Mickey. A looker. Smart." His gaze circled the room. "Bucks don't seem to be a problem."

"What are you, her press agent?"

"Hey, I just know a good one when I see one. Don't tell me you haven't noticed the assets."

Mickey's mouth tightened. He focused on a contemporary painting with hearts in it, above the mantle.

"That's what I figured," Clint said. "Treat her right, Mickey."

Mickey swiveled to Clint. "What's that supposed to mean? She been crying on your shoulder?"

"What do we have here, a little guilt?" Clint's mouth pulled into a smirk. "I can read faces, buddy. She didn't have to say much. You just cinched it."

When Mickey looked away, Clint urged, "So all right, you and Veeta never had much in common; she needed a lot of attention and you had a career to build. You deserved a better partner. Laura's got sensitivity. She's got self-respect. She's not the type to think only of herself and wring every ounce of humanity from you, then leave you for the buzzards. Give her a chance to prove herself, why don't you?"

"Clint, for the love of God," Mickey snapped, speaking sotto voce so she wouldn't overhear. "What do I offer someone like her? My hearth and home? It's sold. My bank account or earning capacity? I'm tapped out. You've seen her. She lives in fairyland where the streets are paved in gold. I'm so close to living with the bums it's not funny."

"Pure paranoia."

"Really? How many of them do you think had it good as kids, like me? Then something went wrong and they ended up on skid row."

The thought chilled him and he veered away from it. "Oh, yes," he said bitterly, as if in afterthought, "then there's my heart. How much of that do you suppose is left after the buzzards, as you call them, picked it clean?"

Clint grinned at him sideways. "You've been a macho idiot, haven't you?"

Mickey felt transparent. Clint had the ability to read him, too. Always had. "We're from different worlds," he said defensively, tired of the cross-examination. "Leave it alone."

Crossing the room, he took a seat on the print sofa facing the fireplace. He gave Clint a cool-it glance. "What'd you find out about Paishon?"

At that moment, Laura came into the room, saying, "Sorry. It took a while to get the financing lined up. Oh—" her glance cut to Mickey and zipped away "—you're both here. Good."

"Morning," Mickey said.

The navy-blue dress and the pearls and that gently pulled-back hairstyle made her utterly beautiful. She was pale, with a chiseled delicacy. She looked like a cameo again, just as she had when he'd first met her in London.

He grappled with his pride and the embarrassment of having to patch things up in front of Clint. "You get some good rest?"

"Yes...." Laura took a seat in the wing chair to Mickey's left, leaving Clint to fetch his briefcase and arrange himself down from Mickey on the couch. "Gregorgi's media information came by courier yesterday," she said. "I've been putting the rough ideas together."

"How's it going?"

She smoothed her skirt, settled herself deeper into the chair. "Fine." She looked expectantly at Clint. "What are we going to talk about? Mickey—what happened yesterday with the Shark Man?"

Clint sat back from his open briefcase. "Shark Man?"

"Paishon," Mickey explained.

Clint grinned inquiringly at Laura.

She shrugged. "Paishon has a big shark swimming around in a tank in his office."

"Nice call, Laura," said Clint, lifting out a typed sheet of paper. "Good alias."

Mickey propped a leg on his knee. The two of them certainly got along, he thought, feeling isolated. What the hell, this was a business meeting, not an admiration society. With a lot to accomplish convincing Clint to help gather the cash for the gem bust, he decided to run the meeting.

"What d'you have for me, Clint?" he asked.

"The black Riviera is licensed to a factory worker in Silverlake. I called him, ostensibly about a Riviera that had been reported missing. Found out he sometimes loans the car to his brother-in-law, a tire store manager in the same neighborhood."

"Who had the car the day we were tailed?"

"The store manager. I checked him out. He did some time for auto theft about ten years back. He's been clean ever since. But there's an interesting detail."

"What's that?" Mickey leaned forward. "He does gems on the side?"

"Nope. At the time of his conviction for auto theft, he was working in a pizza joint owned by The Tape."

Schooled in emotional control, Mickey simply went still, keeping his face neutral. But his empty stomach cinched up and blood rushed in his ears.

Clint was explaining to Laura, "We figure he stole the Garden Emerald."

"You mean NSI figures he did?" asked Laura.

"No. NSI has a sworn statement by one of the Pershing Square locals who says he saw The Tape in that limo Veeta climbed into with the gem. In the alley back of Garth's building. But NSI thinks Mickey put her and The Tape up to it." He sighed in disgust. "Unbelievable. Anyway, Mickey and I think The Tape masterminded the theft."

Struggling to stay in the present, to overcome his choking hatred, Mickey said to Clint, "Maybe they're back in the area. Headquartered here again. Veeta gave me the slip the other day."

"I told him," said Laura.

Clint gave him a chastising look that said, *You* didn't.

"What about the tire store manager?" Mickey said, sticking to the point. "Can you have him picked up?"

"On what?"

"Guilt by association," Mickey said bitterly.

"You wish."

"Yeah, I wish."

Clint cleared his throat. "Look, I have more for you, Mickey. Stay with me."

Clint was reading him again, easily as big print. Mickey shoved the rage and betrayal down deep. "Yeah, all right. What do you have?"

"About the Shark Man." Clint winked at Laura. Her lips curved minutely.

Mickey said, "Go ahead."

Clint flexed a report in his hands and bowed his head over it. "Paishon's close association with the law began when he was ten. He robbed a bakery. At ten and a half, he robbed a dime store and it went on like that for the next seven years—in and out of foster homes and Juvy."

Laura's hand fluttered. "Didn't he have a family?"

"His parents both worked in the Produce Mart right here in downtown L.A., buying fish from the boats in San Pedro, selling it off a table at the market. Meanwhile, Paulo Paishon and his six siblings evidently ran wild. Your typical latchkey situation, only back then they blamed it on the kids and called it juvenile delinquency."

Laura tsked in sympathy. "No wonder he comes off like an overgrown hoodlum."

"A bad past can ruin a kid," Mickey said, glad to have something noncombative to say to Laura. "These streets are crammed with youngsters who don't have parental support because the folks are hustling to put beans on the table. The kids get bored. They develop low self-esteem. In with the wrong crowd, they get hooked on drugs, get into robbery, prostitution, gangs."

"Like Fast Eddie," she said, shaking her head in dismay.

"And worse cases you haven't met and don't want to."

"Well," Clint said with a twist of cynicism, "our latchkey kid landed in jail at eighteen for grand larceny."

Mickey gave Laura a see-what-I-mean look. She nodded.

As he read further, Clint's eyebrows rose. "Sent into the army. Two stints in Vietnam."

"Two?" queried Mickey, surprised at the dedication that implied.

"Yep. Paishon was decorated for bravery, how about that?"

"What else?"

Outside in the hallway, someone tapped at the door.

Laura rose. "That's room service," she said, walking into the foyer.

She returned pushing a cart laden with covered platters and a carafe of coffee. "Come and get it," she said. "Buffet-style okay with you?"

She said it to both of them, but she was looking at Mickey. His stomach was tight, but he figured it would be a slap in the face to refuse her hospitality. She was just beginning to be a bit less brittle around him.

"Great," he said, putting some enthusiasm into his tone as he and Clint rose from the couch. "I haven't eaten today."

"I knew that," quipped Clint. He and Laura exchanged knowing looks.

Laura served generous portions of scrambled eggs and fat brown sausage to Mickey and Clint, and poured three coffees. Laura and Clint took it black. Mickey added cream, a habit he'd developed in the past year of running down leads, when a dollop of cream was better than no food at all.

Laura fixed a lighter plate of food for herself, and brought the plate and a basket of rolls and butter to the coffee table.

"We'd better get rid of this," Mickey said, indicating the cart.

"Bugs?" she asked.

He nodded.

"In the office." She rose and opened the door for him, and went right back to her chair, giving him no time to say something conciliatory.

As he pushed the cart in and closed the door, it occurred to Mickey that Laura was always thinking of his stomach—in London, in New Orleans and in the Biltmore a few nights ago when she'd handed him that croissant wrapped in a napkin. Come to think of it, Clint was the same way. They both looked after him.

Returning to the couch, he sampled the breakfast and realized he was hungry. He tried to think of a graceful way to say thanks to Clint and Laura. But it was awkward with everyone eating, and, anyway, his pride got in the way. The words wouldn't form up. He finished his eggs in silence. Then he decided the least he could do was try to get the meeting over so Clint could get to his golf game and Laura could go back to work on her proposal for Gregorgi.

"Anything else on Paishon, Clint?" he asked.

Clint chewed some eggs, swallowed, leaned forward to read the printout. "Nothing exciting. After his discharge, he dropped out of sight for nine years. Then eleven years ago, he opened Asian Coral Imports. Lives in a big house on the oceanside of Palos Verdes Peninsula. He's clean."

Mickey put down his plate in disappointment, his appetite diminished. "That's all? No link to The Tape?"

"Not to him, but there's a long shot . . ."

"Give."

Clint took a bite of sausage. A sweet, spicy aroma pervaded the room. Clint sighed in apparent pleasure and said, "That grand-larceny deal when Paishon was eighteen? His attorney was a sharp cookie who used to handle all the local penny-ante stuff for an underworld figure by the name of Cagney. There's a little side note here. The reporting officer says Cagney had the attorney bumped off, but they couldn't pin it on him, so they let it drop."

"Why'd he off the attorney?"

"Because the guy failed to plea bargain his way out of a homicide for one of Cagney's henchmen. The thug got life."

"Cagney can't take a joke."

"Cagney can take nearly anything he wants. Including, they say, Fort Knox."

"Cagney...Cagney." Mickey recalled some reports he'd read. "Al 'Woodsy' Cagney? The crime boss from the South?"

Clint gave him thumbs-up. "He has estate strongholds in eight or ten Southern cities and as many warm-climate countries. Half the time he lives on yachts scattered over the world. All the agencies, from ATF to the FBI, the CIA and NSI have been trying to bust him for years. He's too smart. He's got layers of protection thicker than you'd want to sleep under at the North Pole."

Mickey frowned. The Tape was in town, he was certain of it. He'd already spotted Veeta, and the tail in the Riviera had once worked in a pizza joint owned by The Tape. Did that mean he was in town to sell the gem? But if the little weasel had the emerald, why was he having Mickey followed? As a precaution? Mickey tried to think of an angle that linked Paishon to The Tape or either of them to the gem. It was a maze. And they hadn't even talked about Sledgehammer yet.

He mused aloud, "Paishon could be tied to Cagney— might be one of the crime lord's regional bosses. But does Cagney have the emerald? If he got it from The Tape, it was a very quiet deal, because I didn't hear about it on the Jewelry Mart grapevine."

"Maybe Paishon was the go-between."

"I'd love to know. But if I pressure Paishon for information, it'll blow my chances of being included in the sale when it comes down. I have to distance myself from NSI. If Paishon suspects I'm on NSI's side and gets shy on me, I'll have to convince him I turned bad."

"Maybe Paishon is fronting for The Tape, not Cagney."

"Somehow I don't think so." Mickey took a drink of coffee. "No, my instincts tell me Paishon and The Tape would be rivals, not business partners."

"There's a lot of money involved," Clint argued. "Money makes for strange bedfellows."

"Mmm." He shook his head in confusion, still wondering why The Tape had had him followed in L.A.—*if* he had. Maybe . . . He glanced up, leveled a question at Clint. "By the way, is the agency putting heat on me again?"

Clint laughed dryly. "NSI thinks you have the plague. They're not tailing you."

He was probably right.

Laura set down her coffee cup. "Paishon sent us to New Orleans. We were followed there, too."

"Right," Mickey said. "But he said he was checking us out. Seeing if we were serious. The black Riviera was on us before we ever went to see Paishon. Besides, Paishon didn't know we were coming."

"Did the Shark Man decide we were serious?" she asked.

Here it is, Mickey thought. *Time to deal the cards.* He nodded. "Paishon basically said we passed his little test and we're in if we come up with the money."

Laura looked startled. "He said we could have it? When?"

"I don't know. Soon."

Clint had been about to bite into a roll. He let it drop to his plate, his hand stilled in midair. "He name a figure?"

Mickey outlined the terms. He figured it would take six hundred thousand dollars.

Clint whistled. "Where are you going to get that kind of dough?"

Mickey lifted his gaze from his plate to Clint's face and held it there, saying nothing.

Slowly Clint's eyes widened. "You've got to be out of your mind! Forget it."

"If you could talk the Institute into coming in on the bust, they'd put up the money," Mickey urged. "They do it all the time."

Clint stood up, paced to the fireplace. "You don't get it, do you?" His arms rose, hovered, fell to his sides. He faced Mickey. "They'd rather dump your body in the bay than deal with you on this. You're too hot."

Mickey's heart hardened, his lips thinned. "Borrow the money from Logistics."

The suggestion rent the air with tension. Clint's mouth dropped open.

Feeling corrupt, Mickey stared into Clint's soul.

His friend spread his hands in exasperation. "Partner, I can't. Don't ask me."

Mickey steeled himself against self-loathing. "We're on the right side of this situation, Clint," he said, his voice rising. "We're going to bring in the bad guys. We'd have the money back in a day. We can pull the bust ourselves."

Like a storm passes over a plain, changing the character of the land, emotions warred over Clint's features—shock, torn loyalty, abhorrence. "Anything else," he said, his voice thick with feeling. "Intelligence, personal backup, hell—I'd lay down my life if your back was to the wall, man. I've come close to it before, just as you have for me. But I can't forfeit my career—" he waved a hand, "—my *honor* for a lousy expensive emerald and your revenge. I'm sorry, buddy. It's not in me to steal for you." His shoulders slumped. "I'm . . . sorry."

Clint turned away.

Mickey felt as if mud caked his heart. He'd asked Clint to step over the line with him, and he'd refused. The whole thing left Mickey feeling dirty. Desperation clawed at him, and he ran through his options.

Garth was wealthy. Mickey didn't trust his boss anymore, though, and although Garth was willing to let Mickey take time off to trace the emerald, he'd made it clear Mickey had to use his own resources. He'd done that—spent all his savings plus the income from the sale of the home in Pasadena he'd owned for eighteen years.

Then, grumbling about it, Garth had agreed to fund the bare essentials—a cheap motel, fast-food burgers, that kind of thing—as long as Mickey conducted some business for the brokerage on each foray after the gem. Knowing Garth would give him misery over using company funds, Mickey had used his last paycheck to fly to London. Laura had paid for everything since then. He had a few hundred dollars left; that was all that kept him from living hand-to-mouth like the homeless in the square. That thought hardened his resolve.

Paishon's asking price had to be met and Garth's assets couldn't be tapped. The money had to come from somewhere. Laura was wealthy, too, and she wanted the gem back almost as much as he did. Resolutely, he turned to her.

She gave him a questioning look. Then sudden understanding came to her beautiful eyes and they narrowed. She bolted from her chair, searched the room as if wanting to escape, her hands twisting.

"Six hundred thousand?" she said. "I—I don't have that kind of ready cash." She gestured. "I've lost Sutama's shipping contracts. Other smaller accounts have pulled out. I'm going back to London tonight to try to patch things up with Brit Hospital. If I lose the account, the company may go under."

So he'd angered her enough to push her back to England, he thought. Hendley was plenty capable of handling her business affairs, yet she was going home. Well, great. That freed him to do what was necessary on the case—as soon as he got the money.

He'd have to bust the criminals alone—okay, he'd deal with that when he had to. But Paishon would ask to see the cash during the sale. He needed the money, and Laura had plenty of it. He'd have to press her.

"What about Sutama?" he said to her, getting to his feet, spreading his hands. "Wouldn't he advance the money on the gem? What about stocks, an insurance policy you could cash in?"

Obviously affronted, Laura drew herself tall. "Sutama's out of the question. Business relations are on ice. Loss of face is involved. He wouldn't advance any money, and I wouldn't ask. I've already set up a budget of thirty thousand dollars to get the gem back and pay the reward. That's my limit."

"I've run through three, four times that much. Thirty grand's a drop in the bucket."

She gave him a chiseled stone stare. "Even the thirty thousand was a sacrifice, a gamble, but, I felt, worth the risk. With the gem found, the firm's slate would be clean." She had paid out the words in a clipped monotone, and now she paused. She smoothed the sides of her dress as if girding herself. "As for personal assets, that's none of your business."

The chance of getting the gem back crumbling away, his professional veneer crumbling with it, Mickey advanced on her. "I'm making it my business, dammit—"

Clint pursued him, grasped his arm. "Mickey, for the love of the Holy Son Himself, will you stop?"

Shrugging him off, the need to fight one last time driving him forward, Mickey crowded Laura and said sharply, "Paishon said he'd have something for me at the gem show next weekend. A date, a place for the sale. We've got to be ready to deal."

Now she had a betrayed look in her eyes. "Gem show?"

"At the Santa Monica Civic Auditorium. Saturday and Sunday."

"You didn't tell me about a gem show. All these days, you didn't mention it, not even on the trip to New Orleans, when I was telling you I wanted to—" she broke off, stiffened her shoulders. "You knew I would have looked forward to a gem show. It's clear you didn't want me along and would have kept Paishon's meeting at the show to yourself, too, except you needed the money. What else haven't you told me?"

"Nothing. Forget about that." He took her hands. "We're close, Laura. So close. Tell Sutama that. Tell him." He shook her hands, made her look at him. "For the love of God, Laura, we need the money!"

She pried his hands away and stood back. Her eyes told him she felt disgust. "You'd do anything to get it back, wouldn't you? Trade on the loyalty of your best friend...."

His face blanched.

"Use me for kicks. Run me into the poor house," she added, her eyes flashing anger. "What else, Mickey? Sell your own soul?"

Something hot and sick twisted inside him. Veeta's greedy dark eyes blinked in his memory, her lips curved in demand, in derision, and he grated out, "Yes, damn you. I've got no soul left to save."

Laura clutched her hands to her midsection. She glanced around him to Clint—a beseeching, frightened look.

"Hell, Mickey," Clint said, attempting a light tone. "Everyone in our business feels that way sometimes. You know guilt goes with the territory. Take it easy, buddy."

He whirled on Clint. "Take it easy! You can say that, being a lifer. You'll get the pension and all the medals. Me, I got the streets and my revenge. Well, fine—" he clipped the air next to Clint's face, making Clint blink, but he didn't flinch, and he didn't lose the broken look around his mouth.

Furious at the destruction he'd caused, helpless with rage, Mickey dug the spear in deeper. "I don't need you, ol' buddy, ol' pal."

He pivoted, glared at Laura. "And I don't need a conniving, selfish thing like you pulling at my coattails. I don't need anybody."

He stormed past her, sucking in deep breaths that carried the faint lemon-rose scent of her perfume.

As he pulled open the door, he heard Laura murmur a distressed cry, and from the corner of his eye, he saw Clint put a protective arm around her.

Beyond caring, Mickey slammed out.

Chapter Ten

Darkness curtained the square-paned windows of Laura's corner office, and the lamplight outlined her form as she bent over the thick report open on her desk.

Outside the five-story building, cars rattled by on the damp pavement. The wheel-bearings of a double-decker bus creaked. A crowd gathered at a theater down the block, voices murmuring about a Neil Simon play to debut that evening; then they filed inside, the doors closed and the street stilled. Laura didn't hear these night sounds as she worked.

Her eyes stinging from fatigue, she read the last pages and closed the bound volume, pushing it aside. Nothing. Not a bloody thing had leapt at her from the five hundred pages of schematic drawings, performance descriptions and test readouts. The incubators had tested perfectly well this time around. Why had the same units failed Brit Hospital's tests last week? That was the one question Brit Hospital needed to have answered before they would sign off on the shipment.

Her eyes ached and she rubbed them, remembering she and Hendley had a meeting with principals from British Hospital at nine o'clock tomorrow morning.

Laura glanced around at the carved clock on the sideboard beneath the window at her back—8:00 p.m. She'd been studying the report for seven hours now, and would have to go over it again. The glitch she wasn't able to see had to be in there somewhere. After a break, she'd go back to it.

With the first leg of the work behind her, she marveled at her ability to forget the events in Los Angeles two days ago as she delved into the incubator project. Now they crowded her and she gave in to the urge to think about him again.

Mickey had stormed out of the Biltmore. He'd hurt her pride with his final insult, and worse, he'd nearly wiped out a seventeen-year relationship with Clint Moss, his best friend.

Yet despite the abuse he'd taken, Clint had rallied to Mickey's defense, justifying his unspeakable actions, describing the pressure he'd been under, explaining the tendency of agents to want justice at any cost—even personal loss and self-destruction.

After he'd soothed her damaged ego with explanations, Clint had thought of a plan. He intended to have a talk with his wife, Mary, see if she'd be willing to take out a second mortgage on their home. Even reserving college funds for their two teenage children, he explained, he figured they had enough equity to give Mickey some kind of stake.

Mickey might try to use the money to buy counterfeit hundred dollar bills, Clint said; he'd try to dissuade him. A better plan would be to face stacks of ones with hundreds, and pass the stacks off as the full amount. That was risky, too, but at least Mickey wouldn't face federal charges for dealing in counterfeiting. With the sentiment currently against him, if he was caught, he'd be extremely vulnerable to the full penalty of the law.

Clint left the Biltmore directly after that, heading straight home to talk to Mary.

Hours later, en route to LAX in a cab to catch the flight to London, Laura had struggled to understand Clint's reaction to Mickey's manipulations. She felt aghast at Clint's potential for what she considered to be blind loyalty.

Now she sat back in her chair and closed her eyes. Mickey. How could she be missing him? And yet she was.

With time and distance mellowing her anger, she admitted she missed the life they'd led so briefly, the excitement of car chases and unplanned side-trips and high-stakes adventure. She missed the expectation she'd felt each morning knowing she'd see him.

Tomorrows, she remembered thinking in New Orleans. They had no tomorrows. Not in the sense of lovers who meet and fall in love and let love take its course.

A sadness arrowed through her. For the rest of her days, she would long for another sweet, raging passion like they'd known in New Orleans. Always want him again, she thought. Always feel a longing for that demandingly masculine, yet tender, sensitive, enigmatic ex-agent who'd swept her away in a rain storm.

She liked his rangy broad-shouldered body with its cords of strength. She liked his thick black hair, the timbre of his laughter, the gentle way he urged her to talk about the past, and the way his hands fit her arms whether in concern or demand.

When he gazed at her, she was reminded of sun-shot emeralds. His eyes were windows, though he evidently didn't realize it; shifting greens from kelly to forest, depending on what he was feeling. He buried the feelings, he said, but they were there in his eyes. Warmth, desire, barely suppressed rage, determination, sudden humor—all there, all remembered.

Again she glanced at the clock. In Los Angeles, it was just after noon. Was he in the office? What could she say? Gee, I was thinking about you, missing you . . . wanted to call. . . .

Of course not. Ridiculous thought. He'd be insulting, and she'd be angry again. She needed to stay focused on Brit Hospital.

Sure, she argued with herself, he'd made her feel isolated when the demons went to work on him, the old anger, the betrayals. But when he won his war with the emerald, wouldn't the good side rise again?

Among all the mythical creatures, only the phoenix rose from the ashes. Mickey had lost his honor, his reputation, his marriage, his career. The theft of the emerald, in all its aspects, had nearly destroyed him. Would Mickey rise above his past? Were there tomorrows?

Mickey's loss was simply too great to bear without consequence, without a change in his nature.

She realized he'd replaced his original altruistic ambition with a personal vendetta. Revenge and justice had mingled. Get the stone back, bring in the criminals. He would try to close the case no matter what the cost—single-handedly if necessary.

She had not realized until now what terrible stress he'd put himself under, and because she hadn't understood, she'd put roadblocks in his path—chief among them, her attitude. And he'd come close to emotionally mowing her down.

If anyone tried to stand in the way of her solving the Brit Hospital dilemma, accidentally or intentionally sabotaging her work, she'd probably mow them down, too. It was a natural response when your security was threatened.

Suddenly Laura understood Clint's devotion. She wanted to help Mickey, too. But how?

Money. He needed money.

She scanned the pecanwood furnishings, leather wingbacks, ten-year-old rose-and-green Persian rug decorating her office. On this floor, there were three large offices, six smaller ones for the clerks, a conference room and a reception area, plus storage on the floor above, all leased to Marley Enterprises. Thousands of pounds went out each month to pay the overhead on this prestigious location. There was little she could do about that in just a few days.

She thought about Clint's idea. Her home was completely paid off—John had arranged it from the moment they opened Marley Enterprises, and in eleven years, they'd owned the house free and clear. It was put into trust for Jessica and John, Jr., as protection against the death of both parents. She was pretty certain her home couldn't be mortgaged.

A look at the paperwork, still in John's safe in the office next to hers, would tell her. She ought to remove the rest of his things anyway, she thought, realizing she was finally ready to face the task.

But what if she couldn't get a loan against the house? How could she help Mickey?

Jewelry? That was a thought. As the business had grown, prospered, they'd entertained more and more and John had indulged Laura with lavish gifts of jewelry, and she'd had plenty of freedom at the best clothing shops. It seemed shoddy to think of selling off her jewels and gowns; rumors of such an act would haunt her children. She could call them tomorrow and explain, she supposed. She'd tell them she wanted to discard the weight of the past. That, certainly, was true.

Perhaps Mickey could get a loan from his parents. Perhaps, with contributions from them, herself, Clint and Mary, they could scrape together enough so Mickey wouldn't have to deal in the black market for counterfeit money. He'd said himself the powers that be were out to get him. Clint had confirmed it. She had a feeling if they ever got him on any charge, counterfeiting or otherwise, and a judge saw his terrible rage, he'd be locked up for life. The idea was crushing. Intolerable.

Laura picked up the phone and dialed zero.

Midday Tuesday—San Bernardino Mountains, California

FROZEN ARMS OF SNOWBANK passed by the open window of Mickey's Chevrolet as he negotiated the narrow road that twisted through his favorite mountain retreat two hours east of Los Angeles.

Snow caked the slanted roofs of cabins, silvered the pines and blanched the undersides of the great bolders that had lodged along the hilly south shore of Big Bear Lake during the Ice Age. Its edges scalloped with ice, the lake lay placidly, blindingly bright and blue in the five-mile-long cradle of hills.

Past Metcalf Bay, where the land dipped and the road came sweeping through the trees, the evergreens thinned, shaded more homes, provided an iced green backdrop for a liquor store, a real-estate office, a bait-and-tackle shack and the inns and motels of the town.

It was a sunny day with popcorn clouds and that spicy breeze Mickey had come to love in the summers he'd fished for trout and bass. It was the kind of day that made him feel guilty for the stress he carried.

Getting the money for the emerald occupied his energy, his every thought, and this trip to Big Bear might settle the questions in his mind about Garth. Could he trust his boss? Mickey intended to gain a perspective from the agent who'd retired from NSI eight years ago, and who now lived up in these mountains. Clint had said to call Rusty, and Mickey appreciated the tip. Even though he'd never met the former counter-insurgency specialist, in his early years at NSI, Mickey had heard Rusty called one of the best political minds in the Institute.

His hopes high, he'd phoned Rusty, only to discover the man was reticent to speak freely. He'd hinted that Mickey ought to get away for a day, come on up to Big Bear. Mickey hated to lose the time away from work, yet he needed the sage insight of an old-timer like Rusty as to the political leanings of the closemouthed Garth.

The road glistened with runoff, a blue jay darted above the Chevy, and Mickey chafed with the impatience of having to be on business in his favorite getaway. Cars inched along ahead of him, full of locals in no particular rush to shop for supplies, and jovial skiers bound for the slopes at Snow Summit.

Like to be up there myself, he thought. Nice day like this. He could almost feel the bite of the wind at eight thousand feet, the pull in his calves as his skis bit into a steep ridge of hardpack. He imagined soaring over the next mogul, stealing a glimpse of that blue blue lake in the valley.

Even in the summer, Veeta hadn't wanted to come here, he remembered. She hadn't wanted to rough it, camping and building a fire and cooking on a Coleman stove.

He toyed with the question of whether Laura would relish a camping trip. She was a city woman, but then, he was a city man—always had been. How would she react if he built a shelter of blankets hung on rope among the trees, heated water and filled an ice chest with it and after she'd bathed, offered to pour warm rinse water over her from outside the makeshift bath? Would it be adventure to her—or nuisance?

For Mickey, the thought was pure fantasy.

He felt closest to whole, camping in these mountains. Laura willingly with him, enthusiastically sharing the experience, was a dream he scarcely dared permit himself. Yet he was here, en route to a meeting with a reluctant man, a former agent who was living the dream, and the fantasy came in through the window as impetuously as the breeze.

He'd felt the nearest to human among these friendly locals.

"What the devil are you doing, camping in a snowstorm?" a gas station attendant had bawled him out a few years ago, when he'd set up camp right before the first storm of the season and got caught in it. Mickey had grinned at him. Nobody could take away the wonder of crawling toasty-warm out of his sleeping bag, peeking out of the tent and feeling lacy icy snowflakes settle on his nose. Nobody.

How would Laura have fared on that trip?

Why should that occupy his thoughts? She was out of reach in London, out of reach altogether, for the reasons he'd repeated to himself many times. It was a damnable way to have to live, refusing the warmth and affection of a woman like her.

When's life going to ease up? he fretted, skirting the main street of town and heading for the eastern perimeter. *What's the reason for the struggle?*

He didn't know anymore. He only knew he had to decide whether he could trust Garth to help him get the gem back. The rest of his life was on hold.

At the edge of town, he swung right on Moonridge Road and drove up a long gentle slope. He took a rough road leading still higher, its snowbanks gritty with gravel. Around a sharp bend, he saw a coyote fade into the trees at the edge of a meadow, and then, suddenly, he was driving straight toward a weathered log cabin tucked into an embrace of pines.

Smoke curled from a stone chimney, and a huge log pile dwarfed a slight man with gray hair who was wielding a doubled-bladed ax—up-swing, down-swing, *clip-chop*. The log arced apart. His green-and-gold Pendleton shirt balooned as he bent, scooped up the wood, tossed it to the top of a four-foot-high stack. With rhythmic grace, he retrieved another log, set it upright on a stump and swung.

The man knew how to spend a Tuesday, Mickey thought enviously, pulling up beneath the thick prickly canopy of a live oak. He climbed out, approaching the woodsman from the side, well within view. About ten feet away, he stopped and propped his foot on a white-crusted rock, sucking in the good sweet-earth smell of chimney smoke.

He waited silently.

It took two slices before the bumpy, ice-glazed log split apart.

The man's breath puffed a cloud as he glanced at Mickey. He had a piercing gaze as blue as the lake, in a small face mapped with wrinkles. "Stone?" he queried.

"Right," said Mickey, approaching to shake the man's callous-rough hand. "You Rusty?"

"Some call me that. Nice day, isn't it?"

"Good day for chopping wood," Mickey agreed, stepping back.

Rusty grabbed another chunk, set it up. He tapped it with the ax. The blade rose, flashing sun, and dropped with lethal accuracy. *Clip-chop*. The spars thunked to the frozen ground. Mickey picked them up. They were clean-cut hardwood—oak that burned with a slow, hot fire. He fitted them onto the stack. "Lousy day for talking business," he added.

"Enh," Rusty grunted, rubber high-top boots squeaking on the snow as he reached for a log. "Gotta keep at this. Nearly gone through the pile by the door."

Mickey eyed the cottage in its cloak of winter. Red-and-black-checked curtains looked like hunting coats hung in the windows. The split logs stacked on the shallow porch ranged under one window and dipped down sharply by the door. There were maybe five daylong fires left in the stack. Not enough if the snow fell for a week.

"Bum leg acted up on me in the fall," said Rusty, whacking cleanly through the wood. "Slowed down my firewood plans."

"What happened?"

"Old wound. Got in the way of some hot lead in the Amazon jungle one day," he said noncommittally. "Ever been shot, Stone?"

"Nicked in the shoulder in Vietnam. Hit once in the thigh on a mission in Germany eight years ago. Clean hole. NSI fronted for surgery, so I'm good as new."

"That was before you contracted a contagious disease and got put in quarantine."

Mickey smiled grimly, nodded, tossed the chunks to the pile. Rusty chopped and Mickey stacked for a while.

"You called me about Garth," Rusty said suddenly. "I remembered something."

His breath hitched a little in anticipation. Mickey waited.

"Garth couriered some documents to Iran during the Shah's reign," said Rusty.

"Whose flag did he fly?"

"Oh, strictly the Stars and Stripes."

"Well, that's something, anyway." Mickey felt relief.

Rusty scowled at him. "That's a lot, sonny. Woods are full of turncoats."

"'Suppose you're right. What agency?"

"NSI. Otherwise, I probably wouldn't have heard about it. Word is he brought back a jewel-heavy sword of some sort from the Iranian coffers. Duty free, of course. That was the payback."

"It's just rumor, then?"

"Everything's just rumor, isn't it, sonny—in the security business? The guys in the trenches don't know who's doing what to whom, or who has a vested interest, or who really pulls the strings. They just do their job." There was an edge of protectiveness in Rusty's voice. He smoothed it out with a measured, "Heaven's a big town."

At NSI, Washington, D.C., was known as "Heaven." The place from which all blessings flowed in the form of funding for training and investigations. And all authority.

"Lotta secrets in Heaven," Rusty added cryptically. "Lotta favors comin' down all the time."

He was right. Favors and secrecy were the underpinnings of national-security work. You gave favors for information. All nations, all law-enforcement agencies, did it to various degrees. Without favors and secrecy, the U.S. government would crash to the ground like the Eiffel Tower with the rivets removed. But sometimes the ethics of the business had kept Mickey awake at night.

As he worked beside Rusty, Mickey outlined what he knew of John Marley's involvement in the Garden Emerald case and the fact that neither Garth nor NSI had told him about Marley. He covered the personal link to Amsterdam and Laura's report of the unknown documents being couriered with the emerald, confirmed by Garth. He concluded with the suicide. Then he asked Rusty what he thought of the situation.

The ex-agent leaned on the ax handle, his chest burgeoning with exertion. "Maybe Garth teamed up with Marley to do another favor for NSI. You know, under cover of the gem deal. The Institute's not likely to put that kind of thing in a report that's going to get circulated to the FBI or the local police. Opens a can of worms."

If that were the case, Mickey had been considered an outsider, too. Old resentments stirred. Covering them, he asked blithely, "What do you make of the suicide?"

"Maybe the documents couriered with the emerald turned out to be British intelligence. Marley couldn't face being a traitor, so he did himself in."

"Or maybe he was taken out," Mickey suggested. "Got aced out of the deal, tried to blackmail Garth or NSI, and one of them slipped him an overdose."

"What did the coroner's report say?"

"Death by suicide, according to Laura."

Rusty nodded sagely. "The whole thing smells like a top-secret deal that went wrong. They want to cover it up to protect national security. You'll probably never know what happened." Abruptly he peered into Mickey's face. "Something eating you, Stone? You look as if some bad sausage soured your stomach."

Mickey looked away toward the trees, reluctant to tell Rusty the truth. He didn't trust his own government.

"Turn your stomach, does it, getting burned on a possible foul-up by your government?" asked Rusty with needling humor.

Mickey met his gaze. "Yeah, it bothers me some. I've been on cases where the conspiracy and graft lead directly to a big muckymuck in Washington. Whether a politician got Watergated over his illegal, sometimes unethical dealings with other nations was often a matter of clout, not national security. The Garth/Marley link stinks the same way."

"Idealist!" Rusty chortled.

"Maybe. But a criminal is a criminal, in my book. On some of my cases, if the muckymuck had power, no matter how dirty he was, he got immunity. Sometimes my report was declared 'too sensitive' and never filed, the matter swept under the carpet. If they're protecting Garth . . ."

"There are always trade-offs, Stone. In the interests of national security."

The phrase burned Mickey deeply. "Trade-offs?" he demanded, kicking a lump of frozen snow. "A stolen gem means somebody was cheated, my friend. An insurance company had to pay off. A suicide or worse took place. An agent lost his career, his life, dammit!" The emotions roiled in him, and he drew a tight, controlling breath. "If Garth was involved in the theft, he's a slimeball."

"And if he was working for his government?"

Mickey's face flamed. "When is internal corruption too high a price to pay for national security, Rusty?"

Rusty's mouth pinched up. He turned toward his home. Mickey glanced toward the cabin in its ermine blanket and saw it for what it was—Rusty's Alka Seltzer for the heartburn agents got over matters of conscience.

Mickey lifted his arm in frustration, let it drop. "Where's the line between good and evil?" he said roughly.

Rusty stared at him for a moment, hidden feelings playing over the mapped, aged face. "All right," he said flatly, angrily. "It gets to you sometimes. The deals, the tipped scales. But things aren't black-and-white in any government, they're gray. That's right, gray." Rusty pointed the ax at Mickey. "You either go along with the program and do the best job you can for your country, or you let the gray areas sabotage your dedication and eat at your gut. Then you get out. You've done your part. You let the next crop of idealistic, hot-blooded recruits carry on the work. America needs that passion and loyalty."

Mickey's gut felt leaden. His country had betrayed the passion and loyalty he'd given it. As a result, he, Mickey, had begun to betray his own values. He'd even shown that weakness to Clint, his best and loyal friend. He felt dirty, part of the slime, and here he was, the pot calling the kettle black. That insight defeated him.

"Moot point anyway," he said quietly, avoiding those penetrating, knowing blue eyes.

"Why's that?"

"I've been blackballed, remember? I couldn't work in government investigations again if I wanted to. As Clint Moss points out, they'd rather toss me in the bay."

Chuckling mirthlessly, Rusty dragged a red handkerchief from his back pocket and mopped his forehead. "You get that fancy emerald and those documents back, sonny, you might be able to write your own ticket. After all—" he winked "—barter system works both ways."

Feeling moldy inside from the emotions this discussion had raised, Mickey thanked Rusty for his viewpoint and climbed back into his car. The decision about whether to trust Garth still gnawed at him. Garth had once worked for the good guys—maybe had on the Garden Emerald deal—but that didn't guarantee he was clean, honest, trustworthy. Mickey started the car and it rumbled to life. Tomorrow morning, he'd have to decide.

He did a U-turn in Rusty's yard and headed back through town. As he drove down the mountain, the memories came, and the resentment over a career and dreams lost. He was forty and his life was in shambles. He felt guilty for his treatment of Clint and Laura, and he realized that, like his country on occasion, he'd stepped over the line of decency to meet his goal.

Very much alone on the downside of his favorite mountain, he realized he'd lost the idealism that had made him a crack federal agent, and he'd lost the last shred of his innocence.

Suddenly a specter loomed. He thought about Fast Eddie and the other lost ones. Life had tipped the scales against them. How close was he to being one of the indigents of Pershing Square?

Wednesday, January 18—Los Angeles

CRADLING THE TELEPHONE receiver against his shoulder, so he could sign his name to a purchase order, Mickey said shortly, "Garth Gems."

"It's . . . me," said Laura, sounding hesitant.

Mickey put down the pen, grabbed the receiver. He felt a small, almost imperceptible needle of longing. But the resentment he felt around the clock rose up, grappled with the longing, and buried it. "What up?" he said, business-like.

"I—I had an idea last night."

"About what?"

"The money."

Resentment bubbled and hissed inside him, resentment freshly fired by his recent conversation with Garth. "What about the money?" he said.

"I could get together sixty, sixty-five thousand, including the money left in the bank in L.A. Maybe more. I'm still looking into it. With Clint's contribution—"

"Clint's what? I talked to him this morning. He didn't mention any contribution."

"Didn't he? He said you could use the cash to face stacks of small bills with hundreds. He was going to see if he could get a mortgage loan."

Mickey swore.

"I guess he wants to surprise you. And what about your parents? Would they help? Between us, maybe we can do this thing."

Mickey was stunned to silence, the emotions firing charges in his brain, short-circuiting thought, creating a blackout. For a moment, he mouthed words but couldn't get the breath to give them sound.

Too many feelings; explosive feelings. The sound of her voice shoveling down into his gut, the idea she'd tried to help him—sounding like she'd had to scrape the money together, after all—and the fact that she'd swallowed her pride, faced rejection again to call him. Clint helping, too. He felt small, unworthy of such loyalty.

His parents would probably help, too, but they were retired, and he didn't want to risk their nest egg or trouble them with his problems. They'd said 'I told you so' when he'd reported Veeta had stolen the gem and deserted him, and he'd never discussed the case with them again. He wouldn't begin now.

He was lousy at asking for favors, and yet his best friend and the only woman to turn his heart upside-down in twenty years had apparently risked their own security for his sake. They'd been willing to come through for him, even if it was too late.

"Laura," was all he could say for a moment. "Geez, Laura."

"If we don't ever recover the gem," she went on as if he weren't choked up, "I won't have to pay Gregorgi half the reward anyway. Of course, I'm assuming you won't mind using your share for the cause. Anyway, if we do recover it, the sale of the stone will more than pay for the reward. What do you think?"

He gathered himself back together and grated out, "It's too late. Too damned late."

"Too late? Did Paishon call off the deal?"

"No." The frustration, the poor timing drumming at him, he looked out the smog-gritty windows, barely hearing the squeal and clammer of traffic. "I appreciate what you tried to do but—dammit!" He shook his head. "I got the money. All of it."

Silence. Then, tentatively, "Where?"

"Garth's wiring it to our joint account on Friday."

"Garth? But he might be involved with the thieves!"

He ticked his tongue in remorse. He'd wrestled with that possibility for two days before calling Garth. She didn't miss a bet. "I had to take that chance," he said at length. "I told Garth what was coming down. About forty-five minutes ago."

"Ah, God. I'm sorry. Some ideas for raising the money came to me last night while I was working on the Brit Hospital account. I called you right away, but you were out. Your message machine was off."

"I know. I forgot to switch it on before I drove up to Big Bear yesterday."

"You went skiing?"

"No." The sick feeling he'd felt in his gut since Sunday threatened to suck him down into self-pity; he fought it, kept his tone matter-of-fact. "I saw a retired agent for some advice on the case. He said Garth has done courier work for NSI in exchange for favors, duty-free imports, that kind of thing. The agent inferred it makes Garth one of the good guys. Allegedly trustworthy." His tone had gained an edge, and again he resisted climbing back into his pity pot. It felt good to be talking to a civilian who didn't seem to have any vested interest in doing anything but helping him. He wondered what she had been going to do to raise the money for him. "What were your ideas, anyway?" he asked.

The line crackled for a moment. "It's personal," she said. "Too late now, anyhow."

"Yeah, right." Still, he wondered what she'd been planning to do. "The timing's incredible, isn't it?"

"Really is. I'm sorry."

The defeat in her voice was real. It echoed his own and he felt linked to her, close. There was so much to iron out, and the gem still stood between them. "I wish..." he began, and hesitated.

"What?" she said.

He shrugged. "Nothing. Just—how's the hospital deal coming along? Any progress?"

She sighed deeply. "I'm in trouble, Mickey. Calling you took my mind off it, but I'm totally stressed out. Hendley and I met with them this morning, meet with them again in an hour, and the problem isn't solved. Guess I'll have to ask for more time. Beg for it if I have to."

'More time' meant she wouldn't be coming back right away. Inexplicably disappointed, he asked, "What's the problem?"

"I don't know, exactly. In one series of tests, the product failed. This time around, it passed. I asked them to come back for tea at five o'clock, hoping I'd find the discrepancy by then. Still no luck. I'm fit to be tied, Mickey, I really am. They're our biggest account. We may lose them."

"Easy, Laura," he soothed, recognizing her panic. "I've hit brick walls on cases. The more complicated they are, the more I realize I have to look for simple answers."

"Like what, though? I've looked until I'm blue in the face."

"Well, like human error, for example. Maybe on the first tests the technician was asleep at the wheel, so to speak."

A pause; then, "Good Lord."

"What?"

"That may be it!" Her voice peaked and he could imagine a smile making her face sunny—he missed looking at that cameo face. Papers rustled. It sounded as if she were flipping through a big *Webster's*. "Testing January 6, compared to testing January 13," she murmured. "Equipment settings . . . eight-hundredths, compared to . . . eight-*thousandths*. Paydirt!"

He smiled. She'd borrowed his pet phrase. It tickled him.

"What'd you find?" he asked, feeling some of the weight of the world lifting.

"The settings on the equipment that tests the overlimit switches on the heater itself were set wrong on the first run. Wrong!" she said, jubilant. "One tiny number in five hundred pages of detail. This is it, Mickey. This is the key! I've got to ring Hendley."

"This means you'll be home—I mean—" He stumbled. God, he wanted to see her again. He needed her close, if only to see her face from across the room. "Back in L.A. in time for the gem show?"

"Well, I've got to smooth this out, of course," she said. "And I promised myself I'd go through John's office while I'm here. Clean it out. It's long past time, and I feel strong enough now. Still, if all goes well, I think I can be back Friday night."

"Let me know when and I'll pick you up at the airport."

"Okay."

"Good, and we'll drive up to Santa Monica together Saturday morning, if you'd like."

Static on the line while she paused. Then she said quietly, "I'd like it very much, Mickey. And you know what else?"

"What?"

"I miss you."

The longing zinged through him unchecked. "Me, too," he said before he could think about it. Startled, he hung up the phone.

Chapter Eleven

Clutching her briefcase beneath her arm, Laura hurried to the street-level door, her breath mingling with a chill fog that haunted the mews like the mists in a Lon Chaney horror film. Lamplight pooled around her, cutting back the darkness of the enclosed courtyard. She raised a gleaming horse's-head knocker and let it fall.

"Hurry, please," she whispered, edging a wary glance over her shoulder. Her heart thudded against her ribs as she peered among the shadows of the narrow lane across the court. She'd parked and walked into the mews, and she was still not certain whether she'd heard footsteps behind her or imagined them.

Abruptly, the carved door creaked, swung inward. Laura drew a breath, relieved. "Angelina," she said.

The housekeeper's black uniform and her steely hair, pulled into a severe bun, made her look dour. Suddenly a welcoming smile softened the vertical creases in her longish face. "Goodness sakes, come in out of the night, Mrs. Marley," she urged, beckoning to Laura. "We've got a fire blazing and you'll be warm in no time."

"Thank you. A fire sounds wonderful." Laura stepped into the foyer, chilled more from her suspicions and the reason for her visit than from the cold.

"If you'll give me your coat, then, Mrs. Marley, you can go right into the study. Mister's waiting for you."

"Thanks, I'll keep my coat," she said, tugging open the slate-toned lapels, slipping her gloves into a pocket. "I don't expect I'll be here but a few minutes."

"You'll have tea, at least, or sherry. You look positively blue."

"All right, Angelina. Sherry would be nice."

Angelina showed her into a high-ceilinged room that had not changed since the time twenty years ago when John had brought Laura here to meet Jenkins, his family solicitor. The mingled scents of pipe tobacco, burning hardwood and lemon oil reassured her, eased her inner turmoil. Seeing the masculine warmth of the widower's favorite room, with its burnished leather armchairs and bound volumes, its rose-and-emerald carpets and elegantly-aged linen lamp shades, brought to mind the many pleasant hours she'd spent here. She felt a brief thread of longing for the old comforts she'd known before John died. And then her heart quickened because she had come here not for a pleasant visit but for answers—to all the unanswered questions. Jenkins, she knew, would be reluctant to answer them. If only Mickey were here to help her. . . .

Approaching Jenkins's mammoth teak desk, she hugged the briefcase more tightly.

"Here she is, then, Mister," Angelina announced. "Half frozen and in need of some proper hospitality, if you ask me."

"Then by all means, please oblige her at once, Angelina," said Jenkins, lifting his lionlike head. The lamplight glinted in his thick snowy mane. He smiled at them. "Laura," he said, setting aside some paperwork. He pushed up from the desk, buttoning a sport coat that was dark, tailored to perfection.

It made her think of Mickey, who couldn't afford a tailor these days. He'd been on her mind almost constantly since she'd spoken to him last night. Just knowing she was going back to him gave her an edge of determination tonight. She wanted Jenkins's answers to fill that gaping hole of uncertainty about John's death. In addition, she admitted now, she wanted to bring something useful back to Mickey.

Jenkins was approaching her and she switched off thoughts of Mickey, focused on her mission.

Her solicitor came to her, took her free hand, chafed it. "You *are* an iceberg. Let's go to the fire."

"Sorry to come so late," she said, setting her briefcase by the desk. "I wouldn't have if it wasn't urgent. It's just that I'm flying back to the States tomorrow."

"Not at all, my dear. Happy to see you anytime. Anytime at all, you know that."

She wanted to blurt out her fears, her questions. Yet from experience she knew it would alarm Jenkins, who was meticulously the gentleman. She tried to imagine how Mickey would handle the situation. Cleverly, she thought. With subtlety. She let Jenkins draw her to the hearth.

Reaching for a poker, he turned the wood until it blazed. Laura extended her hands to the heat, relishing it.

Angelina was clinking classes at the drinks cabinet. "Will you have a sherry with Mrs. Marley, then?" she asked Jenkins.

"Yes, thanks, that would be swell."

"Your shelter project," Laura said to get things rolling, "how's it coming along?"

"Marvelously, matter of fact. You Americans have a knack for causes. I've learned a great deal from your countrymen." He slid the poker into its rack, dusted his hands. "I'm able to handle the legal end of things, naturally. But there's a whole raft of other considerations. How to recruit the proper staff, solicit patrons, set up house rules that are fair without being discriminatory, that sort of thing. Actually, I was hoping to enlist your aid, Laura." He looked at her from beneath scruffy white eyebrows—the only unruly detail about him. "You've a superb head for organization."

"I'm afraid just now, I—"

He put up a hand. "Not a word about it. You've your hands full at the moment, I realize. Just say you'll consider it for the future."

She nodded. "I will. Thank you for understanding."

When Angelina had brought the sherry and left the room, Jenkins touched his goblet to Laura's, said, "To you, Laura."

"To me?"

"For securing your relationship with British Hospital. Congratulations."

"Oh." She laughed, recalling her phone conversation with him. "I accept on behalf of those who aided me in the campaign. It's been dicey, I'll admit."

"You're entirely too humble, my dear. In any event—cheers."

She smiled, sipped the drink, felt the tingling along her shoulders. Her blood was craving nourishment. Cleaning out John's office had taken hours longer than she'd planned. She'd worked right through supper, then discovered the letter that had brought her to see Jenkins at this late hour. The letter contained an ominous warning, using phrases such as "For Your Eyes Only," "strongly urge you to reconsider" and "proper authorities must be contacted."

She set the drink on a round table, beside a lamp whose base was a carved ebony elephant. John had always threatened to "have off with the monstrous thing" when Jenks wasn't looking. Caressing the dark, polished wood, remembering, she willed the chaos in her mind to still so she could formulate the first of her questions. *I mustn't sound as if I'm suspicious,* she thought. Jenkins might have been involved with the transfer of the documents that accompanied the emerald to America. If so, he might be adversary rather than friend. The thought made her sad, wary.

"I swore I'd have his head if he touched it," said Jenkins behind her.

Startled, she turned to him. "I beg your pardon?"

"John," he said, indicating the elephant. "He was always threatening to nip my memento, wasn't he?"

"He liked to tease you about it, that's all. He knew what it meant to you."

Jenkin's gaze went soft. "South Africa, all those years ago." He was thinking of his wife, who had died two months after they'd returned from safari. "Cancer," he mused. "Who would have dreamed such a happy, lively creature would go so quickly."

Laura stood before him, filled with understanding. "Yes," she said gently. "The shock of it, sudden death. It's terrible. And the guilt. You go for weeks, months, thinking it's your fault, somehow."

"Quite so..." Suddenly his gaze sharpened on her face. "Oh, Laura, you're speaking of John. You musn't ever think—why, no, it was none of your doing. John was—"

He stopped abruptly. Took a drink.

"John was what?"

"Nothing, my dear." He cleared his throat, seeming to collect his thoughts.

In reality, she thought, he was covering up information he didn't want to tell her. She longed to have Mickey with her. He was so clever at interrogation.

"It's better to forget the past," Jenkins said. "It can only hurt you."

The words on the letter she'd pulled from John's safe burned into her mind. "You can bury it," she said. "But that's no guarantee it'll stay buried."

The wise old eyes studied her. "Explain please, Laura."

A quaking began inside her. To cover it, she went quickly to her briefcase. She fumbled the latch, murmured an epithet, put the case on the desk to steady herself. She withdrew the letter. It was expensive cream-colored stationery—and it bore the crest of Jenkins's law firm.

Silently she walked to Jenkins, watched his face, looking for signs of discomfort, of lies. "Do you know a man named Paishon?" she asked.

"No, why?" Not a flicker of emotion.

"Call it curiosity. How about Cagney? That sound familiar?"

"Not at all. What's this about, Laura? What have you got there?"

He didn't know either man, she decided, glancing at the letter. "Just one more name, Jenkins, if you don't mind. Garth. Do you know Garth?"

He bit his lip—a mild sign of chagrin. "Why...he was involved in that gem business, Laura. John mentioned him. Garth was to receive the emerald. Did, in fact, but it was stolen before he could transfer it to your Japanese client."

She felt somewhat better about Jenkins. He'd been straight with her, she supposed. So far. Now there was the last test. She handed him the letter.

He read for a moment.

It seemed to Laura the paper trembled slightly in his veined fingers. Yet she could detect no sign of agitation in his face. She reminded herself he'd had decades of practice at hiding unpleasant feelings. When he was through, he simply raised his head and stared at the flames.

"Explain please, Jenkins," she said softly.

"My dear dear Laura," he said, grating the words, giving her yet another clue to his discomfort. "I had hoped you'd never have to deal with this. You don't deserve the humiliation."

She put an unsteady hand on his sleeve. "I'm afraid I don't understand. I know about the documents, Jenkins. They went with the emerald to America."

His eyebrows danced, showing his surprise, yet he kept his eyes downcast, shaded by the great bush of his eyebrows, so she couldn't read the panic she imagined him to be feeling. She was close, now. The answers were within reach. She touched his sleeve again.

"Please, Jenkins. I need answers. I must have them. I have nightmares—"

"All right!"

He set his glass down blindly, slopping sherry over the rim. It glistened on the elephant's chest. Jenkins took no notice.

"What kind of documents were they?" she asked.

His faded eyes full of remorse, he said, "Intelligence. Something to do with a covert operation of potentially great embarrassment to the Crown if it were to become public."

"Dear God." The quaking inside worked its way down her legs, making them feel rubbery, and into her hands, so that she trembled noticeably. She whispered, "Do you mean . . . are you saying John was a *traitor?*"

"Close to it. Very close, indeed."

She moaned softly. If the children ever knew . . . if the press ever printed such terrible things. She veered away from these new demons. Questions hammered her afresh. Struggling for composure, she wrapped an arm around herself, lifted her chin. "How did John get hold of these documents, exactly?"

"Through Mr. Demude in Amsterdam. Demude was being blackmailed into supporting the effort. He had agreed to do so in order to keep under wraps a rather nasty scandal involving his son, which was also why he needed the money from the sale of the emerald. Demude pressed John into service. Out of loyalty, John agreed."

His voice came to her remotely. She stared at the fire, seeing John as the kindly, calm-tempered father and husband she'd once known—unable to envision him mixed up in espionage.

In a moment, she felt Jenkins's gaze on her. She turned to him.

"Drink your sherry," he said gently. "Steady now."

She went to the table, took a drink, felt the spark of the liquor. It didn't warm the cold knot in her midsection.

"*Traitor* is a rather nasty word, Laura," she heard Jenkins say in a soothing tone. "Perhaps a bit too harsh. There are mitigating circumstances. The intelligence wasn't government-sponsored, for example. It was developed by a special-interest group."

"What kind of intelligence was it?" she bit out.

"Code names, dates, logistics."

"For what?"

He scrutinized her. "What would you say if you learned that a certain faction within the British government was actively supporting white rule in South Africa?"

"But that's ridiculous. The world's going forward to democracy."

"Still, the roots of colonization run deep, Laura. Just think of the prejudice you deal with in your Southern states and that'll put you in the picture. There are factions. There are always factions who don't like progress."

Laura felt weak. "Why?" she whispered. "Why did John do this?"

"As I've said, to help an old friend. One does that, doesn't one? We're trained from the cradle to be loyal to our old chums."

She turned her head, looked at him, pleaded with him. "Must I be ashamed of him, Jenkins? Must I tell the children their father was a traitor?" She gestured. "I mean, is there a chance he took the documents, gave them to the U.S. to help the cause in South Africa? Perhaps he hoped to stop the injustice that might be prolonged if the operation were a success."

"Exactly so!" he said, and came into his own then. Decades of experience in advising, protecting, soothing his clients made him courtly. He took her glass, set it down, eased her into a leather wingback. He slid his hip against the upholstered arm.

"Now, old girl," he said, very paternal, smelling faintly of spice and pipe tobacco. "The authorities have let the case go dormant. No need for it ever to raise its ugly head again, is there? Not in the least. And I happen to agree with your deduction about John's motives. When he told me about his actions, why, he expressed outrage that such a conspiracy could foment within his own government, even if the faction had almost no political clout and certainly little chance of gaining support. Fortunately, Laura, having the documents stolen in California must have scared the devil out of the conspirators. They haven't been successful in disrupting the progress of the antiapartheid movement."

"But if the documents fall into the wrong hands, things could go in any direction."

"That's true. There's a lot at stake. You must be very careful, Laura. Don't take any undue risks in California."

If only Jenkins knew what they were up against in California, she thought, nodding obediently.

Stronger now, Laura felt a niggling resentment that John had shared such deeply personal secrets with his solicitor and hadn't seen fit to tell the woman who had raised his children, succored him, loved him. She stared at the dying fire. "Why couldn't he tell me? I was his wife."

"It was because he wanted to protect you from this business that he came to me, Laura. He feared there might be repercussions to the family. I gave him immediate and strongly worded advice—bring the documents to the proper authorities. But he'd given his word to Demude to see the thing through. He refused my advice."

Apparently Jenkins noticed the spilled cherry. Withdrawing a white handkerchief, he wiped up the liquid. "Legally," he added, folding the cloth and leaving it on the table, "John faced serious charges if he'd been caught out."

"But you said the government wasn't officially involved."

"Yes, but John had aided and abetted the operation by passing the documents. What if the operation had been a success? What if certain of our highly placed officials had been proved culpable? Do you think they would have protected the name of a mere courier like John? He meant well, rest his soul, but he'd have been thought of as a threat to national security." Jenkins swore softly. "I tried to warn him of the risks, both to himself and to his family. He seemed, well, tortured but bent on doing the deed.''

"So you wrote him the letter.''

"Thinking it would scare him into contacting the proper authorities, getting rid of the damned documents, yes. He gave me his word he would destroy that letter, by the way.'' He sighed again, sounding regretful.

"As to the children,'' he said, evidently pulling back his presence of mind, "I shouldn't think you'll need to discuss this matter with Jessica and John, Jr. It will only upset them, as it has you. They would be plagued with the same questions about his motives and scruples.''

She nodded. Her children had been through enough. Perhaps in a few years, when they were well set on their paths to happiness, she mused, she would sit them down, have a chat. By then, maybe the emerald would be delivered to Sutama, the documents returned to the British authorities and the mystery would fade into the past.

"I think you're right,'' she said, pressing his hand in gratitude.

"Good girl. One more thing, Laura. Your husband was a man of utmost integrity in his dealings with those he loved. You must remember that above all else.''

It was true. At least she had that: John had been a good family man.

"Thank you, Jenkins,'' she said.

She rose, picked up the letter. "I was just wondering—'' she went to gather her briefcase, closed her coat "—why do you suppose John took his own life?''

Jenkins paled. "Oh, Laura. I don't—out of remorse? Perhaps he was being blackmailed, like Demude? That can get very unpleasant for a lovely family like yours. I truly don't know, Laura. I'm sorry. You must carry on, not torture yourself with why. We simply don't know.''

She nodded again. She felt he had told her nothing but the truth tonight, and she was grateful. When she'd searched John's office, she realized she'd hoped to find a clue, a note to explain his death. The evidence probably never existed. But tonight's meeting with Jenkins had given her greater insight. *Guilt*. It was a powerful drug. John had overdosed on guilt. Poor, well-meaning, heart-of-gold John.

At that moment, she heard again, in her mind, Mickey's low, "Me, too." He missed her, too. He was waiting for her in California. She smiled slightly, despair beginning to lift. He would be proud of her for going through with the interview tonight, persevering. And the information might help their cause.

"Jenkins," she said, feeling more alert, more in control. "It was good of you to go through this with me. You were very kind. I hope you understand I had to have some answers."

"Yes, of course."

"May I ask one more favor?"

"Anything."

"Will you walk me to my car? I've been working with an agent in California and I think some of his paranoia is rubbing off on me. It's terribly dark out tonight. Only a sliver of a moon and all that fog."

"Delighted." In a moment he'd gotten his overcoat, thrown it around his great aging shoulders. Solicitously taking her arm, he lead her to the heavy carved door.

Friday Evening, January 20—Los Angeles

LAURA STOOD ON THE CURB outside Baggage Claim, watching the limousine Hendley had ordered nudge through traffic to get to her. Six car lengths away, its headlights jerked, the brakes squeaked. The maroon stretch Cadillac was wedged between a Toyota sedan full of teenagers, who were waving at someone emerging from the baggage area, and three cars blocked by a Hilton shuttle bus.

I'm back, she thought with wry humor. No place like LAX for traffic snarls, even with the construction of new approach and exit corridors.

She smelled the familiar acrid bite of exhaust and a frail salty scent of tide flats from the nearby coastline, heard the swish of hundreds of tires beating through rain puddles, and felt both eagerness and trepidation at being so near Mickey.

She had news about the documents to share with him, so that gave her an excuse to go to him straightaway, to talk business. But Laura didn't kid herself. She couldn't wait till tomorrow, when he'd pick her up en route to the gem show. She wanted to be with him tonight. In truth, despite having been hurt by him in the past, she wanted to be in his arms.

A pulse beat that always rose exclusively at the thought of their New Orleans interlude fluttered. Oh, yes, she admitted, she couldn't wait to set eyes on him.

But he didn't need to know her reasons were personal. On the phone two days ago, she'd told him she missed him. Okay, but that didn't mean he needed to think she was rushing back to his arms. Friends said those things, she reasoned. If he pressed for an explanation, she would say she was getting hooked on his roller-coaster life-style—the action and tension of investigations—and wanted to discuss the case. She'd tell him she was going to give him one hundred percent in the bid for the gem. Whatever it took. No holds barred.

The limo edged up, a moon-faced driver in a burgundy Nehru-style uniform climbed out and came around to open her door, and she thought in panic, *What if Mickey takes that to mean physical involvement, too? What will I do?* And it came to her. All she had to do was remind him that they couldn't afford to jeopardize the case again. He'd respect her for reminding him.

Her mind at ease, she climbed into the limo. "We've got a few stops to make," she said when the driver had taken the wheel. "First, the Hard Rock Café on Beverly Boulevard...."

AN HOUR AND A HALF LATER, they nosed into the sinister alley alongside Mickey's three-story concrete-block office building.

The driver eyed a display of X-rated lingerie in the corner shop. A raucous whistle shrieked through the night, and they both glanced back at the busy corner of Broadway and Olive, where locals crowded a bus bench and lounged against nearby walls.

"You sure, lady?" the driver asked, full of skepticism.

Glancing above her, she saw the squares of murky light cast by Mickey's windows on the third floor and her insides jittered.

"Very sure," she said. Stacking her packages and pulling some bills from her purse, she handed the money forward. "Thanks for the tour. It was fun."

"My pleasure," he murmured.

She accepted and pocketed a receipt he handed her. He climbed out to open her door. Purse and packages in hand, she asked him to go around the corner with her and open a door printed with chipped gilt letters that read GARTH GEM BROKERAGE. The man complied and stepped back to let her in.

"Thanks," she said.

He closed the door behind her, leaving her to stare down a dim tunnel of a hallway, lit by a bare bulb at the far end. She took a few steps, lost heart, stopped. Craning forward, she tried to see if there were signs on the three doors fitted into the length of the hall. There were none. Edging warily into the gloom, she tried the first door, the second, the third. All locked. That meant the access to Mickey's quarters was through that door lit by the light bulb, seemingly miles into the distance. Her heart clutched in apprehension.

She'd convinced herself that she hadn't been followed in London. She'd seen no hulking shape, no peering eyes. On the plane as she was drifting to sleep, she'd laughed at herself, put her suspicions down to simple paranoia. Now the possibility of being followed into this dungeon of an office building sent chills up and down her body, and suspicions became downright fear.

This is a bad idea, she thought. The Biltmore was only a block away. She ought to go back there and call him.

Coward, said a niggling voice. *Does Mickey have a coward for a partner?*

Hating to be defeated by fear, urged on by the prospect of seeing Mickey, she firmed her shoulders and walked crisply to the end of the hall.

Juggling her packages aside, she twisted the knob and pushed. Evidently the hinges were well-oiled; the door opened soundlessly. Musty smells wafted to her: iron corrosion, damp cardboard, the dust of decades.

Cringing at the possibility of coming face-to-face with an assailant, an indigent disturbed from sleep, a wild and woolly beastie, she stepped through the door.

A cavernous room stretched to her right, the rows of empty metal shelving reminding her of the skeletons of prehistoric creatures lined up in a natural-history display. Here and there a box formed the head of a beast, concrete pillars the legs. An aisle stretched like a flight path ahead of her, and somewhere beyond, another yellowish light put the skeletons in relief.

Nonsense, she told her overactive imagination, and quickly sought out the source of the illumination. This light bulb highlighted another door. It led to a stairwell with a wooden banister angling out of sight. Climbing up, Laura felt gravity and lack of sleep pulling at her legs, her back muscles. At least the second-floor landing was lit, as was the third.

Catching her breath, relief canceling exhaustion, she pushed open the door to what she supposed were Mickey's offices.

A scarred oak floor much like a roller-skating rink spread away from her. It must have been where they held the dances the overhead sign outside his building announced. Back in the Dark Ages, she thought, slipping the door shut. *Safe at last.*

In the far corner, framed by windows, stood the rudiments of a Spartan office: a large, ancient wood desk cleared of paperwork, a bank of two-drawer file cabinets, a chair, a floor lamp with an ornate wrought-iron stem that curved over the desk to light it.

From the grillwork of the lamp hung a prism that sent rainbows over a wardrobe, bureau and cot—and the sleeping, half-naked form of Mickey Stone.

A new thudding commenced in Laura's rib cage. Tiptoeing across the floor to the desk, she eased her gifts down with admirable silence and crept around a set of stainless-steel barbells to the side of the trundle bed.

It felt treacherous gazing at him, registering details she'd never noticed during their intimacy in New Orleans. One hand lay open beside his face. His dark lashes swept against high cheekbones, making him look vulnerable and boylike. His magnificent shoulders were roped with muscle. A sickle scar marred his right shoulder, another the tapering cobblestones of his ribs. His belly, taut as a drum, angled into the cradle of sharp hipbones. Dark hair bristled from the confines of a forest-green towel secured around his hips, and with one of his legs draped over the edge of the cot, the terry cloth had fallen away to reveal a thigh that had been honed by hard workouts. Slightly to the right of center on his thigh, a circular scar the size of an egg yolk dipped faintly into his flesh. It looked like an old bullet wound.

Gazing so openly at him, Laura felt a mixture of emotions—a longing to touch that seasoned, slightly battered body that had conjured the fiercest pleasure of her life from her; compassion for his exhaustion and the monkish way he lived; curiosity to know the whole of him, intimately, from the thick black hair on his head to the tips of his tapered feet.

There was no shame in her perusal, only that tugging of emotions that urged her, against her better judgment, to bend toward him to kiss him while he slept.

Suddenly he moved, forestalling her kiss. He clamped a steel trap of a hand over her wrist, twisting it behind her to force her around to sit on the cot, while his free forearm closed like a vise against her throat.

She saw white flashes. Pain darted through her twisted arm. The vise went away and a cold tube of metal pressed against her cheek. His gun! She croaked in panic.

"What the devil—" He craned around to look at her. "Laura!"

Abruptly, he let her go, shoved the gun under his pillow. "I heard you come in. Thought you were one of the thugs who's been tailing me," he said.

She blinked, scooped in some air, rubbed her arm. "More shadows?"

He nodded. "I thought I saw the guy who was driving the Riviera—minus the car—following me to the bank today. And a beefy guy who looks vaguely familiar. He was fading around the edges of Pershing Square last night, but I couldn't intercept him. He must have had a car stashed nearby."

"Why'd you stay here on the cot, then? They could've killed you."

He searched her face, touched an apologetic, gentle hand to her throat. "I woke up to the sound of someone opening my door. No time to create an ambush. Faked being asleep."

"You ought to have locks."

"And so I do. I only intended to be here for twenty minutes, long enough to shower and dress. That was two hours ago." He yawned, rubbed his eyes. "I figured I'd get a call when you got to LAX, since you didn't phone from London."

"I wanted to surprise you. Remind me never to do it again."

He chuckled. Traced her cheek. "Anytime, beautiful. How about a kiss hello?"

"Mickey," she admonished, starting to rise from the bed. She felt herself stayed in midflight, snatched back and curled into a boa constrictor of an embrace. His lips tasted hers, gently, tentatively.

So close to her mouth that his lips teased hers, he said softly, "I meant it when I said I missed you. Did you?"

Again the butterflies inside. The going-to-nothing weightlessness of her legs, arms. She forgave herself this one breach in her plans to keep things platonic and brushed her lips against his. "I meant it," she said, arching away. "But I've got so much to tell you."

"All right." He feathered her lips with kisses. Between them, as a concession to her, he asked, "How's the hospital deal going?"

"Brit Hospital's—" Disruptive thought: Mickey seemed changed. Was there anything more than sexual attraction in his game? Or was he simply acting on the natural impulse of a man waking from a sensuous dream to find a woman practically in his arms? Did she have the willpower to deny her own feelings and reject him physically, to protect her heart?

"You were saying," he prompted, nuzzling her cheek— distracting her further, but she fought it.

"Brit Hospital's all settled, thanks to you."

"We aim to please," he murmured. "How're your kids?"

"Much better, now that I'm healing up. Jessica took me to the airport. We talked. My problems about the death had been a source of pain to her and my son. I think they felt guilty about the social events and friendships that helped them get over losing their father. She really opened up to me again."

He pulled back, grinned. "Did you tell them about our...'friendship'?"

"No. That is, yes, I told her we were working together."

"Ah." His emerald gaze held hers for the longest moment, and it was her chance to explain why they needed to stay focused on the case; or maybe to ask if he felt something more than friendship. But he gathered her against him, kissed her, and this time the kisses were insistent, building to passion, and she couldn't resist giving her pent-up longing expression. She kissed him back, tasting him, reveling in the feel of his weathered, seasoned body. His hand stole to her midriff. Snuggling beneath her jacket, he played a dance on the white silk blouse, the circular motions sweeping up to tease her breasts and down to slide under the waistband of her skirt. His breathing grew heavier. She struggled, then, to regain her willpower, to put him off, to contain her own mounting passion.

"Surprise," she managed to get out between kisses. She pushed against his chest. "Don't you want your surprise?"

He finally drew away. "A surprise for me?"

She slanted a suggestive glance at the desk.

He sniffed the air. She'd picked up pizza and beer before coming to his office. No one could mistake the sharp, spicy aroma of pepperoni that perfumed his quarters; especially not an aficionado. He'd only been sidetracked. Now he shrugged away from her and stood up, clutching the loosened towel to his hips. "You didn't," he said, binding the towel as he headed for the goodies piled on the desk. "You shouldn't have, Laura."

She swung to her feet, retucked her blouse, brushed a strand of hair into her chignon. "I know it," she said, charged emotions making her tone saucy as she came up behind him. "Not after the insults you heaped on me last time I saw you."

He grimaced. "Sorry about that. I was an ass."

"True," she said. Reaching into the stack of T-shirts she'd bought at the Hard Rock Café, she handed one to him.

He looked longingly at the square white box with the pepperoni and cheese scents issuing forth, but he dutifully opened the shirt and held it up to himself. "Nice," he commented. "When did you get it?"

"On the way here. Jessica begged me for it, and I decided to buy everybody one."

He pulled on the shirt, looked down at himself.

She was sorry to see the scarred, muscled torso disappear from view, but maybe it would keep her mind out of the bed. They ought to talk about the case, the documents, the money from Garth, the gem show . . . their feelings.

He destroyed her hastily constructed defenses by pulling off the towel. The shirt rippled dangerously at his upper thigh.

She fixed her gaze on the stained plaster ceiling.

He laughed mischievously. "Don't worry," he said. "Dinner first. Who's 'everybody'?"

"Jessica, my son, you." *"Dinner first"* reverberated through her brain. "Me," she added as an unsteady afterthought, glancing his way.

He captured her gaze for a lengthy assessment.

Suddenly she felt transparent. She feared he would feel cornered, trapped by a scheming female. Matching T-shirts were too blatant a signal of her interest, even if it was ostensibly platonic.

He simply nodded. "Thanks, Laura. It was thoughtful."

She inched a shoulder up and slipped past him to open the pizza box, letting out a controlled breath. "Do you have some plates?" she asked. "Napkins?"

"Sure." He went to the bank of file cabinets, crouched down and pulled open a drawer. The slowly-turning prism sent red, purple and yellow wavering over a curved muscular thigh. *He's right out of an art book on classic sculpture,* she thought, reluctantly turning her attention to the food. *A bit too lean, but beautifully carved.*

He brought out paper plates and napkins and set them on the desk. Burrowing a hand into the paper bag, pulling out two beers as she put slices of pizza on the plates, he said, "I'm starving."

"You're always starving," she said.

"Comes with the territory," he said, a somber edge to his voice—a first glimmer from his dour side. He twisted the tops off the beers. Seeing she had the plates and napkins in hand, he surveyed the room, presumably for chairs. There was only one. "How about the bed?" he said, going to it and folding his long legs to sit down.

Laura averted her gaze from what no doubt would have been a glimpse of a Michelangelo work of art and hurried to sit beside him. He was the most uninhibited man she'd ever been around.

They were companionable enough as they ate, Laura telling him about her meeting with Jenkins and Mickey saying something obtuse about, "'Embarrass the Crown,' huh? That's why NSI let me go. I knew it had to be more than a stolen gem. The stakes are higher than I thought."

When they'd hashed out the subject of the documents, they went on to less-important topics. Mickey told her about his work week and the recent rain shower.

Eventually Laura relaxed enough to enjoy the anticipation—never quite satisfied—of glimpsing Mickey's male anatomy as he made forays to the pizza box.

She finished her second slice and was sated. He maintained he could eat a fourteen-inch pizza singlehandedly. She believed it.

He was downing the last bite of the last piece when the phone jangled. "Answer machine's not on," he said, getting up. He went to the desk and palmed the receiver, cradled it against his shoulder, wiping his fingers with a napkin.

"Garth Gems," he said in that familiar no-nonsense baritone. In a moment, he said, "Oh, hi, this is Mickey." After he'd listened, he said, "Hold on a minute."

He glanced at Laura, his mouth curving. "Hendley of Marley Enterprises in London," he mimicked in an Oxford accent. "He's concerned because he couldn't reach you at the hotel. Secondly, he has urgent business with you. Are you in, madam?"

"Of course I'm in," she laughed, going to him and rolling her eyes in mock exasperation as she took the phone. "Hendley?" She paused to hear her managing director say he'd been worried about her whereabouts. He asked if everything was all right.

"Sure," she said. "Just relaxing, having some pizza with Mickey, why? What's the problem?"

GRUMBLING INWARDLY AT HAVING their reunion disturbed by a business call, Mickey trashed the bottles, soiled napkins and pizza box in a container under the desk. Okay, so he'd fallen back on his resolution to keep her at bay, and had prickles of something close to happiness running haywire inside at just seeing her again. So what? That didn't mean he was going to marry her. He was human. He had needs. He was happy to see her.

Anyway, being close to Laura wasn't going to compromise his work, he reasoned. He'd see that it didn't. He could keep a clear head.

He watched her talking animatedly to Hendley, and made plans for when she got off the phone. He had to restrain an impulse to hurry her.

As he was dusting his hands, he felt a tug on his sleeve. He turned to see Laura staring at him—through him—seemingly riveted by what Hendley was saying, her fingers absently grasping his shirt.

"When did you get the call?" she asked, sounding breathless. She nodded in apparent understanding. "I was airborne by then."

"What is it?" Mickey interrupted, his intuition clanging a warning.

"Another call for L.J.M.," she whispered, excitement animating her eyes. She mouthed the words "Paper, pen?"

A thrill of surprise and curiosity went through him as he retrieved them from the desk drawer. Was Paishon putting their backgrounds together, trying to decide whether to trust them? Or was that dastardly slimeball The Tape creeping out of his lair to try to sell the gem to Laura? Maybe the heads of the Hydra were coming together at last.

Slipping into Mickey's chair, taking up the ballpoint, Laura said crisply to Hendley, "What's his name?"

She wrote "Edouard" on the tablet. "When does he want to meet?"

She wrote "Saturday, January 21."

Mickey cursed inwardly and began to pace. The name was unfamiliar and the date was a major conflict. Saturday night after the gem show closed, the industry would do the major part of their networking at cocktail parties in the new Hilton Hotel near the show. The exposure was vital to his work for Garth. And Paishon was due to tell him when the emerald was coming on the market. He had to be open to the moment when Paishon would approach him. He couldn't miss the show. And yet he couldn't permit Laura to meet with a virtual stranger alone. Not with thugs coming out of the woodwork, and comparative innocents like Delarein, in New Orleans, starting to get hurt.

"What's his phone number?" he heard Laura ask.

Alarmed, Mickey listened intently. She was proceeding with a meeting with a stranger as if none of the danger she'd experienced had made the slightest dent in her. He mimed a request for the phone. Laura held up her palm.

"Let me talk to him," Mickey insisted.

"Wait a minute," she responded distractedly, and said to the man in London, "Nothing, Hendley. What was his number?" Her eyebrows arched. "He wouldn't leave a number? But why?"

She listened. "I see." She wrote down "Mtg. behind The Arches Rest., Newport Beach, 8:00 p.m. Come alone."

Mickey bent to take a second look at the note. Sure enough, the meeting place was in a prestigious beach town an hour and a half south of Santa Monica. It had been scheduled for *behind* The Arches Restaurant? What was the point—darkness, no witnesses?

Edouard knew his battle strategy, Mickey decided, feeling tension creep into his shoulders. No way to call back or trace him.... "Come alone...." Meet after dark behind an intimate restaurant near two connecting freeways.

It smacked of danger, and Laura was blithely walking into it. He stuck his hand directly under her nose, demanding the phone.

"Hold on a sec, will you, Hendley?" Laura said. She clasped the receiver in her lap and frowned at Mickey. "What is it, Mickey? Please let me conduct this phone call the way I see fit. I assure you, I've been doing it success-fully for years.''

Ignoring her irritation, he demanded, ''Why's the meet-ing to take place behind the restaurant?''

''Because it's in a limo.''

''Why Newport Beach? Why not New York or Dallas? Or Paris?''

''Because Hendley told this Edouard person that L.J.M. was in Los Angeles on business.''

Mickey frowned. ''Okay, but you can't get into a stranger's limo, Laura. You know you can't.''

''Of course not. I intend to insist Edouard, whoever he is, come out of the car to talk. Go into the restaurant, pos-sibly.''

''Fat chance of that.'' His sarcasm made her eyes glitter. He changed tactics. ''What about the gem show? Don't you want to go?''

''Yes, of course, Mickey. I assumed it would be over by five or six o'clock. Most shows are, aren't they? I assumed you'd drive with me to Newport Beach, stand in the shad-ows or something while I talk to this man. All right?''

''No, it's not all right.'' He paced restlessly and came back to give her a commanding look. ''You're in over your head, Laura. Let me handle this. The Arches is at least an hour and a half south of Santa Monica and the gem show; more, if there's traffic. It's nowhere near our own turf, so to speak, and the timing's lousy. Postpone the meeting with this character until I'm free to go in your place.''

She started to object, said, ''Now, wait just a min—'' And then she hesitated, had what appeared to be an argu-ment with her inner self, clamped her mouth shut and nodded. ''Very well. I'll see what I can do.''

She went back to the phone. ''Hendley, have you indi-cated to his man that I'm a woman—referred to me as Mrs. Marley or anything?''

Hendley's voice crackled faintly.

''Good,'' she said. ''Mickey will act as L.J.M. and go in my place.''

It was the most abrupt switch in gears he'd seen from her, Mickey mused, feeling relief. She'd been about to bite his head off, tell him to mind his own business, and then *pffft!*—she was a pussy-cat, agreeing without a whimper. Who could explain this woman?

Even now she was saying they couldn't possibly make the meeting this Saturday, giving him further respite.

Then, evidently, a glitch cropped up. She pursed her lips. "He won't be calling back?" she asked. "You mean we simply are to move heaven and earth to be there or we can forget about what Edouard has to say?"

In a second she said, "I see. His way or the freeway— what? Oh, just an American expression, Hendley. You can use it in your teleplay." She chuckled, and Mickey heard the weariness in her voice.

She concluded the conversation with a promise to keep in close touch, praised Hendley's dedication and hung up. She sat there a moment, head bowed, rubbing her forehead.

Moved to sympathy, Mickey knelt in front of her. "Tired?" he asked, caressing the shining brown hair that swept into a loose bun at the back of her head.

Without looking at him, she nodded.

"Somehow we'll manage to cover all the bases," he said. "In fact, I'll go see Harry. He'll help."

She raised her head. "Harry?"

"The big guy who owns the fish-and-chips place on Olive. He's the fellow who slapped Fast Eddie silly for mugging you in Pershing Square that first night."

"What can Harry do to help?"

"He never misses the Santa Monica show. Likes to keep in touch with the pulse of the gem-and-jewelry business. I'll ask him to give us a hand."

"'Give us a hand,'" she repeated. Her eyes gained a spark that didn't bode well for Mickey. Suddenly she pushed up out of the chair and strode twenty feet into the room, keeping her back turned. "So you'll ask him to chaperon me, is that it?" The anger in her voice reverberated through the empty reaches of the warehouse.

"Well, yeah, something like that," he admitted, his ire piqued by the reverse in her mood. He schooled himself to patience. "I can give you a crash course on what I need to accomplish Saturday night, you can stand in for me and Harry can back you up. He's savvy on gems. You two can handle things for the three or four hours I'll be gone."

"To Newport Beach, you mean?"

"Yeah." He stepped close and tilted up her chin. "Hey," he said. "What's this anger all about?"

She twisted her face away and showed a snapping spirit in her eyes. "What about the Shark Man?" she said. "Aren't you supposed to meet him at the show? So he can tell you when the emerald will be for sale? Wasn't that a priority?"

"Yeah, sure. It'll work out." Keeping his temper dampened down by sheer self-control, he said, "If I don't see him before I have to leave for Newport or after I return to Santa Monica to pick you up, Paishon can see me Sunday at the show. Besides, he knows my phone number. He can set up a meeting anytime."

"So you intend to meet with Edouard alone, then?"

"I can't see any other way."

She canted her chin at him. "You get off on it, don't you? Being a hero. Taking risks."

Affronted, he spun away, then whirled back to say harshly, "I do what I have to, Laura. Why the third degree?"

"Because I care, damn you!"

Her eyes glistened brightly and he couldn't be sure if it was anger or tears. It sounded like anger. It looked like tears. Either way, he felt hamstrung with conflicting feelings.

"Ah, Laura," he sighed, shaking his head. "You can't keep playing Ping-Pong with me. You know? It takes too much out of me. Are you with me on this or not? In or out?"

"You could take me with you to Newport," she said stubbornly.

"I've lost so much time away from work. My income's suffering. I need the access to possible sales at the show and the parties afterward. Newport may be dangerous. It may be a dead end. You can't go alone, and I need you in Santa Monica. I'm sorry if you feel left out of the action, but that's the bottom line."

"Take Clint with you."

So that was part of it. She feared for his safety. A new emotion arrowed through him, a lightweight dart of pleasure at her concern, and he took her hands. When she tried to pull away, he held them firmly and tipped his head, following her evasive gaze until she couldn't look away. "I'll call Clint. Ask him if he can back me up. Okay?"

She glanced at his hands and up at his face, searching his features. "Okay," she said in a tiny voice.

He brought her stiffly erect body into his arms and hugged her until she relaxed against him. He didn't deserve the kind of caring she offered. Man without a country, a decent livelihood or even a sane outlook. He cared, too, dammit. He just couldn't put it into words. He could only put tenderness in the embrace and hope she felt the underlying message.

She sighed, letting him hold her. "I promised myself I'd do whatever it took to help you, and I've done it again, haven't I?"

"Done what?" he asked.

"Given you a bad time. Argued. I'm so used to running things. I really do believe you know best in this situation, Mickey. I'll try to be less of a . . . liability."

"Ouch," he said, remembering his insult.

"Well, you were right. My pride gets in the way sometimes."

"Shh." He caressed her neck, felt its delicacy, and cradled her head against him. "You're bright and beautiful and you have a heart as big as Africa. Don't ever let me tell you different again."

She nodded, childlike.

He swept his hands from her shoulders to her waist, fingers tucking tightly around her slender form, marveling at the granite strength he seemed to feel when she was in his arms.

Perhaps he'd been too hasty in merely wanting to make love to her. There was a fragility about her now, a vulnerability, that made him reconsider. She wasn't the love-'em-and-leave-'em type at all. Not by a lifetime.

She moved slightly. "I should get to the hotel," she murmured against his chest.

"I'll get dressed and walk you over," he said.

But for a long, long moment afterward, he held her, needing her warmth, aching to make love. Yet knowing both the timing and his motives were all wrong.

Chapter Twelve

Saturday, January 21—Santa Monica Gem Show

Her head crammed with facts about emeralds, sapphires, diamonds—the stuff of Mickey's trade—Laura tried to settle the information into some kind of order in her mind as Mickey pulled the car into a slot in the packed parking lot. He turned off the ignition and pocketed the keys, opening his door.

"Show time," he said.

She smiled nervously, collected her purse. No more time for catechism. Now it was the experience of the show itself that would ready her for tonight. She had to do it, had to be good at gem dealing—for Mickey's sake.

They climbed out, and Mickey went to the trunk to retrieve his briefcase.

Her sleep had been troubled last night by the secrets Jenkins had revealed, and she thought about them again now. She'd made a decision about the lost documents and Jenkins's letter, a decision she needed to discuss with Mickey. There hadn't been time yet, however. During the drive, he'd taught her all he could about gems. Yet the subject needed to be aired. She needed to get it off her mind so she could concentrate on the gem show. She would ask him before they went in.

Laura breathed in the salty taste of the Pacific, two blocks downhill from the Civic Center, and took in the palm trees and brick-and-concrete office buildings of old Santa Monica.

Across the street, the shell configuration of the Civic Auditorium fanned into a leaden sky. In front of the main building, the many spikes of a white tent cropped up, the people of the gem trade filing in through the open flaps.

Laura was reminded of a carnival. Paishon would be one of the sideshow giants, she thought. He was to bring Mickey news of the gem sale. So much at stake today. So many factors to make her feel uneasy. Her fingers were cold. Her mouth felt dry.

Giving herself an edge in appearance, she'd worn her loose chignon high to clarify her features. Her low-heeled pumps were oxblood with a slash of black, the design repeated in the sling-strap purse into which she'd put the Garth business cards Mickey had given her this morning. Her black slacks were tucked at the waist for easy movement; the jacket coordinate, while it fit perfectly at the belt line, had a roominess about the arms, and the puffed shoulders and sweetheart neckline were trimmed with oxblood kid. A small heart of rubies and diamonds, slung from a delicate chain, emphasized the neckline. She felt comfortably elegant, if not entirely capable of handling her new responsibilities.

Mickey came up beside her. He carried a battered case of ebony leather. Even if his charcoal suit was a bit roomy on him, he looked handsome with his black hair brushed back to show a fine brow and a bold, sensuous jaw. She wanted to stare at him, memorize him, relive the romantic moments of last night's homecoming. Instead, as she knew she must, she reverted to business.

"Before I forget, Mickey," she said. "Did you reach Clint yet?"

"He's not expected back to the office till late this afternoon. I'll call him again."

"Great." She paused. "I wanted to ask you something else, too."

His eyes, a mysterious jade green with the weather the way it was, cut restlessly back and forth over the stream of people entering the tent. Now he looked at her, somewhat distracted. "What's on your mind?"

"The documents."

He cut a glance behind them, stepped closer, lowered his voice. "What about them?"

"I want them to go back to England. To the government."

His eyebrows rose. "Bit premature, don't you think?"

"Well, if we get them back, then. I want us to take them to the British authorities. Or get them there somehow. Do you understand why, Mickey?"

He gave her a thoughtful look. "To make amends," he said. "Set a good example for your kids."

Gratitude for his understanding put a husky note in her voice. "Yes. If we get the documents back and your buddies at NSI want to put them in the deep freeze—as political clout over Great Britain—I'll expose everything. John's part, Garth's, all of it. The Brits may never find any evidence besides Jenkins's letter, but at least they'll be alerted to the situation. They may not want the press to get wind of it, but I realize that's a possibility, too. However, if I don't insist on this, many more than just myself and my children may get hurt. In South Africa."

He gained an expression of new respect. "You've gotten very wise these past weeks, Laura. Very aware."

"It's just—I don't believe John would have compromised his own government willingly. I believe he thought he was doing a double favor, one for Demude, the other for the apartheid movement. When the emerald was stolen, he realized he should never have taken on the responsibility for such an act. Realizing the prideful error he'd made, he succumbed to guilt."

Mickey pursed his lips in thought. "You may be right. But it's not your fault, Laura. You don't have to atone for your husband's actions."

"But I do. For Jessica and my son. For their sakes, for mine, for others."

Another penetrating look, and Mickey nodded. "If it ever comes up, I'll do what I can. That's all I can promise."

"That's enough," she said, grateful the topic was out of the way and glad Mickey was on her side.

Setting down his briefcase, he luffed the lapels of his jacket and buttoned it—but not before she'd glimpsed the leather holster under his arm.

Thinking of tonight's meeting with Edouard, she felt a chill of apprehension run through her. At least Mickey was far more qualified than she for an interview with a stranger in the darkness of an unknown city, she reassured herself. And Clint would be with him.

For a brief moment as she turned back to face the crowd, she replayed the fantasy of continuing to see him after they'd settled their debts with the Garden Emerald and its contraband intelligence. He'd given her no encouragement except his warm reception last night, his understanding today, and yet the dream persisted.

"I've got to get to work," he reminded her, and took her arm to bring her across the street.

"Sorry," she said, hurrying beside him. "Just one more question. Did Garth send the money?"

"It was a wire transfer. I did the banking yesterday. I have it in a safe place, ready to go."

FOR THE NEXT SIX HOURS, Laura had no time to think of hidden guns or secret meetings. Even the menace of Paishon slipped her mind.

Mickey took her on a whirlwind tour of the show, from the tent to the connecting building; hundreds of curtained booths, aisles thick with jewelry retailers, collectors, dealers and dabblers, entrepreneurs looking for a new opportunity, and free-lancers like Mickey, who wholesaled his gems to the tradesmen in the booths.

He introduced her as his associate to thirty, forty dealers, one after the other, and closed two deals of his own, selling some opals and sapphires from Garth's last trip to the Philippines.

Fascinated by the wheeling and dealing taking place beneath the scrutiny of beefy armed guards at each entrance, Laura analyzed the huddles, the furtive looks, the conservative, assessing greetings of the vendors. These reactions contrasted sharply with the cavalier manner in which they displayed their caches of riches and memoed rare gems between them as if they were jellybeans.

Gradually she gained insight into the balance these traders struck between caution and paranoia.

She listened intently, eyes wide, when one of Mickey's clients, a heavyset redhead in a pale tent-dress, launched into a diatribe against two Colombians who'd held her at gunpoint in the underground parking lot beneath Pershing Square last month. The thieves had forced her to give up fifty thousand dollars in diamonds—wholesale. The gem trade always spoke in wholesale terms, Mickey told her. She doubled the amount to figure the retail value, but that, he said, was often conservative.

Appreciating the risks the traders faced, she looked more carefully at the scene around her.

Spread out before Laura in glass cases and laid in velvet trays according to size and brilliance, were gems that looked as grand and gleaming as the crown jewels in the Tower of London. Natural pearls the size of nickles glimmered on black velvet. Eastern sheikhs riffled through ropes of rare corals. Petrified woods, sliced to reveal highly-polished, fantastic landscapes, intrigued a boy of ten who wore strands of gold on his chest. Jars of amber sat next to bowls of amethyst and aquamarine and topaz. A wizened Chinese woman watched over ancient figurines, priceless and locked behind glass. The color and intrigue and action were intoxicating.

Eventually, strands of hair unraveled from Laura's chignon. She no longer bothered to tuck them up. Her skin felt sticky, filmed by the sweat of the crush of people in the aisles. The leather trim on her suit felt as heavy as armor; too hot for such physically, mentally exhausting work.

Trade shows were sweatshops for the exchange of goods and services, she thought, unnerved by the experience. How had John stood it, year after year? It had all sounded glamorous, secondhand. It wasn't; it was sheer hard work.

Her head spun with the figures Mickey and his prospective clients had bantered about. Even now, his briefcase lay open next to the long glass case of an emerald dealer who spoke with a Spanish accent, and Mickey was withdrawing something from a pocket inside his jacket. Out came a familiar-looking small white packet, much like the packets she'd seen in BBC television specials on drug busts. Gem dealers used folded papers to identify and carry gems.

"The *jardin* is extraordinary," Mickey was saying, handing the packet across. "I have fifteen that are graded fine."

While the dark eyes of the South American perused the gems sparkling in the fold of paper, Laura remembered her lessons. Emeralds had internal imperfections the trade called *'jardin';* translated, it meant *'garden.'* Flecks of organic matter, traces of iron and the like gave the gem its character. Chromium gave the emerald its green color—without that metallic chemical element, the crystal was a common aquamarine. Mickey had said a normal emerald, flaws and all, equalled or surpassed the value of a diamond of the same classification.

In Bogotá, where ninety-five percent of the world's emeralds were mined, the rough stones were graded, appraised and classified. A stone's brilliance, character and color classed an emerald as poor or fine all the way up through very fine and exceptional.

Mickey's emeralds were fine. The Garden Emerald was exceptional, and rare because of its size.

The Spanish language began to flow between Mickey and his client, indicating the heightened interest of the South American. Laura caught only pieces of the conversation, her Spanish being limited, but she understood that the dealer had asked permission to look at the stones more closely.

"*Sí, sí,*" Mickey said in approval.

The man took the stones to a table at the back of his booth and sat before a magnifying viewer. Placing one stone beneath the magnifier, he put his eye to the lens and adjusted the focus. She heard him draw a sharp breath.

She glanced at Mickey for interpretation, but he was gazing half-interestedly at his nails. So cool, she thought. His financial security was at stake and he was inspecting his manicure!

The client poked delicately at each stone in turn, viewing the crystals from all sides. When he came back, he said, "*¡La materia verde*—the green stuff! *Qué muy bonitas*— how very beautiful. But perhaps too rich for my humble clientele, Señor Stone."

Mickey shrugged as if the decision were of no importance to him. But Laura noticed he did not rush to take back the gems.

Thoughtfully the dealer folded up the precious package. "Let me consider this, my friend." He pursed his lips, thinking aloud. "*¿Este noche, queréis...su regresa en la noche?*"—you'll return tonight?

"*Sí, pero—*" Mickey turned to Laura, introduced her, explained that she would be available this evening should the dealer want to make an offer.

Respect shone in the man's eyes when his gaze came to rest on Laura. She could only presume the emeralds were vastly expensive and that he was impressed at her being trustworthy enough to handle them. Inwardly she felt the pressure of conducting a possible sale without the knowledge to conduct it wisely. But she nodded formally, as she had learned to do from Mickey, and shook the vendor's hand.

"Tonight," she said, smiling conservatively.

He gave her a slight bow.

In a moment, Mickey was urging her toward another booth down the aisle, and she had the presence of mind to protest.

"Mickey," she said, laying a hand on his sleeve. "I feel faint. I have to have some food."

His hand pressed to her forehead. "Probably the rushing around," he said, frowning. "There's a hot-dog stand at the far side of the tent. Get yourself something to drink and sit down for a few minutes. I'll be there shortly and have something to eat with you."

It was on the tip of her tongue to say, *Hot dogs*—in this kingdom of jewels? But she kept her vast disappointment to herself and nodded, squeezing his arm. "I do need a break."

It had sustained her a little to touch him, she realized as she watched him move away. Even the thought of going it alone tonight with just an overgrown stranger as her companion didn't seem impossible. Difficult and disappointing that Mickey wouldn't be with her, but not impossible. As she wove among the attendees, searching for the hot-dog stand, she reflected on her growing attraction for him.

And tried not to think of the danger he might be facing in Newport Beach.

Newport Beach

EVERY NERVE TUNED LIKE RADAR to details of the setting, Mickey curved down off the Newport–Riverside Freeway and onto Pacific Coast Highway. His headlights picked through gauzelike swaths along the road. The lighted areas of Newport Beach's main drag had a fuzzy, unreal look. A quick left just after the underpass would take him into the parking lot of The Arches Restaurant, but Mickey slipped on by the prestigious hideaway to gather what impressions he could of the scene.

Established in 1922, the place practically jutted onto Coast Highway. It looked romantic, the kind of place Laura would enjoy, with rustic wood siding and shingles, a white brick chimney and scalloped white eaves. A shingled turret bore the neon script, Dining Room. A couple, she in red lace, he in black tie, stepped under an awning at the front entrance and went in. Mickey envied them briefly as he drove on, turning his head to see if he could spot the limousine.

The paved lot stretching alongside and behind the dinner house was ill lit, but Mickey glimpsed Italian sports cars, a Mercedes sedan with gold trim, and three or four high-end American cars. No limousine. It might be out back.

Mickey glanced at his watch. Ten minutes to eight. He was glad he'd been able to leave Laura and Harry kibitzing with his colleagues at the Hilton Hotel. He'd left in time to arrive early for tonight's meeting with Edouard, gaining a slight mental advantage by familiarizing himself with the territory.

He drove past the Mediterranean-inspired Villa Nova and other watering holes of the rich and famous. The mast and rigging of a huge sailboat poked out of the fog on the harbor. Mickey ducked into the driveway of the mariner-style Rusty Pelican Restaurant, where he made a U-turn. He returned to The Arches and pulled slowly into the lot.

A hundred yards beyond the building, he could hear the rumble of traffic on the Newport–Riverside Freeway, the vehicles heading for night spots on Balboa Peninsula or north through Orange County to Riverside in the high desert. Some of the traffic fed on or off PCH itself, the main artery connecting the beach towns of the California coast. It was a perfect spot for secret meetings and quick getaways, he thought, wondering what kind of man he was about to meet—wondering if he'd be glad that he was packing the Walther.

Although he drove at idle speed through the collection of expensive cars, he could see no limousine.

Mickey backed up to the rear of an adjacent liquor store and parked facing a shed, where he could watch the restaurant lot.

Leaving the dash lights on, he pulled out the Walther, jacked a round into the chamber, clicked off the safety and holstered it again. He killed the lights and pocketed the keys.

While he waited, he tried to imagine Laura doing this meet. She was naive about the underworld, thinking she could entice Edouard into the safety of the restaurant for a chat about one of the world's most coveted stolen gems. But maybe being chased by thugs, seeing Delarein mauled, coming up against tough cookies like Paishon—maybe she had put two-and-two together finally. He supposed she had, because she'd stopped demanding she be involved in every aspect of the case. She'd not given him another ounce of trouble about his standing in for her as L.J.M. She hadn't even asked again if Clint were backing him up, and he'd been relieved, because his friend was still out on a case.

He admired Laura. She was a trouper all the way. He doubted there were many women who would go as far as she had today, battling heat and crowds and a whole new vocabulary and culture to learn how to stand in for him for a single evening.

She'd kept a brave face, too, when he'd handed over his briefcase full of purchase orders and given her a brusque kiss, telling her to stay close to Harry. He could see the concern, the uncertainty in her eyes, but she didn't cling to him in fear, as Veeta would have done in the same circumstances. Laura had simply said, so softly he barely heard, "Be safe, Mickey. I'll be here when you get back."

A strange and startling emotion rose in him, remembering Laura and her thousand ways of being there for him. He let the new feeling pervade him for a moment, wondering about it. It was a protectiveness, he supposed. A gratitude for acts of generosity by a woman that he'd never experienced before. A female operative—and he'd worked with a few—didn't give as much. What on earth did he give back to Laura? Just a warm hug or two, a joke now and then, and plenty of bad attitude. What did she see in him?

There was something more he felt. Something about the grit it took for Laura to put others above herself. Maybe about the way she stuck to her values—the business of getting the documents back to officials in London, at possibly tremendous personal cost—that reminded him of himself as a younger, less-jaded officer of the law. In addition to arousing a protective, sensual, sensitive side of his nature, Laura made him question his values and actions like nobody he'd ever met before. While it was uncomfortable at times, he had begun to value the changes she was evoking in him.

Though he struggled to identify deeper feelings, put a name to them, he ended in a blank.

Frustrated, he climbed out of the car to walk toward the hill at the north edge of the lot. Now wasn't the time to dwell on Laura, he reminded himself. He needed to stay alert, clearheaded.

Immediately he could taste a salt residue in the air he breathed. The mist clung to his skin, lay heavy in his chest, dampened the thunder of nearby traffic and obscured details in the black shadows at the back of the dinner house, thirty yards away. For a time he leaned against a coppertone minivan with a sign reading The Arches, arms folded, belying the tension that made the wait seem endless.

Then, out near the boulevard, he heard the crunch of footsteps. He turned, peered into the darkness. A dark shape came hulking behind the garage along the foot of the hill, hatless, long winter coat flapping with the rapid gate. The hulk stopped, faceless and silent, ten, twelve feet away.

Mickey let his hands fall to his sides, loose limbed and ready for action. Inside, he felt that familiar blend of anticipation and paranoia that came to him on a stakeout, right before the bust.

He said quietly to the shadow, "Looking for someone?"

"Could be," said a gutteral voice that sounded disembodied. "You waitin' for somebody, mister?"

"Edouard, if it's anything to you."

"Who're you?"

"L.J.M."

A brief pause; then, "Come with me, please. The boss is waitin'."

So the brute had turned polite. That meant there would be at least a semblance of civility about the meeting. Mickey didn't presume it would last.

He allowed himself one grateful final thought that Laura was safe in Santa Monica. Then he followed the hulk toward Newport Boulevard.

Rounding the corner, heading away from PCH and the relative safety of illuminated civilization, they walked uphill on a poorly-lit side street called Santa Ana. A pickup truck approached from the rear. The headlights swept briefly over the big man ahead, highlighting a crew cut, a huge round skull and the brownish tweed of his coat. Nothing about him was familiar. Then the truck overtook them, passed the older view homes at the top of the hill and turned off. Mickey again heard only their footsteps crunching on gravel.

Suddenly his guide heaved up over the shoulder of the road and dropped down a steep sandy bank. The guy scrabbled for footing in the dark, cursed, got his legs under him. Expecting this detour, Mickey followed in silence, circling a half-dead patch of ice plant, picking his way around a pothole, angling downhill.

A polite chat in a restaurant hadn't been a realistic expectation at all, he thought, recalling Laura's plan. That kind of thing never happened when surprise and darkness were allies and when somebody had something to hide. His pulse began to jump. He felt as if he had fleas under his skin. He was glad for the hike; it gave him a chance to work off the heebie-jeebies.

They leveled out on a strip of dusty lane bordered by a wire-and-post fence. About six feet down on the other side of the fence, a service road paralleled the back ends of the retail establishments facing Coast Highway. In another minute, Mickey could see across the highway to the multi-

level facade of the Villa Nova, and he knew where he was.
A sea gull keened down at the waterfront among the mil-
lionaires' yachts, and Mickey's instinct for trouble deepened. His right hand itched to grasp the Walther, heft its
comforting weight.

Ahead of the bodyguard, the hill on the left dropped
precipitously to the lane, and a stark white complex—a
huge Jaguar dealership—rose straight up on the right,
forming a perfect canyon. There was only one way out—
and it was blocked by a pristine black Lincoln limousine.

Like a black beetle, it hunkered at the mouth of the alley,
its headlights doused, its windows inky. Ambient light from
the dulled crescent moon winked on the immaculate hood.

Here, apparently, waited Edouard, who had something
to say about the Garden Emerald. Mickey's heart leapt at
the prospect of solving the mystery—perhaps tonight, moments from now. Still nervy but in control, he eagerly followed his companion.

Abruptly, the henchman stopped. "Gotta pat you
down," he said, turning to face Mickey, blocking access to
the car.

The tone was respectful, half apologetic, but firm. Interesting, thought Mickey. Whoever was hosting this rendezvous wasn't attempting to insult or intimidate him. They
were obviously only being cautious. And they didn't know
who he was, because anyone who was expecting Mickey
Stone under these circumstances would have assumed he
was armed. Then the instruction would have been, "Let's
have your weapon." The polite request to frisk him told
Mickey it wasn't Paishon waiting inside. Who, then? The
thoughts sped through him in an instant and he decided on
a mild protest.

"The instructions didn't say anything about coming un-
armed," he said.

"Just a precaution," said the bodyguard. "No offense."

"I get my weapon back after the meeting?"

"Yeah, if everything's copacetic."

Mickey shrugged, turned his back, put his arms in the air. "Check my left armpit," he said. "Easy. The safety's off."

The big man patted him all the way down to his ankles and inside his legs. Then he reached in and feathered the Walther from its case. He laid it gently on the hood of the car. "Stay the way you are and wait here, please," he said.

Footsteps told Mickey the man went to the rear of the limo. A door opened almost soundlessly. Voices murmured. The door closed, another opened. The footsteps returned.

"Okay," said the man, "just climb in and sit facing the back."

Mickey went to a door cracked open about midway down the car, and climbed in. It closed after him. He sank into the plush seat. It was midnight dark and he could see nothing, not even his hands.

Suddenly Mickey went rigid with disbelief, with recognition. Carried to him on the warm air was a perfume he would remember until his death and hate with a passion that surpassed any feeling in memory. Veeta! His ex-wife was in the car!

Either that, or by pure, twisted coincidence, the woman across from him wore the same rare French fragrance that Veeta insisted was her exclusive brand. She'd taken a Hovercraft across the English Channel with her mother when she was thirteen, the only vacation in an impoverished childhood, and her mother had given her a bottle of the exotic stuff. She'd never worn anything else since. It was one hundred eighty dollars an ounce, he knew, because each time he'd left home to conduct a mission that took him anywhere close to France, she'd reminded him to bring her home a bottle of it. And he had, he remembered, resenting her again for the cavalier manner with which she demanded the scent as soon as he walked in the door. Without a greeting of any kind, she had always waited silently, palm out, looking bored. When he gave it to her, her fingers closed over the bottle and she turned her back to covet it like a greedy child. It had always disgusted him.

The events of the past hit him like a hard slap in the face. He felt instantly violent, his muscles locked in readiness, aching to act. The thick air closed in. He found it difficult to draw breath.

His heart thudding heavily now, Mickey gripped the seat and held himself in check.

A man's voice snaked out of the darkness, nasal and terribly polite. "L.J.M?"

"Yeah," he murmured, low. "What do you have for me?"

There was a feminine gasp of recognition.

"Shut up!" snarled the man.

"But, it's—" came Veeta's familiar whine. It was cut off, ending in a yelp.

Mickey felt an unpleasant sensation. Hearing her voice galvanized his hatred, while her cry of pain touched him. He stirred uncomfortably on the seat. Veeta had gotten herself a cruel keeper. The Tape? Was Mickey sitting three feet from his arch-enemy? Did they have the gem? His gaze bored into the darkness as if that could bring the coveted stone and his enemies into focus, and he tried to figure a way to get to his gun.

"Now," interrupted the nasal tenor voice casually, as if the man were going to the next item on a business agenda. "You'll pardon the unorthodox manner in which we meet. I have my reasons for it."

"Yeah, sure."

"You don't have the stone?"

"Have it?" Mickey retorted, wanting the confrontation. "You're supposed to have information about its whereabouts. Why're you asking me if I have it? What is this?"

Veeta piped up, "It's him, I tell you!"

"Shut—" Silence. "What are you complaining about, 'him?' Who's 'him?'"

"Mickey, it's Mickey!"

Another silence. A metallic *flick,* and a lighter's yellow glow filled the limousine. Mickey saw Veeta first, eyes narrowed against the sudden glare, the dyed black hair ratted and wild looking, the bare shapely legs tucked into a tight leather skirt. He couldn't pull his gaze from her. She looked exhausted, used up. Her skin was pasty. A thin scar ran the length of the right side of her face, and Mickey felt his gut wrench in pity. The emotion surprised him.

When she opened her eyes and saw her ex-husband, that smirk that had often driven Mickey crazy curled up the side of her bright red mouth. "I knew it was him," she said, derisive.

"Yes," said her snakelike companion, "I see that it is."

Veeta's dark eyes glittered crazily, and she said, "You deserved what you got, Mickey."

"You like what you got, Veeta?" he snapped, indicating the scar on her face.

"It's because of you!" She pressed a self-conscious palm to the defect and her voice rose. "You and your precious cases and missions and secrets. It was prison, living with you. I couldn't stand it!"

The serpent next to her let her rave, a cruel smile wavering over his pocked face, lit by the unsteady flame of the lighter.

She gestured. "That's right, you're to blame. Some husband! Gone all the time."

"Thank God I had my work. There was nothing at home but selfishness and sniveling and greed."

Her eyes widened. "And what about you? Savior of the world! And all along, the person you could have saved, you ignored. Quiet as a crypt, you were. No fun in you. No talk, unless it was about your precious cases. And then you passed me off to that schmuck, Garth." She chortled. "Sticking me in that mausoleum of a brokerage was the best thing you ever did for me, Mickey. Did you know that?"

A pearl of rage formed in his gut and whirred there, burning like hot metal. He didn't trust himself to answer.

"Cat got your tongue?" she taunted, giving him a grotesque, mock-sweet smile. "It was no big deal to get close to Garth, you know. How could he *not* trust me, being the wife of a federal agent? He had to travel, and I had to mind the store. Right, honey?'' She looked at The Tape, laughed shrilly.

"All right, you've had your fun," he said.

As if she hadn't heard the warning, she looked back at Mickey haughtily, and said, "Yes, and when the courier had me sign off on the emerald, all I had to do was walk downstairs with it and—"

"Enough!" The Tape's voice stopped her in midsentence, and she cowered before his glare.

It went dark in the limousine, and brightened again when the slimeball switched on a light. A rich navy-blue three-piece suit encased his trim body, and a two- or three-carat diamond glittered on the pinky of his left hand. The dark brown eyes stayed narrow and secretive, calculating, while a lethal-looking smile curved his thin bloodless lips.

"I find it interesting to contemplate, Stone," he began slowly. "If you're not L.J.M., who is?"

"Go to hell." Mickey felt hamstrung without his gun. The situation was ludicrous, unreal, deadly.

Soft, mirthless laughter filled the compartment: "Let me guess," said The Tape. "Your new girlfriend..." In this pause, panic bolted through Mickey. *Laura. He meant Laura!* The Tape waved an effeminate hand. "This dame is really L.J.M., and you're Mickey Stone, is that it?"

Mickey's face whitened but he said nothing. How much time would it take to choke the life out of this weasel? Time enough, before his bodyguard came back with guns blazing?

"Don't consider it, Stone," said his enemy. "Don't think you can do me in and get away. There are several more along the lines of Bruno, whom you've met, watching from the shadows. You come busting out of my limo without my permission, they'll blow you away. Simple as that."

"Since you know I don't have the gem, why don't you have them put me out of my misery and be on your way?"

"It's a thought, Stone, it really is." He pursed his reptilian lips. "But you may be able to vindicate yourself...with cooperation."

"Such as?"

"Well, there's your girlfriend to think of. Let's see, now. She hangs out at Grosvenor House in London, evidently. Currently staying at the Biltmore. These are high-roller digs, my friend. She's worth her weight in English guineas, I would guess." His expression approached innocent curiosity.

"I thought she was loaded, too, but I was wrong. She's scrimping to stake me, get the gem back." Mickey hurried to switch the subject. "What do you want, you little weasel?"

The thin pointy face purpled with sudden rage. "I want the emerald!"

So he wasn't selling, he was buying. "Get ripped off, did you?" Mickey chided gently to goad him. "How does it feel?"

"I don't like being made a fool of, Stone. I can have you killed!"

Mickey met the flashing gaze with aplomb, but he realized The Tape held all the cards. "What's the alternative?" he asked cautiously.

The Tape reeled in his presence of mind, nudged his tie. "There's a guy by the name of Cagney—ever heard of him?"

Paydirt! The heads of the Hydra were starting to merge. "Yeah, I heard about him."

"He's got the stone. I want it."

Mickey absorbed this bombshell quietly. Then he said, "How'd he get it?"

"He *stole* it from me, how do you think he got it? Cheap lousy two-timer. Said he was interested in making a buy, down in Fort Lauderdale last summer. Yeah," the man said ruminatively, "I was about to head for a real cushy life in the islands, if you want to know." His eyes blazed again, and his voice pitched high. He raised a hand as if to strike

Veeta. She pulled back, whimpering. "This lousy chit—she got careless. Cagney suckered me, stole the emerald right off her when she was bringing it to the meet!" The desperado's emotions crescendoed, and he took the name of the Virgin in vain. He clutched his hands together and shook the fist at Mickey. "I want it back or there'll be hell to pay! And you'll pay it!"

Mickey felt the presence of insanity in the car. The hair on his nape bristled. His life wasn't worth a dime if he didn't play along. Besides, there was a way he could bust the lot of them, there had to be. He just had to play his cards right.

He leaned back, cupping the back of his head with his hands in a show of confidence. "Where is he—Cagney?"

"How the hell do I know where he is? He could be anywhere, anywhere in the world. All I know is, he's selling the stone. Soon. Here in L.A. or Orange County. That's all I know."

"How do you figure me in the deal?"

"I thought maybe this L.J.M. thing was it, the sale coming down. But you cheated me. You double-crossed me, Stone." The dark eyes gleamed ferally. "I ought to have you killed now!"

"Honey, what about the emerald?" Veeta reminded him in a tiny scared voice.

"Shut up!" The Tape leaned forward, locking gazes with Mickey. "I've put two and two together about you and your girlfriend, see? You're going to set me up for the sale, you got it? With her dough."

"What makes you think I can find out where it's being sold? I'm an ex-federal agent."

"You've been busy, see? You've been in and out of town a lot lately. I figure you're close. You're going to find out about the sale and tell me about it!"

"What if I don't?"

"Ever heard of a thug named Sledgehammer? Looks like he ran into a brick wall a few times?"

The shadowy figure at Pershing Square the night of Laura's mugging came to mind. The Tape had had a tail on him for two weeks, maybe longer; Sledgehammer was one of them. The puzzle of the black Riviera fell into place, too.

"Yeah, I've seen him around," Mickey said with studied nonchalance. "You going to have him break my ribs or what?"

"All I have to do, Stone, is make a call on this phone right here—" he poked at a phone in the armrest "—and have him pick her up."

Laura again. His Achilles' heel. Apprehension coiled in Mickey. Slowly he put his arms down, tugged at his tie, struggling to appear unconcerned. "You don't know where she is," he said, bluffing.

"Don't I?" The Tape sat back, slanted a gaze at his fingernails, looking relaxed. "Hilton Hotel. Santa Monica. Do we have a deal?"

"You *bastard!*"

"You bet." He turned to Veeta, took her chin in a tight grip and forced her face sideways so the light caught the scar from her brow to her chin. She whimpered, but The Tape ignored it. "Your L.J.M. is a pretty thing, I'm told. Be a shame to do this to her." He tsked in mock sympathy and let Veeta's face go. She crept to the shadows in the corner and stayed there.

The Tape looked calmly at Mickey. *"Do we have a deal?"*

Mickey cursed and slammed a fist into his palm. "Yes, dammit, yes! We've got a deal. Now give me my piece and let me go to work."

"I'll be in touch, Stone." The window motor hummed and the glass slid down. "Mr. Stone is leaving, Bruno."

"Yes, sir," said the henchman, opening Mickey's door.

With one foot on the ground, Mickey hesitated, turned to The Tape, Laura's safety uppermost in his mind. "We've got a deal, you bastard," he said in a low warning tone. "But if you touch her, I'll kill you. Like the old saying goes, you can try to run, but you can't hide. Not from me, not again. Not if you touch a hair on her head."

"I can get her anytime I want. You cooperate—" the Tape gave him a grin and a we-meant-no-offense shrug "—nothing to worry about."

It was chilling.

With a glance of compassion at Veeta huddled against the far door, Mickey climbed out, took his weapon and began to run toward the lights of Newport. His first, most urgent priority was finding a telephone.

Chapter Thirteen

Watching his rearview for cops, Mickey hit ninety going back up the I-405. He had to slow down on the Harbor Freeway that cut back into the heart of Los Angeles. It was always busy, but tonight the traffic was thick around the Martin Luther King on ramp, where the crowds from an early-knockout prize fight at the Sports Arena poured onto the freeway. Mickey listened to the wrap-up commentary on KNX Radio as he slugged through the jam.

He'd phoned, reached Laura at the Hilton. She'd been euphoric over the possibility of closing the emerald transaction with the South American, and Mickey had had to be abrupt to get her attention. Although she didn't know he was worried The Tape might decide to take her hostage as insurance against his cooperation, Laura had finally heard the concern in his voice, he guessed. She'd promised to leave immediately, have Harry drive her directly to the brokerage.

He should arrive back at the office close to the same time Harry and Laura would get there. The tension in him was relentless. Until he saw her, he couldn't relax. Images of Laura being man-handled, pushed around by that criminal bulldozer Sledgehammer kept crowding him.

Minutes later, Mickey parked in the alley behind the brokerage and keyed open the back entrance. He took the three flights of stairs at a gallop, unlocked his office, flipped on the lights to the sound of the phone ringing.

"Don't hang up," he said, racing to the desk. He scooped up the receiver and said, "Garth Gems."

"Stone?"

Mickey heard the gruff demand in Paishon's voice. His skin prickled. "Yeah," he said, glancing at the message recorder, seeing the light blink. There were calls. Two of them. Where the devil was Laura?

"I'm winded," he admitted, his brain ratcheting through his many priorities. "Just took the stairs three at a time."

"You're a busy man. Too busy to keep an appointment?"

"I had business down south," he said. "Figured you'd find me if you had to."

"You pussyfootin' with me, Stone? If it's no big deal to you, why..." Paishon let the challenge dangle.

"It's a big deal," Mickey affirmed, ripping his concentration from Laura and putting it on what Paishon had to tell him. His phone line or his quarters might be bugged by The Tape or NSI or the FBI. He'd checked things over last night after seeing Harry, as he did every day now, but that didn't mean the place hadn't been tapped today. "I get third-parties on my line from time to time," he hinted. "Know what I mean? I can meet you later tonight."

A pause. "No need. How's Tuesday for you?"

The sweet, thunderous surge of adrenaline nearly took his breath away again. "Tuesday's okay," he said, regretting the rasp of elation and surprise in his voice. He went through the trickery of telling himself this was a routine call, no need to get excited.

Paishon seemed not to notice or care. "Under the toll bridge in my backyard," he grated. "You know it?"

He meant the Vincent Thomas Bridge on the Terminal Island side because that's where Asian Coral Imports was located. "Yeah," Mickey said, leveling his voice to matter-of-fact. "I know it."

"Midnight." The line went dead.

The impact of Paishon's words made his blood feel freeze-dried. He was in! The Garden Emerald was all but his!

Without a pause, Mickey pressed the replay button on his recorder. It rewound, clicked, and Clint's voice said, "Got your message but I was out on interviews till eight-thirty. No rest for the wicked, they say. By the way. Down at work, word is you picked up a big money transfer. Now you can pay all your old debts, huh? We may be able to go to bat for you, after all, buddy. Call me back."

"Go to bat for you" indicated NSI might provide man-power in the bust, a huge surprise. What changed their minds? A call from Garth, maybe? Garth knew what was going on because of Mickey's money request.

He listened to a brief second message from Clint left half an hour ago. "Just checking back with you, Mickey. Call me at home." Clint was anxious to talk to him. And no wonder, with the news he'd imparted.

Rewinding the tape, Mickey let the impact of the first message sink in. He'd picked up two money-transfers this week. One from a retailer in Phoenix who'd paid a deposit on some opals Mickey had shipped to him Friday morning, and the other from Garth. That was the only one NSI would care about. Who had given the information to them? And why?

The interview with The Tape and Veeta, the call from Paishon, the news that NSI might back him—all of it funneled into Mickey's brain and spun there like a comet on a fast track to glory. The gravity force that kept his elation from spinning out of orbit was his concern for Laura's safety. The heebie-jeebies were back, and worse. He needed to think. He'd call Clint in a minute.

In agitation, he began to pace the length of the hardwood floor, his shadow, cast by the lamp, a great soft blackness against the dim recesses of the far wall. His silhouette diminished to a small fuzzy blur as he reached the perimeter of the room, turned and headed back.

Where was she? He felt saddled by his worry. He longed to plunge headlong into the kind of free thinking he needed to do to bring the tangents of the case into line, yet she was out there somewhere, and he kept visualizing the struggle she'd put up if someone tried to scar her lovely face.

Unable to reduce the tension by pacing, Mickey strode to the desk and uncapped the mouthpiece of the telephone. It hadn't been bugged. Screwing it back together, he dialed Clint's number and walked out into the barren warehouse to the limit of the twenty-five-foot cord.

Clint answered on the first ring.

"It's me," said Mickey, and he began to lay bombshell after bombshell on his old friend, about The Tape and Veeta, Sledgehammer, all of it. He said he'd considered having The Tape traced through the plates on his limousine, but that it would be wiser to play him along, bust him at the gem sale. Mickey said the sale was coming down Tuesday night, and Clint said, "Oh, *really*"—amazement falling away to nothing.

Then Clint told him he figured Garth phoned the captain, because a message had come in from Bogotá as Clint was passing the message desk on his way to his office this morning.

"I was running late for a flight to Tijuana to do some interviewing on that Russian arms case," said Clint. "Got orders to go before the captain. I went in, he asked me what I knew about you and the emerald, you believe that?"

"What'd you say?" Mickey asked, amazed.

"After I got my chin off the floor, you mean? What do I usually say? That you're killing yourself to get back the gem and clear yourself, etcetera."

"And...?"

"For once, he listened instead of blowing his top and warning me to stay clear of you. I told him you'd had some luck lately and had a line on the gem. He's a changed man, Mickey. I couldn't believe it. He said to keep him informed and when the deal came down, he'd do what he could to send some backup."

For a long moment, Mickey felt a hole where his heart should have been. He stood there staring sightlessly at the dark windows of the warehouse, his pulse loud in his ears, emotions jammed.

Like a distant beacon, the thought came, *If I go back to work for the Institute, what about Laura?* They'd live in two different worlds.

If he didn't go back, he had nothing to offer her—no real goal, no status, no money.

"Hey, buddy," Clint said.

"Yeah," Mickey breathed. "It's just such a shock."

"You remember those documents?"

"The ones with the emerald?"

"Right. I figure NSI wants them pretty badly."

A chink fell out of Mickey's newly formed hope that the Institute wanted him back. "I agree," he said, stepping off the roller coaster and back to firm ground. He briefed Clint on the information Laura had brought back from her meeting with Jenkins.

Finally, he asked if Clint had gotten anything incriminating from his research on Sledgehammer.

"Escaped from prison three months ago," Clint said, and Mickey whistled. "Yeah," said Clint. "He was up for thirty years for armed robbery, aggravated assault on a police officer, some bad-guy stunts while he was doing time. They want him back. Badly."

"Maybe we can arrange it. Tonight he was allegedly in Santa Monica at the new Hilton. I don't know if he's still there. At any moment, he might even be lurking around downstairs. You want to do some PR for me with the good ol' boys at the Bureau and let them know?"

"You bet. He tailing you?"

"Not me. Laura. It's a long story." Mickey glanced at his watch. What was keeping Harry and Laura?

"Holy cow," Clint was saying. "We'll snag them all, buddy. It'll be a good day for the old justice system, won't it?"

"Yeah. It will. Meanwhile, I'm taking Laura and going undercover. Can I give The Tape your private number?"

"Sure. When he calls in, I'll tell him the good news about Tuesday."

"Okay, and I'll call you to check in and give instructions on where I want The Tape to meet me. I'm not just going to hand him the site information. I'm going to deliver him myself."

"Right," said Clint.

"And pick up my messages for me, will you, Clint? That way you'll know as much as I do about who calls. You know the retrieval code."

"Yep." Ice clinked in a glass. After he'd evidently taken a drink, Clint came back on the line and said, "So...how was it, seeing Veeta again?"

"Mixed reactions." Mickey glanced down at the pin-striping of the floorboards at his feet. Somehow he couldn't imagine putting Veeta behind bars. She needed professional help, not incarceration. Hell, maybe his values were all messed up. On the subject of Veeta, he felt turned around.

He'd felt the first twinges of a bad conscience, listening to her spit at him in the limousine.

One, he should have been above belittling her. She was to be pitied.

Two, there was something of truth in her charge of neglect. If he'd found her shallow and conniving during the early years of their marriage, if he'd felt disillusioned, the decent thing to do would have been to break it off. Instead, he'd resented her, felt caged; reacted to her growing demands by giving her the silent treatment or being gone all the time. He'd buried his feelings and dug deep into his work, justifying it like the other men of his era who opted for the American dream at the expense of their marriages. Moles hiding from the light, he thought in self-disgust.

"So," Clint prompted, "did you take her head off, or what?"

Before he could muddle through an explanation, Mickey heard footfalls on the stairs below. "Gotta go," he said. "Someone's here."

"Need some help?"

"Thanks, but I'm hoping it's Harry's big number twelves I hear stomping up." He paused. "I owe you, Clint," he said brusquely, with feeling, and hung up the phone. He set it where he stood, in the middle of the floor. One of Paishon's beeves wore clodhoppers, too. Wing Tip. He wasn't taking any chances.

Unsheathing the Walther, he crossed soundlessly to the door. It was unlocked. The gun cocked at shoulder height and braced with both hands, ready to be leveled at an unfriendly face, he flattened against the wall and waited.

"MICKEY?"

It was Laura, calling him from the other side of the door. Mickey let out his breath in a whoosh, clicked on the gun's safety and sheathed it. He pulled open the door, stood back.

She popped in, gave him a big smile and a breathy, "Hi."

Black coat billowing, Harry trudged in behind her, wheezing heavily. Closing the door, Mickey gave a sympathetic nod to the big man. Pink hot spots daubed his cheeks, perspiration on his forehead caught the light from the office lamp.

"Any trouble?" Mickey asked, his thirsty gaze going to Laura, drinking in the sight of her loosened curls and wide blue eyes and happy-looking face.

It was she who answered—Harry was wiping his brow with a white handkerchief.

Handing Mickey his briefcase, she said, "No trouble at all, and to top it off, your client signed on the dotted line for the emeralds. I told him you'd see him tomorrow to deliver the stones and pick up the rest of the money."

There would be a change in plans, but she didn't know it. Meanwhile, she'd disobeyed orders. He frowned at her. "You stayed to finish the sale?"

"Yes, sir, I sure did. You don't think after what I've been through today I was going to let him get away?"

Mickey sent an exasperated look to her bodyguard pro tem. "Harry?"

"Huh?" Still catching his breath, Harry took a moment to get turned around. His eyes widened in self-defense. "She didn't even tell me you'd ordered her back here until after she'd signed up the dealer. Didn't mention the big guy, looks like he rammed face-first into a Mack truck, till we're in the car. I figured she was actin' racy and skittish, you know—lookin' over her shoulder and stuff—because she was green at the gem trade." He tucked away the handkerchief. "How was I to know some thug was waitin' to nab her?"

Setting down the case, Mickey faced her, his tone stern. "I appreciate the deal you made, but I won't tolerate my instructions being ignored. This isn't a game we're playing, Laura. It's serious stuff."

She lifted a shoulder, smiled at him. "Yes, sir," she said—softly, with mock humility. "I'll remember next time."

There was a fine fire in her eyes. The gloom couldn't hide it, and he felt arousal spiral through him, even as his mind raced through the preparations for their escape.

"Harry," he said, back to business. "Thanks for all the hassle I put you through tonight. It wasn't your fault she didn't relay my message right away."

"That's all right, Stone. Glad to help you out. You need anything else, let me know. Miz Marley." He touched his forehead in a so-long gesture and shuffled toward the door. "I'm beat. Gotta get my beauty sleep, be ready for tomorrow. The show is buzzing with a strange vibe, ain't it? Something big's comin' down. You goin' to be there?"

Cutting a glance at Laura, then Harry, Mickey decided to put a little more trust in the heavy man. He shook his head. "We have to lay low for a while, Harry."

The look Harry sent him was wise. He nodded. "It'll cost ya cash flow, Mickey, but you could lose worse. Take care, hear?"

Mickey went to the door and shook his hand. "Appreciate everything, Harry. Watch those stairs going down."

Harry dismissed the solicitation with a wave and started down more or less like one of those wire Slinky toys that pour-and-thunk down steps.

Mickey returned to Laura, stopped a few feet away. She was having none of it. She came straight into his arms and hugged him. Hard. Slowly he put his arms around her, an inner resistance to the giving it required splintering a little at a time. He put his chin against her hair, tightened his embrace.

"Don't do your own thing again until the case is solved. I mean it. But—" He pulled away, waited until her dusty-blue gaze locked with his. "You did good, Laura. You did one heck of a job for me tonight. I've got cash flow again, thanks to you."

She smiled, seeming very pleased with herself. "I wanted to help you. And you're okay, too. What more could a girl ask?"

He bent close, feathered her lips with his. At the contact, his groin tightened. Flashes of recall from New Orleans urged him to take this moment far deeper than mere kisses.

She forestalled him by whispering between breathy gasps at each kiss, "I want to know...what happened in Newport and...where we're going next."

The phone shrilled, on the floor a few feet away. "Damn," he muttered, inching apart, seeing her eyes closed and her lips waiting for him. "Damn," he said again.

Her eyelashes fluttered up. "Who's calling at this hour? Hendley again?" She turned toward the sound of the telephone bell.

"I'll go see. Relax on the bed if you want. You must be exhausted."

" 'Said the spider to the fly,' " she quipped, voice sultry as she followed him to the telephone.

He cast a glance laced with desirous intent over his shoulder, then picked up the handset. "Garth Gems," he said.

He could hear the nasal breathing before the weasel spoke. "Having a joyous reunion?" asked The Tape with nasty insinuation. "Seeing you whisk her away in the night made me feel good, Stone. It tells me you take me seriously. I like that in my hired help."

"Look," Mickey said, exasperated and angry. "Let's stop playing good-guy, bad-guy shall we? The number you just called isn't clear, if you get my drift. It's only good for messages and lightweight chitchat. Here's my mobile number." He fed out Clint's private number and calling code. "Give the code number to the operator who answers, and she'll page me to pick up the call." He'd let Clint handle the fact that Mickey wouldn't answer.

"This better be copacetic," The Tape warned.

"It's as copacetic as you get," Mickey said flatly. "Now, where can I reach you if things start heating up?"

"Oh, right." The sarcasm dripped. "I'm going to give you a number you can trace to me, is that it? Feds come down like buzzards, guns blazing? I don't kid myself, see? You'd rather have a birthday party on my dead body than get the emerald back." His voice gained that edge of insanity. The Tape snarled, "No deal, Stone. I'll be in touch." The line went dead.

Mickey slammed down the receiver. He muttered a curse and strode into the warehouse. Laura came after him. "Who was it?" she said. "Was it Paishon?"

"No, he brightened my evening a while back. It was The Tape."

"*The Tape!* What's happened?"

"He and Veeta were in the limo in Newport."

And he outlined the events of the evening, his voice giving a brutal edge to the facts. He finished with his plan to go undercover until Tuesday night and to use Clint's mobile number to coordinate the coming together of all the parties. Laura heard him out with a stunned expression, her pretty mouth curved into a bow.

"You'll have to wear the clothes you've got on," he finished, speaking low. "I'll bring a few extra shirts you can sleep and lounge around in. Meanwhile, I've got to go down and get the money."

"Down?" She glanced furtively, worriedly around the room.

"I won't be three or four minutes." He hurried to the door. Garth's money and a set of legal documents Mickey had been holding for nearly a year and a half were stashed in a safe in one of the dark corners of the warehouse on the ground floor. Veeta would damned well sign the papers or she and her ferret boyfriend could forget about going to the emerald sale. He was angry enough, right now, to blow it all if she refused. He'd get the money and papers, then check the streets for tails before coming back up to pack.

"Mickey?" Laura's voice sounded shaky.

He turned around.

She was twisting her hands. "Promise me you will *not* get in the way of any bullets or lead pipes or anything in the next few days. If you promise, I think I can trick myself into believing you, and then I'll do whatever you ask. Give me some hope, Mickey. Nothing will happen to you—to us."

Somehow "us" meant the two of them, a male-female unit, and it put top spin on the vague, half-formed feelings that had been spiraling through him tonight. He put his hand to his head.

Tell her lie or truth? *Lie,* he decided. Then she'd do anything he told her, and maybe she wouldn't get hurt. He looked across the gloom to her, trying to get eye contact. "I promise," he said solemnly.

"Swear it."

"I swear."

She bit her lip, tilted her head in acknowledgement. He watched the shadowed features of her face, trying to instill faith, until he closed the door.

Chapter Fourteen

Sunday, January 22—Ontario to Costa Mesa

Laura was glad she'd been able to talk Mickey into driving back to the Hilton to give the South American his emeralds and pick up the rest of the money before going into hiding. It made the deal clean, complete. She felt good finishing a difficult job.

Mickey knew how to deal with the likes of Paishon and The Tape, Laura thought, settling back into the passenger seat. He was going to bust them all, and she was going to back him one hundred percent. It made her feel needed. She could finally understand his devotion to his former job at NSI. For the first few hours of the trip, she felt a strong sense of acceptance, of destiny, and she willingly put her faith in Mickey's instincts.

Mickey drove the rest of the night along a circuitous route that—when the detours were subtracted—took them north into the foothill towns of Azusa and Glendora, south on the I-57 to the San Bernardino Freeway and east into the high desert.

Toward dawn, her enthusiasm for the adventure waned a little under the lethargy of exhaustion, but Mickey seemed stoic and determined. She took her cue from him and sat quietly on her side of the car.

To the northeast, a cerise glow poured over the snow-capped peaks of the San Bernardinos and tinted the valley floor through which they drove a sandy pink. A warmish dry wind originating in the desert, called the Santa Ana, buffeted the car as they took the Vineland Avenue exit into Ontario.

"Food," she said in a monotone, expressing her thoughts.

"Soon," said Mickey, and he reached over, took her hand. "Thirty minutes at most."

He looked at her with his bloodshot eyes.

They were traveling south, and the early sun warmed her face, putting details in clear view. She knew her hair had raveled down in spots. Her lipstick and blush had long since faded. About now, the lines of forty-two years of living were no doubt tracking deep furrows in her face, but she hadn't the energy even to duck his calm perusal.

"You look beautiful at sunrise," he said. "With the light all soft and pink."

A thread of amazement wound through her weariness. It lifted a wan smile to her lips. The light fanned out behind his profile, masking the experience there, making him look Indian exotic, and she found a lost remnant of appreciation for his rugged presence.

"You, too, *kimo-sabe*," she said in Pidgin. "You damned good-lookin' even if you do starve your women."

He chuckled, squeezed her hand, let it go. "There'll be Mexican food stands open at this hour. I'll try to find one."

That small intimacy had to last her the rest of the journey.

They rented a white sedan at Ontario International Airport, stashed Mickey's car in a dusty lot in a run-down barrio and found a street-corner stand where they bought food. The tacos, refried beans and rice were rich in food value and as tasty as any Laura had had in her youth. Revitalized, they headed toward Costa Mesa, an hour and fifteen minutes southwest and, Mickey told her, only minutes from The Arches Restaurant where he'd met Veeta and The Tape.

Relying on a hunch that the pair were headquartered in Newport, Mickey was heading for a motel in the area so a last-minute rendezvous with the "slimeball," as he called

him, would be convenient. Then they could all head for San
Pedro and the gem bust together. A nice neat package, she
mused, feeling proud of him. He thought of everything.

The morning was bright, breezy, warm. Mickey rolled
down his window, propped his arm on the frame. She could
almost believe they were vacationing together. She began to
visualize the sleeping arrangements.

Five miles from the Pacific Ocean, the Newport–Riverside Freeway traced the eastern perimeter of the Orange
County Fairgrounds. Here, pedestrians and traffic pouring into vast parking lots surrounding a Sunday-morning
swap meet slowed their progress on the road. Mickey let out
a long-suffering sigh.

"Hell's bells!" he said suddenly, craning forward.
"Laura, get down."

"Wh—"

"*Get down on the seat.* Fast."

She hunkered down into the cockpit. "Why?" she said.
"What's wrong?"

"There's a limo up ahead," he said, sounding as if he
were talking out of the side of his mouth. "I think
it's . . . hellfire, it is. I recognize the plates. Just stay down.
Don't even think about taking a peek."

His urgency was such that she thought better of pressing
for an explanation.

With the poor treatment she'd been giving her body
lately, her back muscles protested at the odd angle she'd
taken. Her purse poked into her midriff. She seesawed it
loose and squirmed around, finally bracing her knees on
the rubber floor mat, her left hand on the back of the seat.

The rattle and hum of car engines floated in through the
driver's side window, and she knew Mickey was creeping
forward in the traffic.

Her tired brain finally conjured a notion of who he was
worried about, in the limousine. It had to be The Tape.

"Stone," said a sniveling male voice that gave her the
shivers. "You get a new car?"

"Not that it's any of your business," Mickey said out the window, his tone one of bored disgust. "Mine's in the shop."

"In the shop, huh?" The response was laced with suspicion.

"Yeah."

"Suppose I go with that. What brings you down here again?"

"A lead," Mickey said. "You want the emerald, don't you? The sooner I find it, the sooner you'll be off my back."

"If you mess with me, Stone..." It was a quiet threat that carried faintly, yet thundered with lethal meaning.

Mickey didn't respond, and the creature said, "Where'd you go last night?"

"My nighttime activities are my business, not yours."

"I'm making it my business. Where's the dame?"

"At the Biltmore, I presume."

"Look, flatfoot—" Laura heard the man choke, presumably on his own anger. "Nobody's seen the dame since she got to your place last night. If you're skipping out on me, think twice. There're always your folks in San Francisco. Get my drift?"

Mickey's face darkened but he laughed. It came out kind of strangled, but she supposed it approximated unconcern. "You're going to have to hire better help," Mickey taunted. "That jerk you had posted at the Olive Street entrance was sawing logs when we walked by last night, right under his nose. I took her back to the Biltmore. About now—" he calmly read his watch then craned to look over his shoulder, presumably to gloat at The Tape as they passed the limousine "—about now, I'd say she was calling room service."

The creep threw him some kind of threat about "better be straight with me, Stone," but Mickey called back almost gaily, "Gotta go, now. Phone that mobile number in the morning. Maybe I'll have something for you."

He sped ahead, evidently taking an opening in the traffic. "Straight is right," he muttered. "Straight to jail."

He honked at somebody, obviously giving his irritation free rein. "Move it!" Rolling up his window, he said, "One chance in a million we'd run into him in this crowded metropolis, you know? Renting the car is wasted. Hiding you will be chancy. We're going to have to be very careful."

"Okay by me," she said, humbled by the incident.

The usual quick turns and fast acceleration ensued, as it always did when they were racing away. Laura saw an El Taco sign go by the window. Soon he turned into a bumpy area and stopped.

Laura's head buzzed. "Where are we?" she asked, feeling queasy.

"At a motel," he said. "Stay down. I'll go inside and register."

He left, returned in minutes, a plastic key holder in hand.

Backing the car, Mickey drove around to the rear of the building. "I wish it was dark," he said, "but at least the place is hurting for business. It'll give us some anonymity. The plumbing doesn't work in the ground-floor apartment, the manager says, so I took the one above it in back. It isn't exactly the Ritz, so prepare yourself."

"Where are we?"

"Harbor Boulevard, Costa Mesa. It's not Knob Hill, but it is the kind of neighborhood where nobody asks any questions. We'll need food and something to drink. I'll do that after dark. Sorry about the accommodations, but you'll have to stay holed up here until Tuesday night. I don't want The Tape getting even a hint that you're in town. If he spots me again, I can fake it like I did a while ago."

At least they'd be together, she thought wearily. That was something.

She eased up onto the seat. Looking out, she let go of the last of her romantic fantasies; dismay quelled her spirit. Metal-grid stairs led to the second-story balcony of a run-down two-story structure. Iron railings bowed out along the length of the upper porch and the steps. What once had been a garden at the foot of the stairs held only a low palm, its single indication of life a spike of green rising from a spread of fronds that looked like tan fans. *Great,* she thought dismally. *I wonder if the place has hot water?*

She could hear traffic thrumping by on Harbor Boulevard, but she had no view of the surrounding area. She felt as if she'd been kidnapped and brought here blindfolded.

Keeping to the shadows, they crept up the stairs, Mickey carrying a small duffel of clothing and a canvas flight bag stuffed tight with cash. He unlocked the first door off the landing and they went in, locking the door behind them.

The first major disappointment, besides the musty smell of the place, was that there were two double beds. Unable to stop herself, Laura's tired mind took it to mean that Mickey preferred some distance. Fine, she thought in exasperation, tossing her small bundle of borrowed clothes to the bed nearest the door. He could think up more neat strategies; she could get a bath and some rest.

The good thing about the place was that it had been built in the days when space wasn't at a premium. The bedroom was a large rectangle. With practically a football field of distance between each bed, they wouldn't be bumping into each other, and that was probably a plus since they'd be virtually caged up for two days.

An ancient TV was bolted to the dresser, covering up half of a cracked mirror. A small writing table and chair were niched into the corner near some sad-looking pale green drapes.

Mickey went down the hallway, opening doors and, she imagined, peering into dim corners for thugs. Evidently he found none because he returned to her, gave her a nudge on the chin and a smile that was more of a grimace, and went to the TV. He turned on the news, unlaced and removed his shoes, moved her bundle to the other bed and flopped on the bed nearest the door.

Fine, she fumed. *You're the boss.*

Left to herself, Laura made her own tour of the castle. Down a hall, a bath opened to her right. A roomy though stained tub beckoned her, but she forestalled the relative pleasure of a good soak to check out the rest of the *suite dismal*. At the end of the hall, she found a kitchen surfaced in cracked green linoleum, a ministove with greasy black burners, and rough-hewn Early American cabinets. Oh, goody, she remarked with silent sarcasm. She could cook him chicken *cordon bleu* and maybe it would improve his mood.

Adjacent the tiny table and bench of a breakfast nook, a door led to a shallow porch draped in dusty cobwebs. She stepped outside, put her palms gingerly against the wooden railing and felt it give way. The fright of nearly crashing through to the ground hurt her head and she stepped back.

The rickety veranda hung over a courtyard whose former glory had faded from lack of water. Below her were brambles, dry grasses and dirt.

Behind her, the door squeaked. She turned just as Mickey's hand whipped out, caught her wrist. He pulled her bodily inside and shut the door.

"What are you doing?" he demanded, throwing darts with his eyes.

Too late, she realized she'd breached security. Even so, his brusque tone picqued her ire. "Just looking," she snapped, twisting her arm free. "Sorry. I forgot about the thugs."

"Dammit, Laura, be more careful. I've gone to great lengths to hide you."

"I've gone to those lengths, too, thank you. Take it easy. Nobody saw me but the mice and rats."

He scowled.

Giving him no chance to chastise her further, she edged into the hall. "I'm going to take a bath," she tossed at him. "Okay with you, boss?"

"Do what you want. Just try not to let the whole world know we're here."

"Fine."

He pushed on past her to the bed, his attention drawn to an auto race on TV. The whir of the car engines and the whine of the announcer's voice followed her, as irritating as a hive of buzzing bees, until she'd collected her borrowed clothes and shut herself in the bathroom.

She felt cheated of her romantic dreams, headachy, lonely as a child who'd been scolded by a beloved parent. It only vaguely occurred to her she'd lost the desire to keep things platonic. She felt like crying. Instead she took the pins out of what remained of her coiffure, stripped off the wrinkled designer suit and bent over the tub. Ugh, she thought. She'd have to clean it with bar soap before she got into it.

But that wasn't the worst of her problems. Struggling to turn the corroded faucets, she twisted this way and that, grunting with the effort it took. With a mighty lunge, she threw her weight into the turn and heard a groan from the rusty pipes. Brown water trickled out of the spout and pooled in a kind of soup at the mouth of the drain.

Great, just great, she thought in disgust. Welcome to the life of the adventuress. Welcome to life with Mickey Stone.

LAURA WOKE TO THE SOUND of the apartment door closing. Groggy for a moment, she cast about the room, seeing the cheap bureau, the cracked lampshade near her shoulder. Rubbing her eyes, she glanced at the TV on the dresser; only then did she realize where she was. And who had gone outside. He was leaving!

The canvas bag with the money in it was gone.

Bolting from the bed, she pulled open the door. The landing and top of the stairwell were empty. She stepped gingerly onto a worn doormat, glancing this way and that to be sure no strangers were about.

The steps angled out of sight, and she strained to listen, hearing Mickey's tread grow fainter while the metal rungs of the steps vibrated with his descending weight.

"Mickey!" she said sharply, panicked that he'd lied to her about Paishon's date, that he'd planned all along to go to the gem bust without her. "Mickey!"

The footsteps came back up the stairs. Before he reached the landing, she dashed back inside and stood beside her bed. She wasn't about to earn his wrath again for breaching security.

He stuck his dark-haired head through the door. Setting the tote full of money inside, he straightened and watched her for a moment. His gaze took in the wild cascade of her hair, the bare feet, the exposed thighs where the sides were scalloped out of the white dress shirt he'd loaned her. Her skin looked pink through the shirt; the material was that sheer. She hadn't worn a bra to bed. He noticed, she supposed. His eyes gained an intent, hungry spark.

"What...?" she said, pushing back her hair—feeling as if he'd stripped her.

He arched his eyebrows, a smile tugging at the corners of his mouth. His mood had certainly improved. He was freshly bathed and looked ready for action. The black windbreaker with the collar flipped up was a stab at a disguise, she guessed; the running shoes were made for quick getaways. He'd put on jeans and a red polo shirt that showed the cobblestonelike ribs and wide shoulders.

As if he knew how appealing he looked, he flexed, winked—very macho and cocky. "Miss me already?" he queried.

"Where were you going?" she asked, her tone skeptical.

"Grocery shopping at Lucky's. I was going to buy us a feast."

"Why did you take the money with you?"

"Habit," he said. "A precaution. Not that I think the room'd get broken into while I'm gone, but if it did, the money would be one less thing you'd have to worry about."

"Oh." Her hands found themselves and twisted guiltily. She'd assumed the worst.

"Think I was skipping out on you?"

She bit her lip, looked at him, nodded.

Shutting the door, he came to her. After the barest hesitation, he slipped his arms around her and gathered her against him. He nuzzled beneath the heavy fall of her hair and found himself a tender spot to sample with his lips. Little nibbles, kisses.

"Mmm," he murmured next to her ear. "You're a feast all by yourself."

There was nothing like intimacy from Mickey to make her forget she ever doubted him. Flighty darts of pleasure winged through her. She leaned into his kisses, molded against his body, the beginnings of passion licking and smoldering along the edges of her nerves, giving a weightlessness to her limbs.

He found her mouth, kissed her deeply, and when she was swaying against him, trembling, heart beating out of control, wanting him desperately, he pulled away.

In shock she realized she was breathing hoarsely. The sound of it rushed in her ears. "What . . . ?" she asked in confusion.

He leaned down to taste her lips briefly. He trembled slightly—he was aroused, too.

His voice, although low, had a steady sureness about it. "Back in twenty minutes, love," he said. "Got to call Clint, get the grub. Climb back into bed and wait for me."

Love? He'd called her 'love.' Was the endearment casual—or accidental—or what?

He squeezed her waist and stepped away to the door, locking it before he went out.

Damn his single-mindedness, she thought, watching it close. She glanced at her watch; seven-thirty. Ten-till-eight seemed an age away. She patted back her hair, smoothed the white shirt, took a steadying breath—as if that would calm the molten emotions inside. She turned toward the bed. Her legs were shaky. It was scary to feel like a volcano every time he kissed her. Scary to give so much power to a man.

But oh so yummy, too. She sat down on the bed and hugged herself. Mickey lit a flame in her, there was no denying it. She cared about him and she wanted him. She might as well call it what it was. Love.

Elation kept leaping and cavorting inside her. Unable to be still, she got up to pace the length of the room, hallway to front door and back. She wished she had some nail polish. She felt like detailing herself out, being the best she could be when he came back.

Inspired, she rushed to her oxblood purse, flipped it open to rummage through the pockets. Lipstick, wide-toothed comb, slim tube of scented cream. That was the extent of her grooming kit.

Taking them into the bathroom, she uncapped the cream and smoothed it into her skin. She bent forward and combed the tangles out of her hair, then flipped it over her shoulders and let it fluff down. The lipstick was a cranberry color that darkened with wearing to match the leather trim on the suit she'd worn to the gem show. She pouted, traced her lips with color and pressed her lips to even it out. Then she arched back and looked at herself. The cloudy mirror told her two things—she looked radiant and in love.

She grinned at herself and left the bathroom to put the items into her purse, her mind whirring with plans. She'd ask him, by God—is there any chance for us? He wasn't the kind of man to lie just to get her into bed. She was certain of that. Almost certain.

If he wasn't interested in a future, she'd tell him she'd decided to keep to her side of the room for the two days. What was the harm in telling him, straight out, that she cared too much to be casual about leaping into bed with him and needed to protect herself from getting hurt? Better to be up-front than sorry, she decided.

She felt antsy, waiting the last of the twenty minutes, and reluctant to ruin her concentration by watching TV. Agonizingly, the time stretched to half an hour, then an hour. She turned on the television, watched part of a special on the snow monkeys of Japan, and, impatient, turned it off. She rummaged in the drawer of the nightstand, found a tattered *People* magazine, read about the comeback of John

Travolta. Soon it was ten o'clock and she was downright worried. Had he run into The Tape again? Had to defend himself against one of the thugs? Gone off on the gem bust—lied to her and put her in this dismal rat hole to keep her out of his hair until the bust was done?

She closed the magazine and got up, sat down again, got up. She glanced at the nightstand for the tenth time, wishing the place had a telephone. She wanted to call Clint. He'd be straight with her. What was that mobile number, anyway? If she had the number pad of a phone in front of her, she might remember.

It wasn't as if she were without means, she told herself, pacing again. She had four hundred dollars in cash and a leather booklet full of credit cards. She could take a cab, hire a car—but go where? What the heck was Mickey up to? Was she supposed to be worried or mad? Should she sneak out and try to find him, despite his warnings about the cruel tendencies of The Tape?

She was just climbing into her black slacks when the floor shook slightly, telling her someone was on the stairs. One leg in, one out, she sighed in relief and hopped to the door.

In the silence as she was reaching to unlock it, she realized the shaking had stopped. Someone had come partially up the stairs, then hesitated—why?

Suddenly her heart rocketed crazily. Maybe it wasn't Mickey coming up. Maybe it was—

The grate of footsteps on the metal stairs came once more. Her bare feet picked up the faint vibration. Again it stopped.

Dear God, she said silently, panicked. Fear made it difficult to think. *Rush out now and scream? No, foolish idea.* Mickey had warned her about the neighborhood. Nobody asked questions. Thugs were nasty beasties, she remembered him telling her. You wanted to meet them on your own terms.

What were her terms? she asked frantically, struggling to get into her slacks. It was Mickey who knew about such things. Zipping up and closing the button, Laura shuffled, danced into her low-heeled oxblood pumps. *Money, I'll need money,* she thought, diving for her purse. When she moved, she couldn't tell if the stairs were vibrating, and her fear made breathing difficult, the sound harsh, overpowering all other sound.

She paused for a second to listen. Something scratched across the landing outside the door, and then—stillness. Mickey would have no reason to sneak back to the flat. He would unlock the door and come bustling in, cheery-voiced, arms full of groceries, eyes full of that spark that meant he wanted her. A piercing loss tore into her midsection. *Please be okay,* she thought. *You promised me.*

Out on Harbor Boulevard, a horn honked, brakes squealed. There were people out there. Police. Help.

She tiptoed down the hall, across the linoleum to the kitchen door. The knob warbled a bit—she froze—then she disengaged it. The door swung toward her, silently, eerily as any Hitchcock cinematic technique. She had to overcome the fear that someone waited for her on the porch. It was nonsense, she told herself; there was no access. Only the straight-down drop to the brambles; the way she had to go. She stepped gingerly onto the creaky boards.

Dampness from the sea made the air chilly, goose bumped her skin under the thin shirt. That couldn't be helped; a stuffy second-rate motel room wasn't any place to come face-to-face with a thug. She would have to go over the side.

Outside the living room, a loud pounding commenced. It gave Laura a start. She slung the strap of her purse around her neck and scaled the rail of the porch. It wobbled, and she clung to the sticky circumference of a telephone pole rising past a railing. Down below, it was black. What was the configuration of the supports below the porch? she wondered. Carefully climbing past the railing, she clung there for a moment, one foot feeling the creepy shadows for a crossbar. Her shoulders stung with the pressure of her weight. Tiny moans escaped her. Suddenly it was this moment she knew she'd forseen, in Grosvenor

House when she'd felt she'd stepped off an invisible cliff and was groping for something to cling to. The memory came rushing back, darkening her spirit. *The way must be found,* she railed, muscles beginning to quake. *The strength is in me!*

She found the pipe on the backside of the pole first. Her fingers gripped the cold metal and she slid down by inches, praying for purchase, for strength.

The tip of her shoe struck solid wood—a brace running at a forty-five-degree angle to the upright of the porch. It wasn't much, but it was enough to allow her to shin down, braced between the telephone pole and the struts.

Above, a gruff voice shouted. They were in the kitchen, seeing the open door, coming for her. *All right,* she said to herself, *do it.* And she let go, falling in the dark.

"MICKEY," AN URGENT VOICE pleaded.

He was being shaken, pommeled, prodded awake. "Mickey, you promised!"

It was a wail of despair. Mickey opened his eyes to slits— the throbbing in his head would allow no more—and saw that cherished cameo face. Only it was scratched and damp with tears.

"What's wrong?" he mumbled; his words sounded slurred.

"Oh, Mickey!" Laura flung herself on his chest and hugged him. "They hurt you but you're all right."

She pulled back and looked at him, grinning and crying.

He eased up on his elbow, shook his head—it hurt and he put his hand to his eyes. "Mmm," he moaned.

It came to him in a jolt that he'd been bushwhacked, and Laura was safe. He reached to brush away some moisture beneath her eyes, caressed a dark splotch on her chin. "Did they come for you?" he asked.

She winced, nodded. "I went out the back." She grinned, but it was crooked, and, he thought, painful. "It was convenient that the Lucky market was just across Harbor Boulevard."

"You mean you went over that rickety porch? Two stories up?"

She waved. "Not to worry. I took the elevator."

Even injured, stunned, he appreciated her courage. "Wow," he said in amazement. "The elevator?"

She was as tough as a seasoned operative. Maybe she *could* play the part he and Clint had discussed on the phone tonight. It might work.

He got slowly to his feet, Laura helping him to stand. "Where'd they hit you?" she asked, concerned because he wobbled.

"Conked me on the head as I was putting the groceries in the backseat of the car."

She glanced a few feet away to a trash Dumpster and the white sedan with its door open, a bag of cookies and some apples spilled on the pavement. The car was a gray shape in the shadow cast by the grocery store, but it was visible enough from Harbor Boulevard for The Tape's henchmen—and later Laura—to identify.

"They must have been waiting behind the Dumpster. When I bent over to put the groceries away, they hit me—not hard enough to kill, just to stun. They must have wanted me out of the way so they could get to you. You're the bait to secure The Tape's bargaining position for the emerald."

"We should get out of here," Laura said, taking his elbow. "They might decide to come back for you."

They hobbled to the passenger side of the car, where Laura insisted he climb in. She took the wheel and drove them out of the lot onto Victoria Street.

"This goes to the Newport–Riverside," he said, pointing ahead. "Go on through the light."

They passed Newport Liquor on the northeast corner of the split highway, and beyond, a church, its lot filled with cars. "Turn left," he said.

They passed the pale bulk of a set of cream-colored town houses at the corner of Virginia and Elden, and single-family homes alternated with new condo developments along a street in the process of being reclaimed from obscurity.

"Where are we going?" Laura asked.

"I'm trying to decide. I want to stay in this area. Need to,
with the change in plans."

"What change?"

A burr of anger roughened his voice. "Paishon was
double-crossing us. I figure he's on to the fact that I was a
federal agent. Had to happen eventually, I guess. I was just
hoping he'd find out when we put the cuffs on him."

She glanced at him. "Tell me what happened."

He eased more comfortably into the seat and said,
"When I picked up my messages, there was a frantic one
from Harry."

"Harry?" she said, surprised.

"He went to the show today, remember?"

"That's right. Did he pick up some more strange vibes?
He said something big was coming down."

"I owe him. The guy's a prince. The grapevine was
buzzing about the sale."

"*Our* sale?"

He nodded yes. "Harry's ties in the gem-and-jewelry
business run deep. He's been around Pershing Square for
twenty-seven years. He might do a shady deal now and
then, I don't know. I've never caught him at anything.
Anyhow, Harry's always been straight with me and I trust
him for that. When I called him tonight, he told me he
bought a Coke for a friend of a friend. One of those deals.
The guy told him about a big private sale coming down in
Newport Beach."

"Newport? I thought it was set for Terminal Island."

"That's what Paishon wanted me to think. Anyway,
Harry says word is out it's a rare emerald for sale in Newport. By invitation only. Bids start at three hundred thousand. You seal your bid in a plain envelope with just your
initial on it."

"Those are the same instructions Paishon gave you."

"With two differences. The auction is tomorrow afternoon, not Tuesday night. In Newport Beach, not Terminal Island."

"My God, Mickey!" The dash lights showed him the whites of Laura's eyes. "He was going to take you out!"

"Yeah," he said, appreciating her use of the vernacular. "How about that?"

"Did The Tape know all along about the sale?"

"No way. He's running a damned good hunch, but if he knew, he wouldn't need to kidnap you to make me cooperate. No, the slimeball still needs me to get to the emerald."

"How are we going to get into the sale—get invited?"

"Harry's working on it."

She sure was a smart one, he thought, gritting his teeth as the car bumped over a rut, jarring his skull. He was taking a big risk, putting her in the game. But he was so close, now. He needed her just this once more, and then it would be over. She had to go in. There was no other way.

"Turn right on Mesa Drive," he said, trying to think of a way to break the news so it didn't sound mercenary. "We'll go over to one of the classy hotels near John Wayne Airport, where the security's good. We're playing in a whole new ball game now, Laura. It's the top of the ninth, the bases are loaded and the score's tied. And you, my dear, are up to bat."

Chapter Fifteen

The *Gloaming* nudged the floatdock, its white one-hundred-eighty-foot hull turning amber in the late afternoon, its flying bridge jutting into the deepening cerulean sky. Cagney had the effrontery to conduct the illegal sale in the midst of the most prestigious collection of private pleasure craft on the Southern California coast.

Wearing evening clothes on the slim chance security was so lax he could slip aboard, Mickey hunkered down behind a gear locker on shore. Two hours ago, it had been tough to hand Laura the keys to the rental car and turn her loose to make her way to the waterfront alone, while he dealt with The Tape and Veeta, but he'd done it.

He watched with held breath as Laura walked toward the open gate to the docks. It wasn't really too late, he thought in panic. He could still shout her back, tell her to forget the infiltration idea. It was a lousy plan. It was too dangerous to put her in against the crime boss, hidden somewhere below, and his louts, bristling in whites on deck, weapons bulging beneath their jackets. He'd been wrong, thinking she was as tough as an operative. She was as naive as they come about the underworld.

What have I done? he thought, hearing the gate squeak as she opened it, his insides tightening in remorse. He tried to form the words "Come back, Laura. Get out now!"

His training stopped him. Or perhaps the siren song of the emerald. He never uttered the warning.

Clint still hadn't shown up. Things were going to be dicey without the back-up of a handful of NSI's finest.

Paishon hadn't shown up yet, either. Mickey had been on the stake-out for an hour, had watched the crew readying the boat for guests, but had seen no sign of Paishon. That was a plus, really. The coral merchant might recognize Laura despite the effective disguise and blow the whole setup.

Veeta's whiney voice drifted down to him. She was arguing with The Tape. After Mickey had forced her to sign the papers he'd brought, she'd turned sullen and spiteful. Now the two of them, she and the slimeball, couldn't keep their lethal claws out of each other long enough to get the gem sale finished.

That pair of squabbling jackals might compromise Laura's part in this unholy drama, he fretted. If she got hurt, he'd never forgive himself.

Laserlike, he zeroed in on Laura. She walked along the dock, her shoulders straight, her gait almost a swagger as she assumed the character they'd evolved for her. Widow of a Canadian grain baron, she was emerging from a quiet life of retirement to live in the fast lane, beginning with the purchase of a coveted gem that would gain her plenty of attention in the arena of boy meets girl.

Harry had arranged the invitation to board and make an offer on the emerald. The restaurateur was to meet her at the gathering.

Mickey was uncomfortably aware that the role she was playing became her. She looked the part of a wealthy, predatory manhunter. The five-thousand-dollar cocktail dress she wore was cut below her waist in the back and low enough in the front to show plenty of cleavage—too much, Mickey had told her, but she'd overruled him and bought it anyway. Diamond dust glittered on the raised shoulders and along the décolletage. Her shoes were simple spiky pumps in the same black slinky fabric as the dress, and the dusky hosiery made her look leggy and elegant. She'd had her hair tinted a dark ash brown. Springy curls fluffed beneath the wide brim of a black hat, suggesting eccentric feminine nautiness. A makeover further enhanced the bad-girl image.

He searched for any fragment of hope she'd succeed in her mission. There was the sealed envelope in her purse. The money was packed into a rich black leather brief-case—obviously heavy, because it canted her slightly to the left. At least the money was real, Mickey thought, the sweat popping out on his brow. Real dough, a lot of it, always carried clout in this kind of crowd. If she had any edge at all in this lousy gamble, it was the six hundred thousand dollars she was carrying. That, and her wits.

They'd spent another seven thousand on the biggest, flashiest brilliant-cut diamond they could find, and it swung just above her breasts from a diamond-studded chain. As she turned and raised a hand in seductive greet-ing to the white-coated attendant ushering guests aboard the yacht, the diamond flashed sun. Mickey felt a stirring of jealousy. Laura knew how to fit in with this millionaire crowd; the diamond was a blatant calling card above those luscious breasts.

But it was too late to worry about Laura's reaction to the men aboard. She was about to join them.

Through the microphone secreted in the bodice of her dress, Mickey had access to every breath, nuance and word she uttered.

"Hello," he heard her say to the steward at the gangway of the *Gloaming*.

Her voice modulated with the correct amount of insouci-ant charm when a rich widow speaks to a handsome hire-ling, she said, "My, it's lovely here, isn't it? Canada is practically in a deep freeze this time of year. I'm hardly thawed out yet."

Mickey clamped his mouth shut. She was too good at the role.

The blond Adonis said something indistinct about checking his guest list.

Pretending to be unsteady on her feet, Laura put her hand on his arm, slid it all the way down to his fingers and clutched, crumpling the list. He passed it to his other hand. She seemed to soften into putty when he looked at her in concern. She teetered, glanced apprehensively at the water a foot away. Mickey's heart skipped. Evidently the jock fell for it, too. He quickly bent forward to help her up the ramp, the guest list crushed between his hand and her arm.

"You're so sweet," she cooed, and Mickey saw the man give her a big, come-on grin. By the time she was safely on board and walking away, the attendant evidently realized he'd been remiss in his duties. He called something to her.

"I'm Vivian Longacher," Laura tossed over her shoulder, walking on. "Mr. Cagney's expecting me."

Mickey doubted the man heard; his eyes were glued to Laura's beautifully shaped back as she tastefully swayed toward a step-up deck and a waiting henchman, also in white.

"Marvelous," Mickey whispered, though she couldn't hear his praise with the one-way system. "Just like you were born to it."

Laura's next security check wasn't so easy. She was dealing with Paishon's beef, Wing Tip. He had a buzz haircut and a tight-fitting white jacket that bulged near his right armpit. That made him a southpaw, Mickey thought, filing away the information.

"Name?" Wing Tip said gruffly to Laura.

"Vivian. Vivian Longacher. I'm just the oldest, dearest friend of Harry's. You know Harry. One of Mr. Cagney's closest friends in Los Angeles? Ooh—" she twisted around, pulling distractedly at her dress "—these garter belts are *such* a nuisance." She demurely presented her legs to the hunk. "Are my stockings straight? I must have them straight, you know. So unposh to have lines going in every direction."

"They seem okay to me. ID?"

Tussling with the dress, Laura pretended confusion. "Pardon?"

"ID. Identification. The boss says you've got to show it."

Laura straightened up, affronted. "My dear *man*. I don't see how you have the audacity—" She peered ahead. "Harry!" Waving furiously, she squealed coquettishly, "Oh, Harry, how marvelous to see you. Darling, tell this nice man I'm with you, and let's go have a drink!"

Wearing a black dinner jacket and bow tie that made him look like a penguin, Harry came waddling into view. He said something low to Wing Tip. The thug frowned, nodded, and Harry ushered Laura into the clinking and music of a party in the main salon. Wing Tip wasn't long on brains. Harry was.

Mickey swallowed tension. She was in!

Momentarily, he was distracted by a threesome from a neighboring sloop. They strolled down the dock toward the *Gloaming,* drinks lifted, laughing uproariously at something. *Go back,* Mickey wanted to warn them.

As if they'd heard, they swung in a hairpin turn and strolled back the other way.

Relieved, Mickey gave his attention to his earphone. Couching her descriptions in effusive, chattering dialogue, Laura gave Mickey the layout of the salon and the company. An armed guard was stationed at the opening leading below decks. Five men and a woman, plus Harry and herself, comprised the guests. Was Paishon aboard? Was he fooled by the disguise?

"I'd love to have a look around this lovely ship," Laura was saying. "One never gets to see such exotica stuck way out on the Alberta prairies, you know what I mean, Harry?"

"Sure, Vivian," said Harry, playing his part. "But they ain't ready for us yet. They said we'd be going below just before sunset."

Mickey glanced at the sky. It looked purplish. Sunset was maybe fifteen minutes from now, at most. Harry had also told him, by his comments, that the sale would be conducted in a room below the salon. Mickey didn't like it. It would mean Laura would be further from his protection. But there was nothing he could do about it now.

Veeta's shrill laughter floated down to him. He whirled and strode up to the concrete shelf where they'd put a champagne bottle. In an ice bucket, no less.

At their meeting an hour earlier, Mickey had forced The Tape to get rid of his henchmen and made Veeta sign the papers he'd brought before he would agree to bring them to the waterfront. The incentive was greed. It worked. Veeta had signed on the dotted line and the thugs had vanished back to their lairs. It didn't seem to bother The Tape any to be without his bodyguards. That meant he was armed.

It was all Mickey could do to keep from pulling the Walther, putting the snake's face in the dirt and slapping cuffs on him in a surprise move. But he couldn't risk it. Not quite yet. Not when Laura's life was in jeopardy.

"Keep it down," he ordered shortly, scowling at their half-empty glasses.

"Hey, we're entitled," said The Tape, sneering at him. "We earned this little party. That dame of yours inside yet?"

"Yeah. She's inside."

In his earphone, he heard Laura saying what a thrill it was to be on the water for the first time in her life.

"Remember," The Tape growled, commandeering Mickey's attention. "You tell me who's carrying the emerald when they leave that boat and let me take it from there. If she's carrying it, fine. We all drive off into the sunset together, got it?"

The Tape hitched his Ralph Lauren slacks in a tough-guy gesture. "You fail me, Stone, I'm going to have my revenge. That little stunt you pulled last night, running with your tail between your legs? You and the dame are going to have to do it full-time, because I'll hunt you until I get her. I got me an army of tough guys. It don't mean nothing, you having Sledgehammer locked up, see? Miss L.J.M. won't sleep at night from now on, you pull something fast tonight."

Mickey stood rock still, controlling his loathing. "No problem," he said stiffly. "Just keep the caterwauling down or you'll blow the whole thing."

The Tape hitched his pants again, indicating he'd heard. He looked off at the water, his dark eyes narrow, calculating.

Veeta curled against The Tape's arm, eyeing Mickey, gloating. "You going to marry her?" she said to Mickey. "Raise a bunch of brats while you scrape out a living in the streets?"

The streets. It was his nightmare of homelessness thrown in his face. He shuttered his anger, said stiffly, "I have other things on my mind right now."

"Why else did you want me to sign the divorce papers? She going to live in your prison, keep the home fires burning while you gallivant off to sunbathe in the tropics—on her money?"

Again it was on the tip of his tongue to retort, something about how sorrowfully pitiful Veeta was. He heard Laura's melodic laughter and clamped his mouth shut. Veeta's nature was volatile. He could touch it off with a sideways glance. Besides, he'd resolved to treat her more decently, treat everyone better.

He was sick of taking out his frustrations about the case on those he cared about. When Laura had told him she and Clint were trying to raise the money for the gem sale, it had been like getting socked in the gut. It had begun the process of change in him, awakened him to a few facts of life—one being how rare true friendship really was. He felt low as a gutter rat for abusing that gift. He wouldn't, not again.

Treating Veeta with more compassion was part of the change in him, too, he thought with sudden insight. Maybe it paved the way for something special with a woman like Laura. Down the road. When he got his life together.

One more time he throttled his anger and said, "Just keep it down until it's time or you'll blow any chances you'll ever get to retire to the tropics yourself."

The message hit home. Veeta pouted.

Mickey turned on his heel and went back to his lookout post.

Laura laughed, the sound floating through the earpiece. Now there was a different breed of cat, he thought, smiling grimly.

"Harry," she said in that lilting falsetto she'd adopted for her new role as fast-laner and international wheeler-dealer in gems. "You're absolutely right. He doesn't eat the proper foods. He'd live on pizza if he could, which is barbaric. He needs to be fattened up with some healthy grain-fed beef, that's what I think. Why, he just doesn't take proper care of himself. He needs a woman like me to look after him, don't you agree?"

"You'd do all right by him Lau—er—Vivian," Harry said. "He needs somebody to treat him right. His ex was a piranha. Now, he might think he's not good enough for you, Viv, but you treat him right, he'll come around."

"Oh, I intend to treat him well, Harry. I surely do. I just wish—"

She was evidently interrupted, and said to someone else, "My gentleman friend—the one Harry and I were talking about? Why, he's in gems. We're all in gems, aren't we, Harry, darling?" The simpering laughter bubbled on.

Mickey frowned. What the devil was she about? She knew the mike was live in a direct line to his ear. Was she declaring her devotion to an ex-federal agent who'd scorned her, belittled her, used her selfishly and without regard for her safety or sanity? Was she talking about him?

Who else fits the mold, said a voice in his mind. And it came to him suddenly, in a brilliant flash of understanding—she was talking about him and it made him feel like a superman. What a woman. He shook his head in awe at her audacity. Warm, loving, loyal Laura Marley. Brave, he added to the list; smart, quick-witted, funny. The list grew and grew, like Pinnochio's nose.

Mickey wanted her, he suddenly realized. If he could just figure out a way to get his life in order, he wanted her for keeps. And he'd put her into a situation that could cost her that precious life he'd come to love.

Something hit his shoulder. He flinched, reached for his gun.

"Relax, flatfoot," said The Tape in a stage whisper. "I just came down to check on my investments. What's happening now?"

Mickey let his hand fall away from his chest. "Waiting for the meeting to start," he said. "Another few minutes at most. Wait—"

Laura was telling him something. "Going below now?" she asked, her falsetto a little ragged with what he presumed was nerves. "Well, wonderful," she said effusively. "At last my life begins."

Pray God it continues, Mickey thought.

Suddenly, in his peripheral vision, several things happened at once. Paishon, the Shark Man, came barreling down the walkway between two adjacent buildings, heading for the floatdock. So he wasn't aboard yet!

And over on the wooden sailboat, a man in a white dinner jacket ambled out of the crowd and came down the gangplank onto the dock. His sandy hair was tinged with sunset. The smoke from his cigarette curled up around his face. Mickey recognized him, nonetheless. Clint, old buddy, he thought with an all-over ringing relief.

Several other guests aboard the sloop joined him, ostensibly for brandy and cigars. The tips of two stogies glowed red in the gathering twilight. Mickey recognized the tall, gangly captain of NSI, plus Johnson, Henderson and three or four sinister-looking chaps he didn't know.

Now he could act. Any second...

"Stone," whispered The Tape, behind him. He pointed a bony finger toward the buffalo bulk of Paishon, who waved aside the young steward and gained the deck of the *Gloaming.* "Who's that? What's he doing here?"

Do it now, Mickey decided. Keeping his movements slow, Mickey reached inside his jacket. The handle of the Walther fit his palm comfortably. "That's the guy who told me about the sale," he said, his pulse a steady throb in his temple. "He set the whole thing up."

"Oh," said The Tape. "Is the dame saying anything? Is it coming down yet?"

"Yeah, it's coming down."

Mickey whirled, pulling the Walther, jamming it hard into The Tape's sinewy midsection and bulldozing him back along the building. The air whooshed out of his adversary. His eyes wide with fear and surprise, the weasel staggered back against the wall.

"Not a word, slimeball," Mickey said low. "You just turn around and poke that ferret nose of yours into the concrete and don't breathe. Breathe, and you give me the chance to get even. Got it?"

When The Tape didn't answer, just rolled his eyes, Mickey jabbed him with the weapon.

The Tape croaked a strangle cry of pain and inched around. He trained his gaze over his shoulder at Mickey, like a dancer spotting a turn. "You double-crossing son of a—"

"Nose to the wall, slimeball!" He relieved him of his weapon, slid it into his pocket.

"I'll kill you, Stone. I swear I'll dice your heart and serve it to the gulls. I'll get your woman, too, that rich chit of yours."

Veeta came tottering around the corner, her mouth a moue.

Working fast, Mickey pulled one of the sets of cuffs he'd bought in town from his back pocket. Shoving The Tape down to the concrete, he cuffed him to a clay water main attached to the building. He watched the man purple with rage, writhing to get free, and his satisfaction was immense.

Piping a protest, Veeta came hurrying up. "What are you doing to him? Why—you've cuffed him. You can't arrest him. You're not a cop any more!"

Mickey stood up, showed her the gun, casually, as if he were sharing a favorite toy. Veeta's face went white. "Why, you two-timing cheap-hearted good-for-nothing cheat,'' she said, coming toward him with her claws bared.

"Veeta, stop," he growled.

Something in his voice reached her. She hesitated, looked down at her fallen mate. "Honey?" she said plaintively. "Honey, what's going to happen to me?"

"Life, I hope, you stupid chit."

Alligator tears formed in Veeta's eyes. She seemed to crumple inside, and she gave Mickey the most pitiful look he'd ever seen. Something went out of him then—the last shred of hatred or bitterness, perhaps.

"If you'll let me cuff you nicely, Veeta," he heard himself saying as if from a distance, "I'll see what I can do for you. You can turn state's evidence on this jerk and get some help."

"Help?" she whimpered. "What kind of help?"

"The kind you need," he said, going to her, holstering the gun as he went. She looked at him like a doe looks at her killer, and the image burned deeply into him, pity and sorrow for past mistakes mingling, gentling his hands as he turned her around, cuffed her to the pipe. "Stay quiet, Veeta," he said, the highs and lows carefully culled from his voice. "There are federal officers crawling over the area. You'll be safe until I get back."

Filling his palm with the solid metal and hard rubber of the semiautomatic pistol, he started away.

"Mickey?"

Still facing the bay, needing to hurry now, he said impatiently, "What, Veeta?"

"You'll—you'll help me, really? Not let them put me in prison?"

He nodded, started walking again. Then he was running because down in the lower salon of the ship, Laura's voice had risen in the faked, preplanned seasickness routine that told Mickey the gem was out for inspection.

"Got to get some air, Harry," she cried. "I feel so faint."

"You'll have to wait," said a stern male voice. "Nobody leaves till we're done."

As PAISHON MOVED DEEPER into the *Gloaming*'s salon, Mickey approached the yacht. He slipped his gun under his lapel, nodded politely to the blond steward as he passed.

"Sorry I'm late," he called to Clint and the boys.

"Better late than never," Clint said, coming to him and shaking hands. Their gazes locked, Clint's questioning.

"Any moment," Mickey whispered. "Can we send somebody up to the west side of the yacht club? Veeta and The Tape need their rights read. Veeta, by the way, will turn state's evidence for you. Tell the boys in the Bureau to go easy on her."

Clint went to kibitz with the captain, who issued orders to one of his men.

"Here," Laura was saying in Mickey's ear. "Take my bid now, will you? I'm really feeling awful. I don't want to ruin all this lovely silk upholstery, really. I have to get some air."

"This is irregular," said the man running the sale, his voice laced with irritation. "Where's Paishon, anyway?"

"Don't know, boss," said another male voice.

"I'll take her topside," Harry offered in an inoffensive, helpful tone. "She's been on the farm too long, I guess. The seagoing life is all new to her. We won't be a minute. By then, maybe your man'll be here."

There was a tense silence.

On the dock, Clint's eyes gleamed palely in the lowering reddish light. The men smoked, belying the tension of having Mickey among them again after the bad feeling there'd been. He and the captain exchanged curt nods. Mickey felt bristly, too, but he was more concerned about what would happen if Paishon got below and recognized Laura.

The planks under their feet rocked with the tide. A sea gull cried. Mickey felt the cry down in his gut, where the new feeling for Laura was churning with his dread that she'd be hurt.

Come topside, he wanted to shout to her. *Get up here, Laura.*

She was moaning now, the cries cutting him like knives.

Other voices were raised, but he focused only on hers, willing her to be safe. "I'm going to be sick, Harry," she wailed. "Ooh, it hurts."

"Get her outta here," the bossman ordered. "Leave your briefcase here, Mrs. Longacher. That way we'll relax a little, won't we, folks?"

A patter of laughter followed.

There was a scraping noise, a grunt of surprise, as, evidently, Laura and Harry collided with Paishon in the companionway. Mickey's face blanched. He held his breath.

A moment of silence followed, and Mickey promised himself he'd never risk her life again.

Laura and Harry burst topside, the diamond-dust on Laura's dress flashing like strobe lights as she stumbled past Wing Tip at the salon door. "Sick," she said, waving him off. Harry went with her to the far side of the deck, where he held her as she made gagging sounds, shielding her body from view. Then her mike went dead, probably dislodged by her movements.

"Now," Mickey ordered.

The captain waved two of NSI's finest forward to take out the blond steward. Seeing the guns, the young man threw his hands in the air and flattened himself on the swaying dock. Someone put cuffs on him.

Gaining the deck, Mickey and Clint went at a crouching run toward Wing Tip. Conveniently, he was busy watching Laura's fine figure at the side rail and never saw the blow that knocked him unconscious.

The men tunneled below decks, Mickey at the lead because he knew the layout from Laura. Clint was right behind him, the captain and other agents running silent as foxes through the carpeted companionway.

"Paishon's mine," Mickey whispered over his shoulder.

"I'll take Cagney," said Clint.

At a closed door, Mickey listened. The hubbub of conversation inside would cover any mistakes. He gripped the brass hardware. The handle turned easily, silently. Through the crack in the doorway, he saw the white sleeve of a guard. Breath sucked in, pulse pinging with adrenaline, Mickey flung open the portal, jammed his Walther into the guard's side and shouted, "Freeze! I'll blow him away."

Guns drawn, Clint and the other agents ploughed in behind him and fell among the blackmarketers. It was almost pathetically easy, the surprise was so complete. Shouts resounded in the enclosed room, but little struggle took place. The agents began cuffing the guests, frisking them, piling weapons on a mahogany table that dominated the cabin.

His eyes on another mark, Mickey put the guard in Henderson's care.

Three feet away, Paishon was inching his right hand toward the inside of his dark evening coat, his pig eyes following the movements of the captain.

Mickey trained the muzzle of the Walther at the Neanderthal's midsection. With deadly calm, he said, "Don't you get it, Paishon? The party's over."

The big head swung toward him. Registering shock, anger, he lifted his hands toward the bulkhead. "You're a dead man," he said, beginning to wheeze.

"Save it. I've heard it before and I'm still breathing." Approaching him, Mickey thundered, "Face down on the floor. Now!"

The Shark Man's prehistoric gaze went to anthracite. And held steady on Mickey's face as he slowly bent to his knees, then settled his bulk on the deck. Mickey bent, withdrew the man's gun, tossed it to the table, where it clattered on the pile of weaponry. Paishon glared up at Mickey.

Clint and the captain had the rest of them lined up facedown. One of the flinty-looking characters Mickey didn't know—it struck him now, he was FBI—went calmly along the row of captives, wrapping their wrists with the plastic bracelets law-enforcement officers were fond of using these days.

When the agent got to Paishon, Mickey said, "Make 'em tight."

Spotting Clint, who was bent over, cuffing the silver-haired Cagney, Mickey went to him, grinning. "Not bad for a lifer," he said.

"Hey, buddy," said his friend, finishing the job with a flourish of his arms, like a steer roper. "Piece 'a cake." He dusted his hands, stood back to survey his captive.

Gratitude came sweeping through Mickey. Miraculously, the words were there for him this time. "I never had a better friend, Clint," he said, so softly nobody else could hear.

Clint eyed him. "What can I say? I love you, man."

Something deep and lasting exchanged in their glances. "Yeah," said Mickey at length. "Same here."

He glanced across the cabin, saw the captain. The tall man spotted a set of legal-looking documents on the table. He scooped them up. A covetous smile creased his hawk-like face.

"Stone," he said, studying the papers, jerking his bony jaw toward the lawbreakers. "You want to read these creeps their rights?"

Mickey felt another zing of adrenaline. *Was he back on NSI's payroll?* He was already so high he barely felt the difference.

He glanced at the table. Weapons, a couple of brief-cases, an ashtray with a cigarette burning in it, and two champagne glasses littered the polished surface. At the head of the table, where the crime boss, Cagney, had stood when Mickey came in, sat a black leather box. Cagney had dropped it when Clint shoved an automatic weapon under his chin. Mickey longed to open it, look inside. But there was a favor he wanted to obtain first.

Mickey pressed Clint's arm in final thanks and stepped toward his ex-boss. "A couple questions, Captain," he said.

The man owled him. "Yeah, what?"

Mickey shunted him into a corner and said low, "What about the Marley link?"

The captain's eyes cut to the bulkhead.

He's going to lie, Mickey thought.

He was surprised when the man waved fatalistically and said, "Marley got in over his head, Stone. Picked up the documents as a personal favor to an old friend and handed them off to the courier. Only he got green around the gills. Died of guilt, I hear. It happens."

Cold-hearted bastard, Mickey thought. He indicated the documents. "That's intelligence that should go to the Brits. What're you going to do with it?"

"Keep it, of course. You lost your touch, Stone?" The captain rocked back on his heels, sucking a tooth. "You going to cuff these perpetrators or stand around jawing? You want the job or not?"

You let the next crop of idealistic, hot-blooded recruits carry on the work, Rusty had said up in Big Bear. *America needs that passion and loyalty.*

It did, and God help the man or woman who tried to breach the cherished borders of his country while he was alive, Mickey thought. Yet he knew the gray areas of law enforcement had taken their toll on the idealistic Mickey Stone.

His gaze flicked over the once-loved scene of the bust. He felt weary of it, saw the jealousies and ambitions of its opposing forces as more human than political, compared to before.

The Garden Emerald case had sapped his idealism the way a worm devours the flesh of an apple, he realized. It was time to turn the protection of the country over to the next generation of protectors. It brought him sadness—a long moment of it while his former boss watched, checking for signs of compliance or weakness or disloyalty.

That's exactly how the captain will view what I'm going to do next—as disloyalty, he thought.

His ex-boss began tucking the papers into his coat.

Mickey reached out, tapped them. "They'll have to go back to London. At least a copy."

The color drained from the captain's battle flush. He jammed the papers out of sight. He seemed to struggle for composure, said tersely, "Dammit, Stone, you're a good agent. You got caught in the flytrap of international politics. It happens. We don't die of it."

"One man did, Captain."

"Don't push this."

"Sorry. Got to. I want the papers to go back to the intelligence community in London."

"Otherwise . . . ?"

"Otherwise, I gotta go see a friend in the prime minister's cabinet. Owes me a favor. He'll be happy to pay his debt and look like a hero at the same time."

He gave the captain an it's-up-to-you shrug.

The captain shot his cuffs, stalling. "Blackmail. Better guys than you have been iced for less."

Mickey let the threat hang. Then, "Others know what I know. It would be a waste of resources on your part."

The captain gave him a belligerent stare. "All right. But this cuts it, Stone. We're through."

"No problem. Gotta decline your generous offer anyway. Like to borrow this, though."

Pulling a white handkerchief from his pocket, he dropped it over the box on the table and carefully picked it up, preserving the prints.

"That's evidence," the captain growled.

"Just borrowing it for a minute," Mickey said, heading for the galleyway. What was the captain going to do about it, arrest him? He smiled, climbing topside.

At the salon door, he stepped over the prone body of Wing Tip and winked at Johnson, who was on his knees, reading the thug his rights.

Johnson gave him a dirty look and kept up the recitation.

Over at the rail, Harry was sheltering Laura with an arm the size of a bear's. A breeze had come up and it blew her curly new hairdo into a tempest around the brim of the hat. It reminded Mickey of how she looked when she was lost in passion. But that was for later, that kind of daydream.

Right now, he had a gift to bring her and some amends to make.

"Harry," he said.

The big man craned around.

"I can never thank you enough," said Mickey, joining them.

Harry beamed at him. "Fagetit. Glad to be part of the action."

Mickey knew that was true. Harry loved the action and intrigue of the gem business. The guys at the square would be hearing about this for months. *Chalk one up for the good guys,* he thought.

Laura began to pull away from the rail.

"Hey, beautiful," Mickey said, a catch in his voice because he felt he was bursting with a strange joy. "Look what I've got for you."

She faced his direction, eyes unfocused, her face pale despite the rich reds of the sunset. Finally she recognized him; and the old fire sparked in her eyes. "Mickey!" she said. "You're *safe.*"

She stepped away from Harry, who grinned at Mickey, coughed and sauntered away.

Mickey barely realized it. He was filled with the sight of her. "You were wonderful," he said. "Really unimaginably brave and wonderful."

She seemed to swell up with the praise. A smile bloomed. "Oh, Mickey, it was fun." She glanced at the shrouded box. "Is that what I think it is?"

Reflected light gleamed on the covers of two hatches near the stern rail. He gently eased Laura around and took her aft. Sheltered from the comings and goings of agents and their charges, he pulled back the covering and opened the box.

Inside, nestled in white velvet, was the huge, incomparable, elusive stone. He'd never seen such a gem. Awed, he extended the box to her. "The Garden Emerald, Laura."

She sucked in her breath. "It's . . . so big."

"One in a million, like you. Take it," he said, foregoing protocol on stolen property.

"Oh, yes," she breathed, "I want to hold it."

Carefully, reverently she picked up the stone and put it into the cup of her right hand. She closed her eyes briefly, and he wondered what she felt. Something wondrous, no doubt. Her face looked radiant.

When she opened her eyes, she held the stone up to the last rays of sunset and the light struck through the magnificent gem, sparkling out in a thousand facets, enclosing the two of them in a multisided pattern of amber.

It was a magical moment. Never had Mickey felt so thoroughly happy. He would remember the courage and goodness and caring in that cameo face, and he would always keep the memory of this moment with him.

As if she felt the vibration of his thoughts, she lowered the gem to the box and closed the lid.

He wrapped it and set the box on the varnished hatch cover. He straighted, turned, found her looking at him.

He had a lot to say. No time like now to begin. "The captain's agreed to get the documents back to London," he said.

She smiled again. "Now there won't be a scandal and the operation will definitely be scuttled." She cocked an eyebrow. "So, Mickey," she said softly, "what about us?"

It felt as if the deck wallowed out from under his shoes, left him suspended about thirty feet above the sea. "I've treated you badly," he began, trying to find his footing, forcing the words past the butterflies in his stomach. "Veeta . . . I treated her worse, Laura. Made some serious mistakes in that marriage. I treated you practically the same way, even though I don't feel the same way about you as I do her. I used you and thought only of myself. I have no right to ask you—" he lifted an arm, thinking he should feel desolate, feeling hopeful instead "—to forgive me."

Her eyes widened. "I used you, too, Mickey."

In surprise, he asked, "How?"

"You were my ticket to a new life. You helped retire my demons to hell. So we're even. What about us?"

It was gratifying to hear her ask, even if she didn't realize what she was asking. The specter of what he might have become if he hadn't snared the emerald and the perpetrators; the thought of what it would have done to him if he'd lost Laura in the process—these thoughts chipped away at the joy he felt, hearing her ask for his commitment. He owed her honesty, he knew; even if it killed the hope in her eyes.

"You have no idea how close I came to being like Fast Eddie," he said, "aimless, lost, living hand-to-mouth on the streets." He cut her a glance to see if it made sense to her. She looked, if anything, doubtful.

"There's a cow pasture right in the middle between right and wrong," he began again, his voice roughening with distaste. "For a while on this case, I was lost in the middle of that pasture."

She came to him, laying a tentative hand on his arm. "But you're through it, back on the right side again?"

"I was there," he said. "I guess that scares me, knowing I compromised my values and tried to get my friends to do the same."

"Have you got your values back again?"

He met her steady gaze. "Yes," he said. "I've got them. But I'm not going back to NSI and I'm quitting Garth. I'm starting completely over, Laura. Square one."

"You have a stake from the gem show sales. I have my own means. This isn't about money, Mickey. It's about us. Do we begin here, too?"

He glanced out over the water—didn't see it. "I thought about working on industrial espionage cases. The discovery process intrigues me. I'd have to look into it," he said, stubbornly holding to the notion that a man took care of his woman, offered her some stability.

Abruptly Laura went to the rail and put her face toward the thin band of orange along the horizon. "John, Jr. wants to run Marley Enterprises one day," she said flatly.

"He's got school to finish first. I want to help him make the transition. In fact, Mickey—" she glanced back at him "—I don't want to quit work. I like my company. It needs me right now. Gregorgi and Brit Hospital and Hendley and the others. I need them, too." She sighed, sounding angry. "*Mickey.* Damn you, this isn't about any of that."

Something *plinged* inside him. *Call it truth,* he decided. She was right. This was about love. Theirs.

"I don't want to lose you, Laura." He let the statement hang in the wind a moment.

"Me, neither," she said more softly. "Mickey, how can we bridge the ocean and the whole U.S.A.?"

The answer was there, unreasonable, crazy, but why not?

He went to her and turned her toward him. Grasping the brim of her hat, he eased it from her. The wind set her curls free. *I couldn't bear to lose her,* he thought. *Ever.*

Her eyes were lavender, sad. He wanted to take the sadness from her forever, though he knew she could only do that for herself. Just as he was about to do it for him.

"I was thinking," he said, caressing her lustrous skin. "I could look for work in Europe, Laura. I could be based in London."

"You could?" The doubt evaporated; a sudden happiness made her features mobile, expressive, hopeful. "Would you?"

He'd thought he couldn't feel more adrenaline. He was wrong. It coursed through him, opening him, cleansing the wounds he'd held inside for years—freeing him from the fetters of hatred and revenge, filling him with a light he would swear later came from the Garden Emerald.

Their gazes locked. It was another crystalline moment he would remember because shining in her eyes was a light that pierced him to the core. From the depths of him came a hunger to hold her close.

"From now on, there's only us," he said, sweeping her up to share that wild feeling of release, of joy, of abandon. Over and over, as he buried his face in her perfumed hair, he said, "I love you...."

HARLEQUIN
American Romance®

RELIVE THE MEMORIES . . .

From New York's immigrant experience to the Great Quake of 1906. From the Western Front of World War I to the Roaring Twenties. From the indomitable spirit of the thirties to the home front of the Fabulous Forties. From the baby boom fifties to the Woodstock Nation sixties . . . A CENTURY OF AMERICAN ROMANCE takes you on a nostalgic journey through the twentieth century.

Revel in the romance of a time gone by . . . and sneak a peek at romance in a exciting future.

Watch for all the A CENTURY OF AMERICAN ROMANCE titles coming to you one per month over the next three months in Harlequin American Romance.

Don't miss February's A CENTURY OF AMERICAN ROMANCE title, #377—TILL THE END OF TIME by Elise Title.

A CENTURY OF
AMERICAN ROMANCE
1970s

The women . . . the men . . . the passions . . . the memories . . .

Everyone loves a spring wedding, and this April, Harlequin cordially invites you to read the most romantic wedding book of the year

With This Ring

ONE WEDDING—FOUR LOVE STORIES FROM YOUR FAVORITE HARLEQUIN AUTHORS!

The church is booked, the reception arranged and the invitations mailed. All Diane Bauer and Nick Granatelli have to do is walk down the aisle. Little do they realize that the most cherished day of their lives will spark so many romantic notions....

Available wherever Harlequin books are sold.

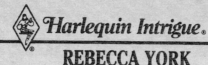

Harlequin Intrigue®

REBECCA YORK

Labeled a "true master of intrigue" by *Rave Reviews*, bestselling author Rebecca York continues her Harlequin Intrigue ongoing series

It looks like a charming old building near the renovated Baltimore waterfront, but inside 43 Light Street lurks danger . . . and romance.

Don't miss the next book in the series when private detective Jo O'Malley finds herself being stalked by a serial killer. Chilling suspense and a fiery romance.

Look for #155 SHATTERED VOWS in February 1991. And watch for more 43 LIGHT STREET titles in the future.